MYSTERY

-ON THE-

PECOS

❧ **THE WILL AND BUCK SERIES: BOOK II** ❧

ISBN: 978 1 683131 816
LCCN: 2018959916

Pen-L Publishing
Fayetteville, Arkansas
www.Pen-L .com

First Edition
Printed and bound in the USA

Cover and interior design by Kelsey Rice
Cover photograph by Kristi Bracewell Photography

MYSTERY
–ON THE–
PECOS

≈THE WILL AND BUCK SERIES: BOOK II≈

BY
ALICE V. BROCK

Ⓟ
Pen-L Publishing
Fayetteville, Arkansas
Pen-L.com

DEDICATION

This book is dedicated to my real-life cowboy, Don Brock, who knew more about a cow than most textbooks, and to the children of Iola, Texas. You have always been and always will be my inspiration.

ACKNOWLEDGMENT

A special thank you to my sister, Sherrill Nilson, author of the Adalta Series: *Karda*—Book One, *Hunter*—Book Two, and in 2019, *Falling*—Book Three. She is the reason I'm still writing. She lifts me up when I'm down and brings me down to earth when I'm overzealous. We are a team.

To Harvey Cannon, a long-time friend and co-teacher, I offer my gratitude for the use of his mules and the 1890 Studebaker buckboard wagon used in my cover photograph. Thank you for hitching Eula and Ida and taking us for a ride.

The cover photograph, taken by Kristi Bracewell Photography, is artfully done and makes for an outstanding cover. Thank you for blessing me with your talent.

If I have developed any writing skills at all, it is due to the instruction I received from the Institute of Children's Literature, the West Texas Writing Academy in Canyon, Texas, and Margie Lawson's Deep Editing courses. They have brought me from unstructured ramblings to winning awards and I thank you.

I appreciate the support of my family and of the family at Pen-L Publishing for their patience and caring during a most difficult year.

DISCOVERY

Will Whitaker had endured enough of Pa's worrying. Enough of his constant watchful eye. Enough of his babying. Will was almost twelve, almost grown, almost convinced he could run the ranch on his own.

Getting away from Pa was the number one plan for the day. Lying to Pa to make that happen was—no. Will swiped lying off the number two spot. The thought of lying to Pa twisted his heart like wringing the sweat out of his bandana.

He tightened the saddle's cinch on Buck, his buckskin stallion and best friend, waited till the big horse exhaled, and pulled tighter. Will stopped his adopted brother, Two Feathers, leading Gray Wolf, his grullo gelding, before they reached the heavy wooden door of the barn half of their cave. They had made a home in the other half of the cave and spent their first winter in New Mexico there.

"This time I'm not going to ask him if we can hunt those heifers. This time I'm going to tell him the heifers got out again. I'll tell him we're going after them."

"Do you think Pa will listen?" Two Feathers's words didn't sound like a question.

"Maybe. We worked all winter helping him make adobe bricks for the new house. We fed cattle, cleared water holes, and helped him collect strays. Maybe that will count for something. Maybe he's learned to trust us. Maybe he's tired of worrying about Yellow Hawk capturing us again."

Two Feathers snorted. "I do not think that will ever happen. And you were the one captured, not me. I had to rescue you from my uncle. Remember?"

Will's mouth twisted into not quite a frown and not quite a smile. "I remember."

The boys led their horses to the creek, where Pa smoothed adobe mud into brick molds.

"Pa, those same two heifers got away again. Me and Two Feathers are goin' after 'em."

Pa unwound his long legs and stood by the tub of mud and pile of empty brick molds.

"No. You're not going by yourselves."

There it was—Pa's ain't-never-gonna-happen face.

Will's eyes squinched, and his teeth stopped a string of cuss words just in time. He started to argue, but the cuss words were in the way. He knew any arguing meant Pa'd glue him and Two Feathers to his side tighter than a tick on a hound.

Pa pointed a finger at Will. "You're not twelve yet, and you," he aimed the finger at Two Feathers, "ain't much older, so don't think you can go traipsing off in Comanche country by yourselves."

"But Pa," Will worked to keep the begging out of his voice. "We helped Charlie Goodnight drive twenty-five hundred head of cattle halfway across Texas and New Mexico, so we can certainly drive two heifers back to the ranch. Besides, we haven't seen any Indian sign all winter. No tracks, no campfires, no nothing. And even if we did, Buck and Gray Wolf can outrun any horse on the plains."

Pa put his hands on his hips and stood silent for what Will began to think was forever. Then he leveled a you-better-listen-to-me look at both boys.

"Okay, you can go. But if you don't find the heifers right away, come straight back."

Will slid a triumphant glance at Two Feathers.

"Be sure to study the country," Pa said. "Study close in. Watch for tracks, scat, and snakes. Study far out for dust clouds outlined against the horizon. Watch for movement and anything unnatural. And listen to the sounds of the desert. Listen the hardest when there's no sound. That's when the desert is the most dangerous. Everything out there will bite you, sting you, or kill you. If you two get into trouble, you'll be making bricks till Christmas."

Will and Two Feathers rode down the creek to the Pecos River before Pa changed his mind. The river looked different without Pa tagging along. Will felt different. Pa hadn't been so crazy about them going off alone during the cold winter months when he let Will and Two Feathers go feed hay. He figured Yellow Hawk, the Comanche war chief and their enemy, was holed up in winter camp. But the weather was warming, and Pa's worry level rose with the temperature.

Riding loose in the saddle, Will's eyes scanned the ground and spotted a track in the damp sand.

"Here's one."

They followed the river and the heifer tracks till the canyon walls towered over them.

"The heifers are still headin' upriver," Will said.

He tapped Buck with his boot heels. The big buckskin stepped farther ahead of Two Feathers's grullo and splashed up the shallow Pecos River.

"Cows are not smart like buffalo." Two Feathers caught up with his brother, and Gray Wolf trailed behind Buck. "Why do they leave good grass and get lost?"

Will laughed. "That's a good question." He twisted his head and spoke over his shoulder. "When you learn the answer, tell Pa. He's been hunting lost cattle as long as I can remember."

They rode along the narrow strip of sand between the water and the walls.

"You missed a track, Will," Two Feathers called from behind.

"I did?" Will turned Buck around. "Where?"

He dismounted, squatted at the water's edge, and studied the ground. Will considered himself lucky. Not everyone had a Comanche teach him to track.

"The heifers walked through the muddy river. We cannot see their tracks in the water." Two Feathers pointed to a hoof print, one side in the water and a sliver of the other side out. "See where this heifer stepped. Only the edge is out of the water."

"How'd . . . you . . . see . . . that?" Will's words pulled apart in frustration because his untrained eye let him down again.

"I watch for the little things. Things not in their right place. Come on. We won't find them standing here."

They mounted their horses and continued upriver. Will, determined not to miss another track, kept his eyes studying the ground.

A fresh breeze met them as they rounded a bend in the winding river. Will took his hat off and ran his fingers through his sweat-darkened hair. The air cooled his forehead and fluttered the turkey feathers in his brother's brown braids that hung on each side of his face.

Striations of red, orange, and tan sandstone colored the canyon walls rising about fifteen feet above them. The water deepened and covered the red-brown sandy bottom of the river. A sandbar at the river's edge gave the two lost heifers a spot to nibble on willow branches, so they'd stopped to enjoy a brief snack. The boys circled wide around them, walking the horses in the water. On the sandbar, they headed back toward the wayward animals. The heifers spotted the approaching horses and headed for home.

Will walked Buck behind the drifting animals. *Two heifers found, and all Pa has to do is open the gate when we drive them into the pen by the barn. That should make him happy.* Will didn't hurry them along, not when plenty of mud, straw, and empty brick molds waited for him at home.

"Will!" Two Feathers called from behind. "Come see."

Will turned around and eased Buck along the edge of the river, farther into the canyon. Two Feathers stood upstream on the end of the sandbar, looking up the canyon wall.

"There is a cave. I see a rope hanging from the rim above it."

Will slid off Buck and walked over. "Where?" He shaded his eyes from the sun. "I don't see anything."

Two Feathers put his hands on Will's shoulders and twisted him a quarter of a turn. "See that juniper tree on the edge of the bluff. It's about halfway down from there. There is a dark place."

"I see it." Will studied the rough sandstone wall. "Let's climb up. I want to explore that cave."

"Dan said to bring the heifers back."

"If we get back too early, we have to make bricks." Will cocked his eyebrows, and mischief twitched the corners of his mouth.

Two Feathers usual solemn expression broke with a grin. "It will not be a hard climb." He pointed out hand and footholds all the way to the cave opening.

The Comanche's moccasins gripped the toeholds better than Will's boots, so he reached the cave first. Two Feathers pulled Will up the last few feet. A coil of thick, coarse rope coming from a juniper tree on the canyon lip wound through a large block and tackle that lay on the flat shelf of the opening.

Hefting the block, Two Feathers asked, "What is this?"

"It's used to lift heavy stuff."

Will took hold of the rope hanging from the juniper. He gave it a tug. It held. He gave it a hard jerk. It held. He and Two Feathers both took hold and gave it a fierce yank. It held.

"What is up there?" Two Feathers strained his head as far back as it would go.

"I don't know. Let's see what's in here first."

Will led the way into the cave and in the dim light stumbled into a wooden crate. He fished a match from the bottom of his pocket and struck it on the cave wall. In the feeble light, he saw large boxes as far as the light reached into the darkness. Holding the burning match beside one, he read, "U.S. Army. Dried Beans." The match burned his fingers, and he dropped it. They walked back into the light at the cave opening. Will walked in a circle on the small ledge, his thoughts in a jumble.

"Something's wrong here. Why would the army store stuff in a cave this far from Fort Sumner?"

"It makes no sense." Two Feathers walked to the rope dangling from the juniper on the cliff edge above them and started to climb. "I want to see what is on the other end of this rope."

Will followed Two Feathers, pulling himself hand over hand up the coarse rope, and scrambled over the canyon rim. He rubbed his stinging rope-reddened hands on his pant legs and joined his brother studying the ground around the tree. A short distance from the juniper, Will pointed to large square impressions and drag marks beside wagon tracks.

"This is where they unloaded the crates. They must be heavy. See how deep they dug into the dirt."

Two Feathers followed boot and wagon tracks mixed with mule tracks that led away from the edge of the cliff to a fire ring.

"Will, look at this. Two men camped here. You can see two different boot tracks." He circled the campsite and found the place where they had tied their mules to a manzanita bush. "Why would the army bring a freight wagon of supplies way out here?"

"They must be stolen. The robbers hid them here. On our ranch!" An uneasy feeling prickled the back of his neck and his palms dampened. He wiped them on his pant legs. "Pa is not going to be happy." The prickles worked their way down his spine.

Eyes on the ground, Will followed the wagon tracks for about fifty yards until they led over a rise and disappeared in the distance. Unaware his hands had clenched into a tight fist, he relaxed and stretched his fingers. *Not good, not good, not good,* echoed over and over in his head.

"Will!"

Two Feathers's urgent voice and frantic motions sent Will racing back. He stopped beside his brother and gagged. Holding his breath, he grabbed his bandana and covered his mouth and nose. Two Feathers pointed to a pile of rocks covered with brush and juniper branches.

"Look." His muffled words sounded hollow through his wadded-up bandana. "A coyote or something tried to get in these rocks."

A sickly, stinking, rotten smell hung heavy in the air and sent Will retching and stumbling away. The pile of rocks covered a grave.

FORT SUMNER

The following evening, with the last pale-pink fading from the sky and shadows darkening, Will—weary, aching, and dust coated—stepped down from Buck behind the sutler's store at Fort Sumner. The buckboard rattled behind him into the wagon yard. Pa spoke to the mules, and they stopped in front of the open barn doors. He jumped from the wagon, rubbed his backside, and stretched the kinks out of his back. A boy of about eight peeked around the corner of the barn. Wide-eyed, he watched Two Feathers ride Gray Wolf next to Buck and dismount.

"Hey, boy," Will called. "Is there a place to get a bite to eat? The mess hall is probably closed by now."

"Yes, sir."

The boy stepped out from behind the door and stared at Two Feathers's long braids hanging to his waist. He watched the Comanche unwind the thin leather strings and pull the turkey feathers out of his hair, place them in the wagon box under the seat, and tuck his braids under his hat. Nervous brown eyes peered from under dark curls that bobbed when the boy nodded.

"The storekeeper's wife boiled up beef and gravy over at the store. If you hurry, you might get some of her biscuits. They're mighty good."

After showing the travelers where to settle the mules and horses in the barn, the boy took off at a run. Will and Two Feathers hurried to catch up to Pa's long stride as he headed toward the store.

"We should see General Carleton first. Don't you think?" Will asked Pa.

"All we've eaten today is jerky and coffee. If we wait, there won't be any food left. Our news will hold for a few more minutes."

Will's growling hunger agreed with Pa's plan.

Full darkness met them after supper when they stepped off the store's porch and crossed the compound for the general's office.

"Well, look who's here." Sergeant Baker greeted them. "How's that new ranch coming along?" He grasped Dan's hand and shook it. "Will, you're a good bit taller than the last time I saw you. How's that big buckskin of yours? Can you mount him without a boost? I recall that was a problem for you last year."

Will laughed. "It's a jump, but I can make it."

Baker pulled Two Feathers's hat off and the long braids tumbled around his shoulders.

"Are you going by your Comanche name or your white man's name on this visit?"

Two Feathers did not smile. "When at the white man's fort, I am John Randall." He tucked his long hair back under his hat.

"Okay, John it is."

Pa stepped up on the porch. "We have news that General Carleton needs to hear. Please tell him we need to speak to him."

"General Carleton is no longer here. Colonel Dowell is in command now. Can I help you?"

"Yesterday, Will and Two Feathers found a cave of stashed army supplies north of us along the Pecos—"

"Army supplies?" Sergeant Baker interrupted, his relaxed attitude gone. "Near the river? In a cave? How'd they get there? We need all the supplies we can get. There isn't enough to feed the Navajo, and they're starving."

"And a fresh grave," Will added.

"A grave?"

The sergeant turned and knocked with a sharp rap on the colonel's door.

"Enter," sounded from inside.

The sergeant opened the door and saluted.

Colonel Dowell's square face showed irritation, and his lips tightened into a frown. He returned the salute and snapped, "What is it, Sergeant? I'm busy."

"Sir, this is Dan Whitaker and his boys, Will Whitaker and John Randell. Last fall they set up a ranch on the Pecos, south of Puerto de Luna. Yesterday, the boys found a stash of army supplies."

The colonel's face changed from forced politeness to serious business. "What kind of army supplies?"

"Sir, they also found a fresh grave."

The colonel shifted his sharp gaze from the sergeant to Dan. "Start from the beginning." His words barked like an order.

"Will." Pa nodded toward the officer. "Tell the colonel what you and John found."

Will watched Two Feathers slip out to the darkness of the porch. *Where's he goin'? Wait till I find him. He's supposed to help tell what happened.* Will swallowed and licked his dry lips. His sweaty hands were as shaky on the outside as he was on the inside. He gripped them tight together. All three men stared at him. He wanted to be anywhere but there. He straightened his shoulders, pulled in another gulp of air, and started talking.

"We found a cave in the canyon wall above the Pecos full of crates branded U.S. Army. A rope hung from a juniper tree on the canyon rim. We climbed up and found lots of boot and wagon tracks and a grave."

The colonel drummed his fingers on his scarred desk. "How far from the campsite was the grave?"

"About fifty yards."

He breathed a long sigh. "Maybe they're not connected. It's not uncommon to find a grave where a traveler met with misfortune. This is hard country." Colonel Dowell, his tone all business again, asked Will, "How many crates were in the cave?"

Will's voice squeaked a little, and he cleared his throat. "I don't know. We only had one match. But I saw at least eight or ten. One was labeled dried beans. The cave was deep. We couldn't see all the way to the back."

"Thank you. That was a clear and concise report."

Colonel Dowell stared out the window for several minutes. Will relaxed his clenched hands and rubbed the blood back into his fingers. Maybe his part was over.

The colonel spoke to Dan. "Have you seen any other sign of wagons traveling through that area? Anything out of the ordinary?"

Will watched his father. His eyes held his don't-bother-me-I'm-thinkin' look. Will waited. Pa shook his head.

"No, only the normal traffic back and forth from Puerto de Luna. But we haven't strayed much from the ranch this winter. It was all we could do to care for the cattle."

The colonel stood and clasped his hands behind his back. "In the morning, Sergeant Baker will take four troopers and investigate the cached supplies and mysterious grave. Will, if you could show him the location, we would be grateful. Those supplies were probably intended for Fort Sumner. We have too many hungry Navajo to be losing food, if that's what's in those crates."

The colonel stepped around his desk and shook Dan's hand, then Will's.

"Thank you for making the trip to report this. You have brought disturbing news. I have no report of missing supplies and will speak to our quartermaster. Sergeant, show Mr. Whitaker and his son out."

With a brisk salute, they were out the door.

The empty compound was dark in the moonless night. The light from the sutler's store was a welcome beacon. Will followed Pa toward it.

"What are we going to do about all this?" Will felt all jumpy inside. "What if the dead person is a soldier? We can't have soldiers chasing murderers and outlaws and hunting stolen army supplies all over our ranch."

"Whoa, Will." Pa put his hand on Will's shoulder. They stopped in the middle of the dark compound. "Take it easy. This is army business. It doesn't concern us. All we did was alert them to the situation. It's their problem now. Don't worry. I'm sure we won't hear any more about it."

Pa's words didn't stop that jumpy feeling. *Where's Two Feathers?* Will's nervousness changed to irritation at his brother's absence. *If he's going to be a partner on the Pecos River Ranch, he needs to do a better job of backing me up.* Irritation replaced the nervous feeling and crept into Will's tone.

"Pa, did you see Two Feathers sneak out? He needed to stay and help me tell Colonel Dowell what we found. He's the one who found the grave."

"I know." Pa's understanding calm aggravated Will even more. "Give him time. Remember, soldiers never brought him anything but tragedy. He feels the same about soldiers that you feel about the Comanche."

Will hung his head and followed Pa around to the wagon yard behind the store, but he didn't roll in his blankets under the wagon like Pa. He decided to wait for Two Feathers. *Where is he? Where did he go?*

A crowing rooster and the loud clucking of hens in the coop behind the store roused Will from under the wagon. Last night, sleep had overtaken him before his brother returned. He scrambled out when he saw Pa and Two Feathers bring the mules from the barn in the predawn light.

"You going to eat breakfast with us or sleep all day?" Pa said.

He hitched the mules to the doubletree. The mules stepped up, and the wagon rolled over the edge of Will's blanket. He jerked it free.

"You're lucky those wheels didn't roll over you, lazybones."

Pa spread Will's folded blanket on top of his and Two Feathers's to pad the wagon seat.

Leading Buck and Gray Wolf, the boys followed the wagon to the front of the sutler's store. The crisp smell of bacon and fresh golden biscuits mingled with the rich aroma of leather and tobacco. Rows of spicy red peppers and sharp-smelling onions hung from the ceiling.

Will found space on a crowded bench facing a long rough-hewn table in an open area at the back of the store. A large buxom woman handed Pa and Will a tin plate apiece and, after a double-look at John, gave him one also. A Navajo girl brought a mountain of biscuits piled on a platter and placed it on the table, followed by a large bowl of speckled gravy. Will caught the startled glance that passed between her and Two Feathers.

Hands—some dirty, some clean—descended on the mountain and soon reduced it to a platter of crumbs. Pa managed to get the gravy first and quickly slopped a spoonful on top of their biscuits before someone grabbed it from his hands and passed it down the table. By the time the bacon platter reached Will, it was as empty as his stomach.

Will devoured his breakfast and wiped his mouth on his sleeve. Following Two Feathers from the store, he stepped onto the hitching rail and pulled Buck's reins loose. Buck turned sideways, and Will slipped into the saddle.

"Let's look around while Pa's gettin' the supplies."

When his brother didn't answer, Will kneed Buck to face him. His eyes slits, his gaze unblinking, Two Feathers stood on the porch, staring across the compound. Will followed his line of sight to see a group of Navajo women gathered outside a low squat adobe building. One at a time, they entered. One at a time, they came back out with a small bundle.

Rubbing his stuffed belly, Will watched the women carrying their meager supplies. When a gaunt Navajo woman walked past, he saw the bundle was only a small flour sack. Suddenly, feeling full was no longer pleasant.

Pa came out of the store. "You boys load the wagon. The storekeeper has the supplies ready."

Pa watched the Navajo woman as she passed and shook his head. Jerking his hat off, he ran his fingers through his hair and yanked the hat down tight on his head. Will knew that gesture. Pa always did it when he saw something he didn't like.

"Sergeant Baker said he'd meet us here."

Two Feathers walked down the porch steps on stiff legs and mounted Gray Wolf. His tight, narrow eyes remained fixed on the Indian women entering and leaving the small building with their too-small sacks of flour.

"What's the matter?" Will couldn't tell if his brother's strange reaction was because the Navajo were enemies of the Comanche or because the women were so thin and their bundles of food so small.

Before Two Feathers answered, the girl who served at breakfast hurried down the porch steps. When she crossed in front of Gray Wolf, she threw a quick glance at Two Feathers. Then she called out to an older woman in line and ran across the compound.

Two Feathers grunted, startled. Gray Wolf stepped up. Reining him in, Two Feathers watched the Navajo girl enter the building. When she came out, she gave her small sack to the older woman and headed back across the compound. When she reached the porch steps, Two Feathers spoke to her.

"Na-es-cha?"

With no friendship in her eyes, she spoke to him in Comanche. When he answered, her face hardened with anger. She ran up the steps and disappeared into the sutler's store.

"What's going on?" Will stepped Buck up next to Gray Wolf. "Do you know her?"

"Navajo." His eyes lingered on the open doorway. "I saw her last night while you talked with the soldiers. It was dark. We could not see each other very well."

"So that's where you went." Will's anger at his disappearance from the colonel's office slid away. "She's kinda pretty."

Two Feathers snorted. "She is angry. She thought I was white. Now she knows I am Comanche. She hates both." He walked Gray Wolf to the other side of the wagon.

A tall, angular captain coming across the parade ground stopped to toss a lost rawhide ball to a group of Navajo children playing in the dirt. Approaching Buck, but keeping a safe distance, he studied him while walking around the horse. His eyes gleamed with admiration.

With a quick glance at Pa, he asked, "This your stallion?"

Pa shook his head and inclined it toward Will.

The man stepped closer and ran his hand over Buck's shoulder. "He's a fine one."

Buck snorted, threw his head up, and sidled away.

"Whoa, Buck." Will stroked the big horse's neck.

The soldier backed away. A smile softened his angular face, but not his eyes.

"You must be quite a horseman."

One long-legged step put him onto the porch. He offered his hand to Pa. "Mr. Whitaker?"

Pa nodded, shaking his hand.

"I'm Captain Stanaway, the quartermaster. The supplies you found in that cave will be well used."

"It looks like they're needed."

"Yes, they are. Sergeant Baker will be here shortly."

"Do you know where the supplies came from?"

"No, not yet. We can account for all our supplies. But I'm sure we'll find out."

Stanaway and Pa walked down the steps. With another admiring glance at Buck, Stanaway said, "This is a fine animal, Mr. Whitaker. I hope to have a line of breeding stock in a few years. I might look you up and buy him from you."

Will gave Pa a not-again roll of his eyes.

"Captain, Buck is my horse, not Pa's, and he is not for sale."

Stanaway turned his back to Will and leaned against the porch rail facing Pa. "I understand you're new to New Mexico. The colonel told me you've set up a ranch on the Pecos near Puerto de Luna."

Pa nodded. "We came up with Goodnight last fall."

"That area is not safe. The Comanche raid through this part of New Mexico."

Will and Pa exchanged knowing glances, and Will's heart did its usual jagged hiccup when he heard the word Comanche.

"I've fought Indians before."

"For the sake of your boys, you should consider moving your ranch closer to the fort. Where you are now is dangerous country. That's evident by the grave your boys found." He shook Pa's hand again. "Thanks again for telling us about those supplies." Ignoring Will, he stepped off the porch and walked back across the parade ground to his office.

Sergeant Baker rode up, followed by a buckboard wagon with four soldiers.

"You ready?"

Will and Two Feathers on their horses, and Pa driving their wagon loaded with supplies for the ranch, followed him out the fort gates.

Tapping Buck, Will rode next to the sergeant. He glanced several times at the man before he collected enough courage to ask the same question he'd asked Pa the night before.

"Sergeant Baker, do you think the person in the grave is a soldier?"

"I have no way of knowing, Will. We'll have to wait till we get there and see the body."

ONE BOOT TRACK

The day passed one step at a time, and when Will finally spotted the juniper tree on the canyon rim, he nudged Buck into a faster gait.

"Come on," he called to Two Feathers, "let's go ahead so we can get this over with."

They waited for the caravan on the outskirts of the campsite. Suddenly, he wished he were anywhere but there. He remembered the sickly smell that oozed from the pile of rocks. He sniffed the air—testing, to be sure he couldn't smell it from there.

The sergeant rode up and dismounted. Will pointed toward the tree.

"The rope is tied to that juniper at the edge of the bluff, and there is a block and tackle down below at the cave. Two Feathers found a fire ring about twenty steps east of the tree."

"Thanks, Will." Baker turned to his men. "Dismount. Leave the wagon next to Dan's. You men walk a circle from here to the rim and about fifty yards out from the campsite. If you find any tracks left after the windstorm we came through, call out." He tied his horse to the back of Dan's wagon. "Will, you and Two Feathers show me the campsite."

At the circle of blackened rocks, Sergeant Baker poked through the remains of old fires but found only ashes and dried coffee grounds.

"Looks like they camped here several times." He walked over the area but found no tracks. "Will, you looked the campsite over, right?"

"Two Feathers did."

Two Feathers pointed out the faint imprint of a boot the blowing dust had not filled. "There were boot tracks. It looked like more than one person. We could see where the wagon had been. It came in from the north and returned the same way. Over by the juniper, Will saw marks that looked like heavy square crates had been sitting there."

Baker followed the boys to the juniper tree and examined the rope that hung down to the shelf and cave.

The troopers returned with Pa. One of them reported, "No sign of any tracks, Sergeant."

Pa swept his gaze up and down the bluff along the Pecos. "You can't see the cave unless you're standing on the edge. I wonder how they found it."

"We saw it from the river," Will said.

Pa knelt where the rope hung to the shelf below. "They must have used this place more than once. Sergeant, look at this. You can see where the crates scarred the rim of the wall."

"Before we climb down to the cave, we better look at the grave," the sergeant said. He turned to a trooper. "Get the shovels from the wagon."

"Sergeant?" The trooper ducked his head and rubbed the back of his neck. "Private Tucker's been missing for several days. We've searched everywhere for him—"

"I know. Let's hope we don't find him today."

Will started after the sergeant, but Pa tugged his arm. "No, Will. You and Two Feathers stay here with me. That's army business, not our business."

Will's shoulders relaxed with a long puff of relief. Not going near those smelly rocks was fine with him.

"Your Pa's right. Wait here. You boys can show us the cave when we're finished."

"Sergeant Baker," Will said, "it's due north. About fifty yards. You'll see the rocks and brush they covered it with."

Will and Pa took off their hats and beat the dust out of them against their pant legs. The water barrel strapped to the side of the wagon was half full, and Will fanned the dust off the lid with his hat before he opened it. He dipped the gourd into the cool water, drank, filled it again, and passed it to Pa and Two Feathers. They hunkered down on the leeward side of the wagon, out of the wind.

"I don't like this wind," Will said.

He sat on the ground, leaned against the wagon wheel, folded his arms on top of his knees, and dropped his head on them. Tired from two long days in the saddle, he dozed. A nudge from Two Feathers woke him. Sergeant Baker and his troopers had returned from their grisly task—their faces hard, their expressions angry.

"Boys, the army owes you a debt of gratitude. You found our missing soldier, Private Tucker. He was murdered."

"Murdered? Was it Comanche?" Will's heart took off like a scared jackrabbit. He leaped to his feet.

"No, Will." Two Feathers put his hand on Will's arm. "I saw no Comanche tracks. It was not Yellow Hawk."

"If they weren't looking for Comanche, then why were soldiers out here?" Will looked to Baker for answers.

"And where were they going with only one wagon of supplies?" Two Feathers asked.

"Those are questions the army will want answered." Sergeant Baker held his hand out to Pa. "I found this forty-four shell in the rocks."

Pa took the brass casing and rolled it in his fingers. "Did Private Tucker come across something he wasn't supposed to see, or was he a part of whatever is going on here?"

"I don't know. Let's go see what's in that cave."

Will, then Two Feathers, climbed hand over hand down the rough rope. Sergeant Baker followed, then Pa, who dropped the last few feet onto the narrow shelf. At the cave entrance, Baker lit a small brass lantern.

"Okay, boys, show me what you found."

Will and Two Feathers walked a short way inside and stopped. Baker held the lamp high, and the small light faded into the darkness of the empty cave. He looked at Will.

"The supplies were here," Will said, his tone confused and puzzled. He walked farther into the cave, and Pa followed him. "They're gone now."

Kneeling, Baker studied the thick dust that covered the floor of the cave. "Dan, look at this. Someone took a brushy limb and wiped out all the tracks. See those sweeping marks? Looks like they were in a hurry."

"They may have been in a hurry, but they took enough time to do a good job." Dan walked around the walls of the cave. "I don't find any tracks. Only scuff marks from the crates."

"Will, how many crates were there?" asked Baker.

"We couldn't tell for sure. It was too dark to count, but there weren't too many, maybe eight or ten. Two men could haul them up and load them on a wagon in half a day."

Will led the way out of the cave, and Pa and the sergeant followed him. Two Feathers waved for Will to go ahead and hung back in the cave opening. He walked out slowly, studying the ground. At the entrance, he knelt behind a boulder alongside the opening for a minute, then rose and joined Will.

Will stood with his hands on his hips and stared up at his father. "Pa, an army soldier was murdered on our ranch. I don't like this one bit."

Pa grunted deep in his throat. "I don't like it myself."

"What are we gonna do about it?"

Sergeant Baker pushed himself off the boulder and walked to the rope hanging down from the juniper tree.

"*You* aren't going to do anything about it," Baker said. "This is army business, and we'll take care of it."

Reaching high, he grabbed ahold of the rope and climbed up the bluff. Pa followed, but Two Feathers stopped Will.

"Come. I have something to show you."

They knelt where the boulder touched the sidewall of the cave, making a narrow V-shaped space sheltered from the wind. Two Feathers pointed to a boot heel track in the space—a track with a distinctive notch in it.

Will jumped to his feet. "Two Feathers, why didn't you show this to the sergeant? Or Pa?"

"No, not yet." Two Feathers stared intently at Will.

"Why not? What's wrong?"

"Sergeant Baker said this is army business. Not ours."

"Yes, but this is important."

"I do not trust soldiers. This same track was at the fort in the wagon yard. It was an old track, faint, but not an army boot. I saw it beside the back steps of the store. The same piece is missing in this track, like it was carved out with a knife."

"So?" Irritation slipped into Will's voice. "It's still important."

"Will!" Pa yelled from the canyon rim, his voice impatient.

"Come on. We need to get these supplies back to the ranch. What are you boys doing down there?"

Will headed for the ropes, but Two Feathers stopped him again at the base of the bluff.

"There may be a bad man in the fort of the whites. We do not know who he is. We must be careful. Soldiers cannot be trusted."

YELLOW HAWK

Two Feathers hauled himself up the rope and Will followed, scrambling over the rim of the canyon wall in time to see Pa step on the wheel hub and settle himself on the wagon seat. They walked toward their horses, tied to the back of the wagon. Sergeant Baker stopped next to Pa, and they shook hands.

"It's a shame we didn't find more evidence of what happened here," Pa said. "This is bad business. The Indians are enough of a worry. Now we have a murderer and thieves."

The sergeant nodded, frowning. He shook Will's hand and nodded to Two Feathers, who hung back away from the soldiers.

"You boys be careful and keep a sharp lookout."

With their empty wagon, the sergeant and his troopers headed back toward the fort.

The mound of rocks with its sick smell of death stuck in Will's thoughts. He couldn't rub that smell out of his nose or clear it from the back of his throat. *Why was that man killed?* he wondered. *Who was Private Tucker? Why were soldiers out here without the army knowing anything about it?*

Buck blew and shook his head, rattling the bit in his mouth. Will pulled Buck's head down and patted his jowl. Buck snuffled his shirt and pushed at Will's chest.

"You don't like it either, do you? Let's get out of here."

Two Feathers mounted Gray Wolf and leaned over to Will.

"This is not a good place. I want to go."

Leaving the place of death behind them, they followed Pa home.

Spring moved into early summer, and while Will and Two Feathers checked their herd every few days they kept a sharp lookout for tracks of horses and wagons moving on the desert or soldiers checking for . . . he didn't know what they'd be checking for. All he knew was he didn't want any more stolen army supplies on the Pecos River Ranch.

One day early in June, he and Two Feathers were working at the creek, making adobe bricks with Mateo, a neighboring rancher who often helped them. Knowing Mateo's younger sons traveled around Puerto de Luna with their herds of goats and sheep, Will wondered if he knew anything.

"Mateo, Pa told you about the army supplies we found. Have you or your family seen any strangers in wagons around here or Puerto de Luna? Maybe tracks or campsites?"

"No, chico. We see no strangers. We see no wagons." Mateo handed Will more empty brick molds. "It is a bad thing to steal. My niños stay close to the hacienda. They do not go far."

After lunch, lying in the creek next to Two Feathers, Will felt the cool water carry away the grit and sweat from the morning's work on the house. It eased his aching body. Every muscle in his arms and shoulders ached from the strain of days lifting adobe bricks up to Pa and Mateo. But brick by brick, the walls of their house rose higher. Will lifted his head to a more comfortable position so the water could flow around his sore neck.

"Pa's been in a crazy hurry these last weeks to get the house finished. He's workin' himself and us all the time. I hope I never see another adobe brick."

There was no answer from Two Feathers.

"He acts like everything needs to be done right now. Telling him to slow down, that we have all summer, makes him push harder."

Still no answer from Two Feathers.

"At this pace, I might not live till August to see twelve." Will splashed a double handful of water over his face. "Do Comanche men work this hard to make their tepees?"

Will lifted his head off the flat rock high enough to see Two Feathers, but not enough to pull his sore shoulders out of the slow current of water. No wonder his adopted brother hadn't answered. He was belly down, draped over a half submerged log, with his head under the water. His dark-brown hair, loosed from its long braids, floated on the surface of the creek.

Two Feathers's head popped up, and he sucked in a huge gulp of air. Then he flopped over on his back and immediately ducked back under to let the water sweep his hair out of his face.

"Did you speak?" he finally said.

"Yes, I did. Do Comanche men work this hard to make their tepees?"

Two Feathers lifted his head from the log, one eyebrow cocked. "Comanche men do not put up tepees. The women set the poles and cover them with the buffalo skins. That is woman's work." He rested his head back on the log, and the water rushed over him. "White men work too hard. I remember Ma scolding Pa when he helped her with her woman's work, but he always said her smile made him want to do more."

The sun broke through the canopy of leaves overhead. Will closed his eyes in frustration.

"I guess we better get busy. Pa wants the brush cleared from the creek bed so we can dig the irrigation ditch to water the garden."

He waded to the bank and stepped out of the water. Two Feathers followed and picked up the machete Mateo had taught him to use.

"It is good to clear brush. Then there is no place for an enemy to hide."

Will sliced his machete through saplings growing along the creek bank. *Enemies. I guess now we have new enemies—murderers and thieves.* He wondered if Sergeant Baker had learned anything about the murder or the stolen supplies. It had been several weeks, and they hadn't seen anyone from the fort.

By the time the sun settled in the orange and deep pink of the western clouds, the boys had cleared several yards on both sides of the creek. Sitting under a cottonwood tree, Will scraped mud off his boots and Two Feathers counted the blisters on his hands.

"If your Pa keeps working us this hard, I may go back to the Comanche."

Will looked up. The crinkles at the corners of Two Feathers's eyes took the bite out of his words.

"You go if you want to." Will laughed and gave Two Feathers a shove that nearly landed him in the creek. "Don't run into Yellow Hawk. I don't want to have to rescue you."

The laughter faded from his voice. "A week as a slave in his camp was enough for me."

Two Feathers braided the turkey feathers back into his long hair.

"I think we have both had enough of Yellow Hawk."

Early the next morning, in the cave house they had lived in all winter, Will woke to the sound of the coffee pot hitting the table with a loud clunk. He opened one eye.

"Pa, what are you doing?"

"I'm making coffee. Get up. The sun won't wait for a lazy boy."

Will groaned. Pulling the rough wool blanket over his head, he curled into a ball.

"But today is *Sunday*. Aren't we supposed to rest on Sundays?"

"We'll have plenty of time to rest this winter. Summers are shorter here than in Texas, and we have twice the work to do."

The blanket was yanked off and dropped at his feet.

"Drink this." Pa shoved a cup of steaming-hot coffee under his nose. "You'll feel better in a bit."

Will took the cup, trying not to burn himself with the hot brew.

"Where's Two Feathers?"

Will stumbled to the table, coffee in one hand, his pants in the other, shaking one leg of his long johns down from his knee.

"He's saddling the horses. Get your britches on and eat breakfast. I want to get the brush corral patched up. We need it to hold the heifers."

He set a plate in front of Will loaded with scrambled eggs and salt pork dredged in cornmeal and fried crisp. Two Feathers walked in the door and slipped into his chair in time to take his plate from Pa.

"It's gettin' dry." Pa put his plate on the table with one hand and pulled his chair under his backside with the other. "The berm to hold the irrigation water in the garden needs to be finished. Fresh corn and squash will be good this summer, and they need a lot of water."

"Pa," Will asked between mouthfuls, "is something bothering you?"

Pa frowned. "What do you mean?"

"You're working like crazy. You don't ever want to stop. It's . . . it's like you have to finish everything right now. Like . . . like tomorrow will be too late."

Will ducked his eyes to his cup and took a sip. He caught Two Feathers's eyes with a help-me-out look. Two Feathers watched Pa.

"I see you staring way off," Two Feathers added, "at nothing. Your eyes not seeing."

Pa held his cup to his lips and blew. Circles spread over the dark liquid.

"Remember when you saw your ma in a dream when Yellow Hawk held you captive in his camp?"

Will's heart jolted when he saw the emptiness in Pa's eyes. He nodded and studied Pa's face. The sun-browned skin was rough under the stubble of his beard, and there was gray in his whiskers and hair. The sight of it startled Will. It was not supposed to be there. Where had it come from? Pa's next words gave his heart another kick.

"Well, she hasn't visited me, but she calls my name."

Will laid his fork on his plate. His head felt woozy. Two Feathers's fork froze in midair.

Will sucked in a deep breath. "What do you mean, Pa?"

"I'll be working on something, my mind busy with what I'm doing, and suddenly she'll call my name."

"You hear her?" Will stirred the eggs on his plate. He'd lost his appetite.

"I don't hear her with my ears. She's inside my head. She speaks my name inside my head."

Two Feathers pushed his plate away. "A vision. Only you don't see—you hear."

"Yes. It makes me stop what I'm doing and look for her." He stood and picked up the coffee pot from the stove. "Grief is an odd thing, boys. It plays with your mind." He filled his cup and sat back down at the table. "We don't have time to sit around talking nonsense. We have work to do."

No one got up from the table.

"Maybe you need a vision quest. Let the Great Spirit speak to your heart. Then you will understand what path you should take." He studied Pa's eyes. "Then you will know your heart."

"What's a vision quest?" Will asked. "What are you talking about?"

"It is a time when the spirits speak to you. A time when a vision appears to you and you learn what path you will take in life. I will soon be thirteen summers. I must make my quest before the cold winds blow."

When Two Feathers left to bring up the horses, Will cleared the plates from the table and tried to clear his mind of visions.

"Pa, you're missin' Ma. That's all it is. We were so busy over the winter, you haven't had time to think about both her and the ranch. There's no need to get everything done right now."

"There's so much you need to know, Will. This is hard country. You need to be able to run this ranch if something happens to me. You need to be able to stand alone."

"I know, Pa. I've wanted to talk to you about that. I don't want you to make a big decision again without talking it over with me."

"I told you I had to sell the ranch in Texas quickly. Goodnight was making the drive in a matter of days, and I had to act fast to be ready to come to New Mexico with him."

"I understand that. I had to grow up when Yellow Hawk took Buck and me. I'll be twelve this summer. I've seen kids my age working on ranches. Even though I'm not tall like you, I'm not a kid anymore. I don't just want to do what you tell me. I want to know what to do *before* you tell me. I want to learn how to run our ranch. I want to be a real partner."

Pa went to the stove and refilled his coffee cup, again. He stood at the window and stared out over the desert.

Will sat at the table with Pa's words about the Texas ranch still in his thoughts. Then "stand alone" popped from the back of his mind. *Why did he say "alone"? I'm not alone.* A sprinkle of uneasiness, like cold fat drops of rain before a thunderstorm, hit him. But before he could think about them, Pa walked to the table, stuck his hand out, and Will grabbed it.

"You have a deal, son. You're now a full working partner and decision maker."

They each gave a firm shake. Will tried hard to keep a serious expression, but his cheeks wouldn't cooperate. The smile felt good.

Will heard Two Feathers bring Buck, Gray Wolf, and Pa's sorrel, Rojo, to the rail outside the front door. He swallowed the last of his coffee and dropped his cup in the dishpan.

"Let's go," he said. "If we don't hurry, the sun will beat us to the brush corral."

Will stepped up onto the rail, swung his leg over the saddle, and rode ahead of Pa and Two Feathers.

By late afternoon, the three returned to the ranch yard. Will noticed weary lines sagging on the others' dust-streaked faces and bet he looked the same. Dark blotches of sweat soaked their shirts. Mateo and his crew greeted them from the shade of a juniper tree.

"Señor." Mateo waved his arm at the adobe house. "It is finished."

Will dropped from Buck, stood with both hands on his hips, and laughed.

"I don't think it's finished. There's no roof."

"Sí, that is so. The walls are finished, but not the roof. We must cut logs for the roof."

"How long will it take to get the logs?"

"It will not take long. But first, we must have the quinceañera for my daughter. She is fifteen. You and your boys must come to the quinceañera. Mucho food. Mucho fun. Mucho dancing."

"To a party?" Excitement mixed with fear added a squeak to Will's voice. "Pa? Are we going?"

Two Feathers took Buck's reins from Will and headed for the barn. Pa flipped Will's hat off and tousled his hair.

"Of course we'll go."

"To a real party?" Panic shrank Will's stomach like a dried apple. "I've never been to a real party?"

"Bueno, amigo." Mateo's booming laughter brought a frown to Will and a grin to Pa. "In two days, you come. We will eat. We will dance with the pretty girls."

Dancing?! Will's ears burned. *With pretty girls?!* Will looked down at his scuffed boots. *I can't dance. What am I going to do?*

Two days later, Two Feathers watched as Will and Pa rode toward Puerto de Luna and left the Pecos River Ranch in his hands. He had laughed at Will's constant complaining about having to go to the dance while working to get his best clothes washed, ironed, and carefully packed in his saddlebags, his boots polished to a bright shine and hanging from the saddle horn, and his hat brushed till no dust could be found. Through all the preparations, he had begged Two Feathers to come with them. And complained about girls.

But the only girl that came to Two Feathers's thoughts was Red Wing, his childhood friend from the village of Yellow Hawk. He remembered the games they played on the open plains and along creek beds when his aunt, Weeping Woman, sent them to pick up buffalo chips and fill water pouches. He had not thought of her for such a long time. Will's fussing about girls brought her to his mind. Where was she? Last fall, the colonel at the fort told them the army took Yellow Hawk and his band to a reservation across the Red River. Yellow Hawk would not live in a place like Fort Sumner. The Navajo might have to stay and starve, but not Yellow Hawk.

Two Feathers shook the thought of girls from his head and picked up his machete. Pa had told him to clear more of the brush along the banks farther upstream from their garden. He wanted to make brush dams in two places, to create pools to hold water in dry weather and to make fishing ponds. *Fish! Why does the white man want to eat fish? It is not food for a Comanche.*

The morning hours passed while Two Feathers worked in the company of two woodpeckers and a very angry squirrel, which chattered and scolded from the safety of tree branches. A rabbit scampered from a log near the creek bank and ran off. Rubbing his sore hands, Two Feathers grinned at the small furry critter.

"Do not worry, my little friend. I will not disturb your log."

He sat on the bank and soaked the heat from his hands in the cool water. Happy sounds returned to the woods—the twitter of birds in the trees, the scurrying of small animals in the underbrush. He lay down in the shade and watched the clouds float by through the swaying, dancing leaves of the trees overhead.

The light splash of water—the clip of hoof on stone—the low murmur of voices stilled the woods. Two Feathers shimmied silently up the bank and behind the rabbit's log. A rider appeared from around the curve of the creek. His horse was wet above his knees, so Two Feathers knew he had come up the creek bed. One of the riders was terrifyingly familiar.

Yellow Hawk! The boy dropped his head into the crook of his elbow to stifle a gasp. *My father's murderer.* Fear froze him to the ground. Hatred filled him and oozed through his skin like sweat. He drew in a long, slow breath but dared not move to get in a better position to watch, for even a small noise might bring the war chief down on him. He knew Yellow Hawk would kill him. Lifting his head enough to see around the log, he watched Running Wolf ride up behind Yellow Hawk. Two Feathers struggled to stifle a growl when Barks Like Coyote also rode up. He lay still, barely breathing, listening.

"No men. No horses. No dunnia. The horse-with-black-mane-and-tail must have gone with the white boy. We will wait. I will kill the white boy. This time, Running Wolf, you will not stop me. The dunnia is a war chief's horse. Not for a small white boy with no strength in his body. I am a war chief."

Hearing the low, flint-hard tone Yellow Hawk's voice sank into when he was angry filled Two Feathers with so much fear and hatred he could not swallow.

The Comanche followed the creek toward the Pecos. When Two Feathers was sure they were far enough away, he rose from the log. Wading into the water, he studied the tracks the three Comanche left in the bottom of the creek before the water washed them away. In Comanche, the words Yellow Hawk spewed from his lips and he spat on the ground.

He who is no longer my uncle.

Two Feathers stood still for several minutes as the cold water swirled around his ankles and fear held him frozen. Stumbling, he waded out of the water and hurried to Gray Wolf, hidden safely around a bend in the creek. Two Feathers followed the three warriors.

From a stand of cottonwoods, he watched them cross the Pecos where the creek flowed into the river. His eyes followed them until they disappeared into the distance. Yellow Hawk was gone, but in the dust of his passing trailed death.

RED MESA

Late the next afternoon, Will and Pa rode into the ranch yard. All was quiet. Will swung a leg over the saddle and dropped to the ground. Pa handed his reins to Will.

"Give me your saddlebags and put the horses in the barn. Brush 'em good and give 'em a bit of grain."

Will looked around the yard. "I wonder where Two Feathers is? Do you think he went hunting? I'm so hungry, I could eat a bear, hair and all."

"Hungry? How could you possibly be hungry?" Pa shook his head and squinched up his forehead. "I don't have any idea where you put all the food you ate at the party last night."

"I burned it up dancing with the girls."

Leading the horses behind him and holding the reins in his widespread arms like a partner, Will danced his way into the barn part of their cave.

After feeding the horses, he latched the barn door and walked into the kitchen area. He pulled a chair from under the table, spun it around, and sat with his arms crossed on its back.

"Pa, Gray Wolf's not in the barn. I don't think he's been here all day. Not only was there no water in the bucket, it's as dry as an alkali flat. I made two trips to the creek to get enough water for Buck and Rojo."

"Bring in wood." Pa opened the stove and stirred the dead coals. "I'll start a fire. If he's hunting, we'll have a fire ready to cook supper."

Will and Pa unpacked their saddlebags, put everything away, and started to make a supper of jerky and leftover cold biscuits when they heard Gray Wolf lope into the yard. Will bolted out the door.

"You should've come with us. I had the best time. There were so many pretty girls. I . . . Two Feathers? What's wrong?"

Two Feathers dropped off Gray Wolf. Sucking in a deep breath, he handed the reins to Will.

"Here, feed him for me. I have much to tell you and Pa."

Two Feathers pulled two jackrabbits off the horse. At the cave door, he dropped the rabbits and scooped a double handful of water from the bucket sitting outside to wash his face and hands. Pa stepped out and handed him a towel.

"You all right, boy? Are you hurt?"

Two Feathers glanced toward Will. "Yellow Hawk! He found us."

Pa blew out a long, slow breath. "General Carleton told us last fall the army took Yellow Hawk's band east to the Nations. Could it have been someone else?"

"I saw him. He either escaped or they never caught him."

Pa picked up the rabbits and handed them to Two Feathers. "Clean these. Will, feed Gray Wolf, and I'll make fresh biscuits. We'll talk about Yellow Hawk after supper."

Will's feet wouldn't move. His eyes wouldn't blink. His lungs wouldn't breathe. *Yellow Hawk! Here!* His heart raced like an antelope.

"Will!" Pa snapped. "Go."

Will jerked, shook himself, and led Gray Wolf inside the barn half of the cave.

After the last cup was washed and hung on its hook and the last plate stacked on the shelf, Will, Pa, and Two Feathers sat around the table in the glow of the lantern. Two Feathers told them he'd seen Yellow Hawk, Running Wolf, and Barks Like Coyote at the creek the day before and what he had heard his uncle say. When he finished talking, no one spoke, no one moved. The silence hung in the room until Two Feathers continued.

"I left early this morning, way before the sun showed any light. I crossed the Pecos and went southeast in a wide circle away from their trail. I did not want Yellow Hawk to see Gray Wolf's tracks. When the sun crossed the sky, past what you call noon, I found a dry creek and followed it east. It started to show water, and I spotted unshod tracks. Yellow Hawk's camp was up an arroyo. I did not get close."

"You're sure it was Yellow Hawk's camp? Did you see his tracks? You said you didn't get close." Will sucked hard to pull enough air into his lungs.

Two Feathers nodded.

The blood drained from Will's head, and his stomach churned as though it had pooled there. No one spoke. The longer they sat, the louder the tick-tock of the clock on the mantel grew. Pa cleared his throat twice.

"Boys, Yellow Hawk is our enemy. We've lived with that since the first day he spotted Buck. But, he doesn't rule how we live."

"That's right, Pa," Will said, his voice strained. A long, deep breath that stretched his lungs steadied him. "I don't want him to stop us from building the Pecos River Ranch."

"We'll take precautions." Pa's eyes focused first on Will, then on Two Feathers with an intensity Will had not seen before. "Never go anywhere alone. Stay alert. Check for tracks."

"We know, Pa." Will reached across the table and squeezed Pa's forearm.

Two Feathers's eyes flared, then faltered and filmed over. Will couldn't decide if what he saw in those eyes was anger or fear or both.

That night Will lay awake for a long time in his bunk. Memories of his captivity in Yellow Hawk's camp tormented him and drove sleep further and further away. The long days of riding Buck bareback without stopping for water or food. His attempts to keep the furious Indian from harming Buck. The beatings. Then, the horror of the race to escape when Yellow Hawk nearly caught up with him and Two Feathers on the desert. The terrifying sound of Two Feathers's wild war cry.

Finally, Will slept. From the void, far in the distance, was the faint sound of hoof beats. A horse approached through the swirling, murky fog—Buck. Paint covered his body. One side yellow. One side black. A painted Comanche rode him. One side yellow. One side black. They blended, as if they were one being. Will whistled for Buck, but no sound came from his dry lips. Buck rode over him, knocking him to the ground. Will jumped up and watched him gallop away. Yellow Hawk pulled the horse to a stop and spun Buck around to face Will, raising a rifle in his fist and shrieking his fierce war cry. Buck reared on his hind legs. His loud scream yanked Will from sleep, and he leaped from his bed.

He raced out the door of the living part and into the barn area of their cave home. Buck stood in his stall, sleeping. Will buried his face in the long dark mane, breathing in the familiar dusty smell. Wrapping his arms around the strong, muscular neck, he hung on. Buck nickered softly.

"You want to know what's the matter, don't you? Well, I had a bad dream."

He let go of Buck's neck and reached up. Buck lowered his head, and Will scratched behind his ears in the horse's favorite spot.

"You know what, Buck? I think I'll stay with you for what's left of tonight."

He spread Buck's saddle blanket on the straw and stretched out. Soon horse and boy slept, secure in each other's presence.

In the weeks that followed, they saw no signs of Yellow Hawk. Will worked with Pa and Two Feathers on the ranch and house, with one of them always on lookout.

The cool of morning faded into the afternoon heat. Will threw another sapling on the travois already filled with trees of various widths. He and Pa had built the travois from two long poles lashed together with three crossbars, and Will pulled it behind a horse. Two Feathers pitched another slim tree his way, and Will sliced off the branches and twigs with a few well-placed swings of the machete. The load on the travois slowly grew until the whole pile threatened to spill off.

"I think I am going back to the Comanche. I will leave in the morning. I am too tired to go right now." Two Feathers dropped his machete and sat in the shade of a cottonwood.

"You say that every day, but you're still here." Will collapsed beside him.

"I would be mad at your Pa for working us so hard, but he works harder than we do."

Two Feathers plucked twigs out of his long braids and smoothed the feathers hanging in his hair.

"I think he's trying to work me to death before I turn twelve."

A large blister puffed the palm of Will's hand. He poked at it—gently.

"We better get back. You know what happens when we're gone too long. Ever since you saw Yellow Hawk, Pa comes huntin' us, madder than a grizzly with a sore tooth."

Will led the horse, and Two Feathers followed behind the travois, picking up fallen saplings and tossing them back on the pile. When they came out of the trees, Will saw Pa on the ladder halfway to the roof of their adobe house, handing a bundle of the slender poles up to Mateo. The grin on Pa's face was a welcome sight. Will hoped it meant they were through for the day. He handed the reins to Two Feathers, unhooked the travois, and helped Lupe unload. The Mexican's "Muy bueno" and a chopping motion of his hands told Will their job was done. Pa and Mateo climbed down the ladder.

"Lupe said we've cut enough." Will plopped to the ground. "What else do we have to do?"

Mateo's laugh boomed before Pa could answer. "Ah, muchacho. Now the fun begins."

Will didn't like the sound of that. "What do you mean, *fun*?"

The man's black eyes sparkled. "We make the barro."

"What's that?"

"Mud," said Pa. "We mix the adobe mud and spread it over the saplings."

Two Feathers's head and shoulders drooped. He led the horse toward the barn.

"I think I am going back to the Comanche."

Pa looked at Will, and surprise popped his eyebrows straight up.

Will rolled his eyes. "He says that every day we work on the house."

Buckets of sweat, too many blisters, and a week into July they finished the house. Mateo and Lupe headed back to Puerto de Luna, promising to return with furniture to make the new house a home. Moving the furniture and belongings from the cave house to the adobe house was short work. The table and chairs fit in the kitchen, but the emptiness of the large living room felt lonely. The beds Lupe made with Alma's new mattresses filled the bedroom. By the time they arranged their belongings on the shelves and hung their clothing on the pegs in the wall, the room felt cozy and comfortable. Pa had taken their quilts out of the trunks where he'd stored them when they left Texas and aired them in the sunshine. The colorful patterns brightened their bunks, and the smooth cotton cloth felt good against Will's skin. He decided a soft quilt beat a scratchy wool blanket any day. Will settled onto his fluffy new mattress. The fresh straw and corn husk stuffing rustled with a crisp sound. Even after sleeping on his new mattress for several nights, the fresh straw still rustled.

Daylight jabbed at Will's eyelids. The smell of bacon nudged his nose. He sat up, rubbed his eyes, and stretched. *A real bed. A real mattress. A real house. It's been a long time coming.* He dressed and followed the aroma of frying bacon and boiling coffee to the kitchen. Pa stood at the stove, and he laughed when he saw Will.

"We've lived in a house now for several weeks. We're not camping on the hard ground or living in a cave like a grizzly bear. Don't you think you could comb your hair? First chance we have, you're gettin' a haircut."

Will combed at his hair with his fingers, smoothing it down.

"Pa, do you know nearly a year has passed since we left our ranch in Texas?"

Pa nodded and took the Dutch oven filled with hot biscuits to the table.

"Yep. We've come a long way in a year. But we have busy days in front of us. Lots to do. "

Two Feathers came in the back door.

"Horses are ready."

He filled his plate, his cup, and his mouth.

"John," Will shook his head at his brother, "you can eat more than anyone I've ever seen."

Two Feathers frowned. "I am Two Feathers, except when at the fort of the whites. A Comanche warrior needs a Comanche name."

"But you ain't no Comanche warrior, yet," Will sassed in a sing-song voice. "You're a cowhand, like me."

He caught the biscuit Two Feathers threw at him, popped it into his mouth, and darted out the back door. With a loud *whoop,* Two Feathers jumped on Will's back, and they spilled to the ground, tumbling in a ball of arms and legs.

"Hey!" Pa shouted. "That's a fine way to start a workday— rolling in the dirt."

The stern expression on his face didn't fool either boy, but they brushed themselves off and mounted their horses. Buck humped his back and pranced in a circle.

"Whoa, Buck. You want to wrestle too?" Will patted his neck. "Pa says this is no time to play, so get serious."

"Listen up, you two." Pa's smile lightened the sternness of his words. "I want us to stay together today. We won't be able to cover as much ground, but it will be safer that way. Charlie Goodnight should be coming in a week or so with the herd from Texas. I want to have our steers ready to ship north with him."

"It will take us twice as long to bring the cattle in if we stay together," said Will. "Why don't we split up but stay within the sound of a rifle? If we find trouble, we'll fire a shot, and you can come runnin'."

"No!" Pa's set eyes matched his firm tone. "Yellow Hawk knows where we are. We never know when he'll decide to come back."

"If I'm gonna be a partner, I should have a say in this. I don't like running into Yellow Hawk any more than you do. We already know Buck can outrun any of his horses. And Gray Wolf is almost as fast as Buck. We can meet up around noon at the brush corral, make a count, and then head out again." Will wished his heart felt as brave as his voice sounded.

"I trailed him east of the Pecos a good way." Two Feathers glanced at Will. "The land on the other side of the river is flat. We can see far."

"Pa, I know you're worried about us. But it's nearly August, and I'll be twelve then. I'm not a kid. You said I had to learn to run this ranch. I can't learn with you doing all the work and me tagging behind you all the time."

Frowning, Pa looked off toward the Pecos and resettled his hat on his head.

"Okay, I'll circle wide to the northwest. Two Feathers, you bring in any cattle you find going due west, and Will, you gather any between here and the corral. If either of you gets into any trouble, you'll be making—"

"There's no more adobe bricks to make," Will said. "You'll have to think of something new."

Will gave Buck a whoop, and the big stallion jumped into a run.

The noon sun found Will and Two Feathers swinging the heavy gate shut as Pa drove the last of the cattle he'd gathered into the brush corral to join those the boys had penned. The longhorns either spread out to graze on the lush green grass of the enclosed meadow or headed for the cool water of the lake.

"I swept the country close in and brought in all I found." Will's confidence in a job well done showed in his business-like voice. "Two Feathers said he spotted a big bunch down an arroyo in a mesquite thicket. We're going to get them after lunch."

Pa nodded. "Okay. I left several grazing in a good-sized buffalo wallow. I'll go back for them."

Two Feathers led all three horses to the lake for water, Will gathered firewood, and Pa dug coffee and the pot out of his saddlebag. It didn't take long for the welcome aroma of boiling coffee to make all three dig in their packs for cups.

"How many more do you think are still out?" Will asked.

He used his bandana to grab the hot handle of the coffee pot and poured each of them a cup of steaming Arbuckle's. Two Feathers handed out cold biscuits, jerky, and cheese from a canvas bag Pa had hung from his saddle horn.

"I'd say we have most of 'em. These last two bunches should be it. We kept them pretty well gathered through the winter. They haven't strayed far."

Pa stood, stretched his back till it popped, and walked away from the fire toward the grazing cattle. Will followed him.

"What do you think, Pa? I think they're pretty good."

Will and Pa watched the cattle spread across the pasture enclosed by the high sandstone bluffs.

"They do." He sipped his coffee. "We didn't lose but a few this past winter. The rest fattened up over the summer."

"Look over there, Pa." Will pointed to a small bunch of heifers. "See that brindle heifer? I think we should keep her. She'd make a mighty good momma."

"I think you're right, Will. There are several here that will make good mommas. Come on." He pitched the dregs of his coffee on the ground. "We have a lot to do to be ready when Charlie comes. Let's break camp and go after those last two bunches."

Will and Two Feathers found the arroyo with about ten cows, some with calves, and several yearlings grazing between its banks.

"Two Feathers," Will spoke softly. "See that cow with the cock-eyed horn? The one holding her head up, sniffin'? She's spotted us. Circle away from the edge of the arroyo and get ahead of her. If that crazy cow figures out what we're doing, she'll spook and take off runnin'. The others will follow her, and there's no telling when or where they'll stop. I'll wait at the end of this gully and turn them south when they come out."

Two Feathers stood in his stirrups and looked down the arroyo. "Those banks are steep. What if Gray Wolf won't go over the edge?"

Will raised his eyebrows. "Are you kidding? Buck won't, but that horse of yours would jump off a cliff if you asked him to. You'll get down. Go! Don't spook 'em and get them runnin'. I don't want them bursting out of here in a stampede."

A short time later, Will heard the plop of hooves in the dust and horns clacking together. He backed Buck away from the arroyo and behind a mesquite bush. After the leader was clear of the opening, he headed Buck at a slow walk alongside her. She veered away from him and headed the way Will wanted her to go. He kept his eye on the crazy heifer, but she seemed to be settled down and moved in the middle of the line. Will let the cattle pass, and Two Feathers caught up with him.

"Will, I spotted unshod horse tracks in that arroyo."

Will stopped Buck and gripped the saddle horn till his hands ached.

"Yellow Hawk?"

"No. The tracks were several days old and faded. I did not see any I knew. We are a long way from where I saw Yellow Hawk's camp. They might be Apache."

"Oh, is that supposed to make me feel better?" Will shook his head, and his mouth twisted into a grimace. "Well, it doesn't. Let's get out of here."

He urged Buck after the cattle. Two Feathers rode Gray Wolf to the opposite side of the bunch. Will's eyes didn't stop scanning the land around them until they drove the cattle to the brush corral. Before Will shut the heavy gate, he heard more cattle coming. Pa pushed the last of their wayward animals through the opening and helped Will drag the gate closed.

Two Feathers stacked twigs and struck a match to start the fire, but Pa said, "No time for coffee now, boys. You're not going to believe what I found near that buffalo wallow. Mount up, and I'll show you."

He started back the way he had come, but Will called to him.

"Wait, Pa. Two Feathers found unshod tracks."

Pa jerked his horse around. "Where? Yellow Hawk's?"

"No." Two Feathers rode up beside him. "Might be Apache. They were not fresh."

"Apache?! That's all we need. Old tracks. Hmm. Can't be helped. We'll keep a sharp lookout. Come on. You have to see this."

After an hour at a steady pace, Pa and the boys pulled up at the buffalo wallow not far from a red mesa rising from the desert floor. Fanning out from the steep wall lay scattered boulders and slabs of rock broken off the sides of the mesa. Pa circled to the back edge of the wallow and pointed to the ground.

"Wagon tracks!" Will tapped Buck, and they followed the trail. "What's a wagon doing out here in the middle of no-where?"

Pa rode ahead of the boys. "That's what I want to know. Come on. See that dark spot at the base of the mesa? The tracks go straight to it."

They rode around and between slabs of red rock and brown boulders. Soon the ground was too cluttered for a wagon, and the tracks stopped. They dismounted and scrambled up a short incline to a broad overhang. And under the overhang, they found piles of flour sacks, bales of blankets and crates stamped U.S. Army.

SECOND STASH

Will pulled the wagon of recovered army supplies to a stop in front of Colonel Dowell's office. The dawn-to-dark ride the day before collecting the cattle, loading the stolen goods on the wagon, and traveling till nearly midnight had left Will exhausted. This morning, he felt stiff and sore from spelling Pa on the wagon seat for the last several miles to the fort. Two Feathers had dozed on the seat beside him off and on during the morning and jumped down when the wagon stopped. Will stomped his feet before he risked climbing down. He untied Buck from the rear of the wagon and tied him beside Rojo at the hitching rail. Two Feathers slipped his turkey feathers between the blankets on the wagon seat and headed to the sutler's store, tucking his braids under his hat.

Captain Stanaway walked out of his office, and the pounding of his boots down the sidewalk made Will uneasy.

"What's going on, Mr. Whitaker? These are army supplies."

Stepping on a wheel hub, he leaned over the side rails. It groaned and squeaked under the additional weight. Each time he lifted, shifted, or shoved the goods stacked in the wagon bed, he shot Pa a hard look. When he reached the tailgate, his lips pressed tight and his jaw clenched. He jumped from the wagon.

"There are sacks of flour and cornmeal, bags of rice, and bales of blankets. Where'd you get this?" Suspicion laced his words.

"In a cut-bank at the base of a mesa about ten miles from our ranch headquarters." Pa's voice held an edge.

"Your ranch again, Mr. Whitaker?" Stanaway cocked his head to the side, leaned his back against the wagon, and folded his arms across his chest. "Mmm, that's quite a coincidence, don't you think?"

"Wait a minute." Will stepped beside Pa. "What are you saying?" He couldn't believe what he heard. It was not only far-fetched but unthinkable.

"First you tell us you found hidden supplies, but there were none. Now you bring the supplies to the fort. Maybe you gave up a little profit to prove you're an honest citizen. You needed to persuade the army to hunt some place other than your ranch for your nest of thieves."

Anger sped blood through Will's body till the veins in his neck bulged, and his face pulsed hot. His hands fisted and rose in a fighter's stance.

"You think we stole these supplies?" Will knew, in Captain Stanaway's mind, the unthinkable had become—thinkable.

"Hold on." Pa grabbed Will's shoulder in a tight grip. Steely flecks glittered in his eyes. "Captain, I'd be careful what I said, if I were you." His words came out in a low, menacing monotone. "What you're saying makes no sense."

Sergeant Baker, followed by Colonel Dowell, came out of the office and down the porch steps. The colonel walked around the wagon and approached Stanaway.

"What's going on out here?"

"It seems Mr. Whitaker brought us army supplies." He shoved himself away from the wagon and stepped in front of Pa. "Just where he's getting them, I . . . don't . . . know." The last three words snapped.

"Stand down, Captain." Colonel Dowell's voice was quiet but firm with authority. He smiled at Will. "Hello, Will. If you and Mr. Whitaker will come into my office, you can tell me where you found them." The look he gave Stanaway told Will the captain would be more cautious with his accusations in the future, at least out loud.

Sergeant Baker offered the two extra chairs in the room to Will and Pa. He didn't bring one for Captain Stanaway. The colonel took his place behind the scarred desk. Collecting the scattered papers into a neat pile, he placed them in a desk drawer.

"Now, gentlemen, tell me how you found these supplies."

"This time I found the cache," Dan said. "We were rounding up stock to be ready for Charlie Goodnight when he brings his herd up from Texas. I saw a bunch grazing in a buffalo wallow about ten miles northwest of the ranch and headed around the backside to get them moving toward our holding area. Imagine my surprise when I came across a set of wagon tracks in the middle of the desert in a spot that is on the way to nowhere."

"There's a big red mesa that pops up out there," said Will, "with steep sides, and the top is as flat as a johnnycake. At the base was a deep undercut full of barrels, bales, and boxes of goods."

Pa shifted in his chair. "I don't understand why the army can't hang onto their supplies. Don't people keep track of shipments coming and going?"

The colonel looked to Stanaway. "Captain?"

"All our supplies come from Fort Union. Captain Inman is the quartermaster there. Ed Franklin is his bookkeeper. The manifests he sends with the supplies match the supplies that arrive. We've never had a problem."

"Thank you, Captain. Have the supplies unloaded from Mr. Whitaker's wagon. You are dismissed."

Stanaway saluted and walked out, his back perfectly straight, his face expressionless.

"Colonel, do you know anything about the other supplies we found or the murdered soldier?" Will asked.

"Not much. Private Tucker was AWOL for days before you found him. I demoted him to private for disorderly conduct over an argument about money. One day he was broke, and a few days later he had plenty of cash. We're trying to find out where he got the extra money. None of his friends seem to know anything about it."

"Or won't say."

Pa stood to go. Colonel Dowell nodded.

"Thank you for bringing in those supplies. They're needed."

Outside, Captain Stanaway stood leaning against the hitching rail where Buck was tied. He stayed just out of the horse's reach. Buck's ears laid flat against his head, and he pawed the ground. His tail swished side to side like a whip. Will jumped off the porch and spoke to the angry horse.

"Whoa, Buck." He stroked the arched neck. "Easy. What's wrong, boy?"

"That stallion is skittish." Stanaway stepped away from the rail and the horse. "I'd sell him if I were you." This time his face held lots of expression, all of it anger. One step up with his long legs, and he stood on the porch. "Sergeant Masters is having Corporal Donley unload your wagon at the warehouse."

The firm clomp of his boots struck the floor as he marched down the boardwalk. He yanked open a door and pulled it shut behind him with a solid thunk.

"Whoa, Buck." Will crooned gently to the horse and stroked his neck. "What happened? What did he do that upset you?" Will looked toward Stanaway's office. "You don't like that man, do you?" He ran his fingers through the long mane. "That's okay. I don't like him either."

Buck's tail stopped its fierce lashing, his ears relaxed, and he dropped his head between Will's raised arms.

"That's better. Come on." Will gave him a quick hug and led him across the compound to the store. "Let's go see what Two Feathers is doing."

He tied Buck next to Gray Wolf, and the friends put their heads together.

Pa finally came out of the colonel's office and joined Will across the compound.

"Pa, I don't like Captain Stanaway. He did something that upset Buck. I want him to stay away from my horse."

"It doesn't matter whether we like him or not. He's in the army and tied to the fort, and we're not. Don't let him worry you."

"He's the quartermaster. Doesn't that mean he is in charge of all the supplies? Maybe he's the one stealing the goods."

"I don't think so, Will. Colonel Dowell and I talked after you left. He respects the job Stanaway is doing."

"I still don't trust him."

They walked into the cool dimness of the sutler's store. Will missed the earthy smell of onions hanging from the ceiling beams. They were all gone. The Navajo's crops had failed once again, this time because of armyworms and their relentless destruction of grass, grain, and crops. Only a few bunches of dried, shriveled peppers hung in the back of the store. The shelves showed bare spots that were not there last spring. Will looked for Two Feathers but didn't see him.

"Pa, my birthday is in a few days. Is there enough money for a skinning knife? I can't do a good job skinning deer with a pocket knife, even one as sharp as mine."

"We've about used up the supplies we bought when we came last spring. Let's see what money is left after we stock up."

"Did you talk to Colonel Dowell about selling the culls to the army? The ones not good enough to go up the trail with Mr. Goodnight?"

Pa nodded. "Yes, I did. We got a fair price." The grins on their faces held a similar slant. "You're right, partner. There should be a couple of extra dollars to get a good skinning knife. A man in wild country needs a good knife."

Taking his list out of his pocket, Pa handed it to the large man behind the counter. Will noticed it was not the same man who had worked there last year or last spring—the one that always looked squinty-eyed at Two Feathers. This one was taller than Pa and barrel-chested. His thick, bushy black beard stuck straight out from his chin and bobbed up and down when he talked.

"Let's see what's here." He took the list and ran his finger down each item as he read. "We're a little short on goods right now, but we can handle all this. I don't believe I've seen you folks in here before. My name is Ben Wallace. I own the place, such as it is."

The man's huge hand nearly swallowed Pa's big one when they shook.

"Dan Whitaker. This is my son, Will."

Will's hand disappeared in Mr. Wallace's enormous grip. Pa glanced around.

"I thought my other son was in here, but I don't see him right now."

"Whitaker? You got a ranch over toward Puerto de Luna, on the Pecos?"

Pulling baking soda off the shelf behind him, he set it on the counter beside a five-pound bag of sugar and five one-pound bags of Arbuckle's coffee.

"That's us," Pa replied.

"Aren't you the folks that found those supplies last spring?"

He checked Pa's list and walked around the counter. With a small wedge, he popped the lid off a barrel and scooped dried pinto beans into a large bag.

"That's us," said Will before Pa answered. "We found another one two days ago while rounding up our cattle. It was northwest of the first one."

Wallace shot Will a startled frown and spilled beans on the floor.

"More army supplies?"

He tapped the lid back onto the barrel, picked up a large sack of flour from a pile nearby, and put both flour and beans on the counter.

"Yes, sir."

"I bet Captain Stanaway is romping, stomping mad about losing supplies."

"No," said Pa. "He said he isn't missing any."

Wallace shrugged his shoulders. "Well, I've never been too sure how good the army keeps track of things." He picked up the list from the counter and read it again. "Let's go to the smokehouse to get the side of bacon. You're lucky. I've got one barrel of salt pork left. Load these supplies in your wagon and come around back. I'll have your meat, and we'll load the horse feed."

Will found the case with the knives. He picked up several and checked their balance and their feel in his hand. One of them wasn't new, but he liked it. The blade was sharp, not too long, and the handle made from bone. He found a basket of scabbards next to the knives and rummaged through them till he found one not too scarred that fit the knife.

Two Feathers walked up next to him.

"What do you think of this knife?" asked Will, handing it to him, handle first.

"Sharp. Heavy. Feels right. You going to buy it?"

"I told Pa I needed one for my birthday, if it doesn't cost too much." He held the knife up to the light. "Maybe we can ask Pa to get you one."

"I have a good knife. Do not need one."

Pa and Wallace came in through the back door. Will showed them the knife and scabbard.

"That's a good knife." The store owner turned it over in his hand. "An old trapper named Badger brought it in here a few days ago." He studied it, rolling it over in his hands, feeling the balance and the sharpness of the blade. "Hmm. I guess I can let it go for . . . two and a half dollars for the knife and four bits for the scabbard."

Pa frowned. Will held his breath, watching Pa.

"Ummm. That's a little steep for me," Pa said. "How about two dollars for the knife and two bits for the scabbard?"

Will's gaze jumped to Mr. Wallace, hoping he'd lower his price. The big man twisted one side of his mouth up, and his beard slid sideways.

"Well, I guess I can let it go for that."

"Add it to the bill," said Pa. "My partner needs a good knife."

Wallace handed it back to Will. "There's no telling where Badger got it. He travels all over this part of the country."

Two Feathers picked up the crate of supplies. Will ran his belt through the slots in the scabbard and slipped the knife in. It felt good against his hip. He flipped the sack of flour over his shoulder and carried it out the back door and into the wagon.

"Boys, Wallace says there's lunch left over. How about we eat, stay here the rest of today, and start back before daybreak tomorrow? We might hear news of Charlie. He should be showing up any day."

"Lunch always sounds good to me," Will said and followed Two Feathers back inside the store.

After finishing a plate of fried salt pork and potatoes boiled with their jackets on, Will sopped up the remaining gravy with several of Mrs. Wallace's fresh tortillas. Then he excused himself and went to the store counter to get stick candy. A Mexican man, who smelled of goats, came into the store. Mr. Wallace greeted him, and a rush of Spanish passed between them. The only word Will understood was "Goodnight."

He waited to buy his candy until the goatherd and Mr. Wallace concluded their business. Before he paid, the storekeeper smiled at him.

"Will, how about a trade?"

"What kind of trade?"

"I'll trade you that candy and throw in another couple of pieces if you'll help us bring in the goat's milk and wheels of cheese from Señor Ortega's wagon."

Will's love for candy was only slightly stronger than his love for cheese.

"Yes, sir. That's a trade."

When he finished, Will hurried back to the lunch table and found Pa finishing the last of several cups of coffee. Two Feathers made a final sweep of his plate with the last bite of his tortilla.

Sliding onto the bench beside Pa, Will said, "I got two kinds of good news. Mr. Wallace got news about Mr. Goodnight." Knowing Pa's love of cheese almost equaled his own, he added with a huge grin, "And you'll never guess what I did."

Pa arched his eyebrows. "Oh?"

"I helped unload a cart of goat's milk."

Pa's nose wrinkled, like he smelled something sour.

"And wheels of fresh cheese."

Pa's face brightened, and a chuckle mingled with his words. "Why don't we add that to our supplies? The cheese, not the goat's milk."

"Good idea."

"Let's go see what Wallace can tell us about Charlie," Pa said and nudged Will off the bench ahead of him. The three of them went to find the storekeeper.

After hearing that Goodnight's herd would arrive within a week, Pa decided to start the trip home that afternoon. They still had a few calves to work, and they needed time to separate the cattle they wanted to send north with Goodnight from the heifers they were keeping.

Pa mounted his horse, and the boys tied theirs to the back of the wagon.

"John, you ridin' in the wagon?" asked Pa.

"Yes, I need to talk to Will."

Will slapped the reins on the backs of the team, and the mules stepped out at a good pace. At first, the boys rode in silence.

"Well," Will finally said, "are you going to tell me what's on your mind or do I have to guess?"

"I saw Na-es-cha."

Will laughed out loud. "So, this is about that girl you met last spring? I told you she was pretty. Where'd you see her?"

"In the barn behind the store."

"Do you like her?"

"What? No! I'm white and Comanche. She hates me. But she's curious about the supplies we brought."

He took his hat off and let his long braids drop. Reaching between the blankets on the wagon seat, he pulled out his turkey feathers and worked their shafts into the braids. Then he secured each with small strips of leather.

"There is something wrong at the fort," Two Feathers said.

"Yes, I'd say that's true. They're losing supplies."

"I saw boot tracks with a chip out of the heel."

Will's eyebrows shot up. "The same one we saw at the cave?"

Will clucked to the mules and flipped the reins. The wagon bounced over the ruts in the road.

"Yes. Na-es-cha likes to be out at night when the air is cool." Two Feathers sat sideways on the bench to face Will. "She knows we found the supplies and the dead soldier. I told her we found more and brought them to the fort. She hopes this means they will get more food."

"Maybe it will."

"One night, a few moons ago, Na-es-cha slipped away from her mother to get biscuits the storekeeper's wife left out at the store. She was afraid to get any earlier in the day because an old trapper was hanging around—a man she had seen in the Comanche camp when she was a prisoner."

"What do you mean a prisoner? Was she captured like I was?"

"Yes, then they traded her back to her people."

Will sat still for several minutes. Memories fought to escape from the corner of his mind, where he kept them locked away. He shook his head, shoved them back down, and said, "What about the trapper?"

"She didn't like him and didn't want him to see her. He came into the store to sell a knife."

"Must be my new knife. Wallace said a man named Badger sold it to him. I didn't know it was a Comanche knife."

"Maybe and maybe not." Two Feathers glanced at the knife on Will's hip. "Na-es-cha stayed in the shadows because she did not want anyone to see her and tell her mother. She started to pass a group of Navajo men who talked around a small fire but feared they'd hear her, so she stopped. One man talked about going across the river and toward the far hills to hunt. He found wagon tracks where no tracks should be."

"Did he say where? Did he tell anyone?"

"No. They do not tell the army anything."

"Did Na-es-cha?"

"No. She fears the soldiers. She told only me."

"Only you?" He poked Two Feathers with his elbow. "Ya know what I think? I think 'hate' is not the right word for how she feels about you."

Two Feathers's gray eyes flashed in irritation. "On the way back with her biscuits, she stopped again to listen to the men. One of them, a young man Na-es-cha knows, talked about slipping away from the reservation. He told the men he wanted to wait a while before leaving because he saw tracks of a band of Comanche warriors. The men talked of the Comanche war chief Yellow Hawk. They thought he might be in this part of New Mexico Territory."

The boys sat stone still on the wagon seat. Neither spoke for a while. The wagon creaked and squeaked down the road.

"Do you think they're right?" Will asked. "Do you think Yellow Hawk's band is back?"

Will slapped the reins on the mule's backs to catch up with Pa.

Two Feathers did not answer for a while. His shoulders slumped, and he sucked in a shuddering breath. His voice dropped to a husky rasp.

"He is back for the dunnia. Back for you. Back for me. Yellow Hawk is back."

P~R BRAND

A week after they returned from Fort Sumner, they started branding the steers for the drive north with Charlie Goodnight. At the brush corral, Will kept the coals in the fire burning and the branding irons a glowing red. The tall walls surrounding the brush corral held the August heat, adding to Will's misery. The constant movement of horses and cattle stirred the dust, and it hung in the air. Will's work gloves chafed his hands, wet from the sweat trapped inside. Mateo hollered. Cattle bawled. A wandering breeze blew during the overcast day, so the smoke followed him no matter which side of the fire he was on. His eyes watered, and his nose ran.

Breaking a branch over his knee, Will added the pieces to the fire. He stepped away to watch Pa and Two Feathers circle the bunched cattle not far from the lake. Their lariats swung in circles over their heads. The cattle moved with wary eyes.

He picked up a branding iron from the coals and stuck it against a branch lying on the ground, burning the P~R into it. At the sight of the sizzling brand, he forgot about the smoke. He forgot about the heat. He forgot about the rank smell of burned hair. Kneeling down and shoving the branding iron back into the bed of red-hot coals, he realized he felt different. P~R—the Pecos River Ranch. His ranch, his brand. Pa wanted just the PR for Pecos Ranch, but Will had insisted on the squiggle in the middle for the river. It made the brand different, harder to change if someone stole their cattle, his cattle—his, Pa's, and Two Feathers's. When he stood back from the fire, pride changed the way the work felt to him. He didn't have to only follow orders. He could do the telling.

Two Feathers rode up on Gray Wolf, pulling a bellowing calf toward the fire. Mateo picked it up by one front and one hind leg and dropped it on its left side. Will slapped the iron to the right hip, leaving their P~R brand. The stench of burning hide and hair assaulted his nose, but no longer made him sick. He raced back to the fire, shoved the used iron in the coals and pulled the hot one out. Pa caught another calf by its heels and dragged it to the fire. With the hiss of the hot iron, Will left his mark. Two Feathers and Pa released their lariats and went after more. Mateo drove the released calf to the gate, and Lupe swung it open. The calves shot through and ran to their mamas, bawling about their rough treatment.

The job went smoothly as long as the calves were small. By afternoon, only the larger steers going north with Goodnight remained. Will didn't think they would like the idea of hot iron and their protesting would be more vigorous—doubly dangerous.

When the last of the smaller calves rushed through the gate, Will walked away from the fire and bellied down on the bank of the lake that filled the middle of the brush meadow. The burn on his wrist, where a protesting calf had kicked the hot iron into his arm, hurt. His face stung from the heat of the branding fire. He buried his head, arms, and shoulders in the cool water. Scrubbing the soot and sweat out of his hair, he pushed himself out of the water and sat up in time to see Two Feathers flop down and dunk his head. Wiping his face with his bandana, he walked to the shade of a piñon tree and dropped to the ground near Pa.

Mateo's oldest son, Cesar, rode through the gate with a bulging burlap sack hanging off his saddle horn. He was taller than Mateo and slim. His arms bulged with muscle, and when he brought the sack to Will and the others under the piñon tree, the rowels in his big spurs jangled when he walked. Tipping his sombrero off his head to hang down his back by the chin strap, he tossed the loaded bag to his father with a burst of Spanish that brought a rumble of laughter from Mateo.

"Amigos, my Alma sent us a feast."

He dug in the sack and pulled out hunks of ham and goat cheese. With his skinning knife, he cut thick slices, wrapped them in big round tortillas, and passed one to each of them. Lupe brought a steaming pot of coffee from the branding fire and filled cups. Between serious chewing and slurping the hot coffee, Mateo bragged about Cesar's abilities as a vaquero.

Way too soon for Will, Pa stood and stretched till his back popped.

"Loafing around in the shade won't get these big boys branded. Shake out your loop, Cesar. Will, stir up that fire. Two Feathers, stay with Will. Our fun is about to get serious."

Will once again manned the branding fire, rotating the irons so that one was always buried in the hot coals, all the while trying to keep the heat and smoke from roasting him. Pa and Cesar worked through the remaining cattle. Pa roped their heads, and Cesar caught their hind legs, stretching them out on the ground. Will raced up and pushed the hot iron to the steer's right hip. Two Feathers and Lupe drove the branded cattle to the backside of the lake.

After watching Cesar on his stout, well-muscled mustang all afternoon, Will decided Mateo's son was the best roper he'd ever seen. Cesar's long lariat seemed magical, with a will of its own, as the loop grew wider and wider each time it circled above his head. Then, when Will didn't think it could stay aloft any longer, it sailed through the air and settled over the hips of a steer. The animal stepped into the loop. Cesar pulled up the slack. Then the steer lay stretched between Cesar's rope on its heels and Pa's on its head. Those big steers didn't have a chance. Even though they fought a fierce battle, the cowboys roped and branded them before they'd figured out what happened.

I thought Curtis was the best cowboy with a rope, but Cesar has him beat.

The afternoon passed quickly, and when the last steer was turned loose, Will was surprised to find the sun sitting on the rim of the brush corral and making the walls a fiery-red stockade. Coughing and sputtering from the smoke, Will and Two Feathers doused the smoldering coals with the last of the afternoon's coffee and dragged their weary feet to the lake. Neither boy spoke. It took all their remaining energy to soak their sweat-drenched bandanas in the lake and wipe the soot from their faces. Pa joined them and splashed water over his head and face.

"You boys look like nine miles of bad road."

Will shook his head. "Nine miles ain't near enough to compare with how I feel. I'm glad we finished this job and can rest for a few days."

Pa picked up Will's hat and plopped it back on his head.

"Rest?! Don't you know there's no such word for a rancher?"

Two Feathers sat up from drinking handfuls of lake water. Suspicion narrowed his eyes, and his gaze jumped from Will to Pa and back to Will.

"I do not like the sound of that. We are not doing this again, are we?"

"These big ol' steers are going to feel better tomorrow." Pa tied the wet bandana around his neck. "I'm not sure we have the brush tight enough in the wall's open spaces to hold 'em."

Two Feathers dropped his heads into his hands.

"Sooo!" Will stood and headed toward the horses. "Tomorrow we get to cut brush."

All morning, the boys took turns clearing brush from the creek bed upstream from the house and dragging it to the brush corral. Two Feathers returned from dragging a load to find Will sitting on the creek bank with his wet bandana wrapped around his swollen left hand.

"What happened?"

"A wasp nailed me. I always swell up." Will studied the creek bank. "I think we need to work downstream from the house. I checked it out while you were gone, and there's a good-sized tangle of scrub brush all along the far side past that bend in the creek."

"I know the place. Good cover for an enemy."

"That's what I was thinkin'. Let's go clear it out."

The boys picked up their machetes and headed downstream. Will's hand burned and itched from the wasp sting. He couldn't grip the big knife, so Two Feathers cut and chopped the brush while Will tied it in bundles to drag behind Buck. The work went slowly. Will wished Mateo, Cesar, and Lupe had stayed a few more days. He looped his rope around the brush, mounted Buck, and wrapped the loose end around his saddle horn.

"Come on, Buck. Maybe we'll get lucky and this will be our last trip today."

He followed the trail worn from all the previous brush bundles.

"You know what, Buck?" The big buckskin flicked an ear back. "Remember I told you the other day about Pa and me having a good talk about the ranch. Well, I kind of like being a full partner. Back in Texas, he said I was, but I wasn't. After all, he did sell the ranch without talking to me. I don't think he'll make a decision like that again. Out here in New Mexico, it takes everybody working together to build a ranch. He's even started listening to me." Buck shook his head and turned his ear forward. "Are you listening to me?"

They crested the top of a swell, and Will pulled Buck to a stop. The big horse shook his head, as though irritated by the delay.

"Let's take a look around. A sharp eye can keep a person out of trouble, you know."

Will studied the area around him, close in and in slowly widening circles into the far distance. He watched for anything out of the ordinary to catch his eye. He sat still and watched for any movement that couldn't be explained by the natural landscape.

"I don't see anything, Buck. Do you?" The buckskin stepped on down the trail, dragging the bundle behind him. "Do you think we will ever have a day we don't have to worry about Yellow Hawk?"

The bundle caught on a snag. Will slid to the ground and tugged it free. While checking the tightness of the rope, Buck stepped up and jerked the bundle from his hands.

"Whoa, Buck. Stand!"

The tall horse stood still. Will moved toward him and, with a running jump, caught the saddle horn, stabbed his foot in the stirrup, and landed in the saddle. The big horse stepped on down the trail again.

"You know what, Buck? Being taller and not having to climb on things to mount is good out here in flat country."

They rode on until the brush corral came in sight.

"Pa!" Will called when he rode through the gate.

"Over here," he called to Will.

Will spotted Pa's hat waving from the far side of the corral. Pa had filled every opening in the enclosure big enough for a cow or even a calf to pass through.

When he reached him, he slid off Buck and, with the rope over his shoulder, dragged the brush to where Pa was working.

"If you think we need more, we'll have to move pretty far downstream. The creek bed is cleared of all underbrush a good ways from the house, both upstream and down. We've been at this for three days. I don't think there's a place even a skinny grass snake could wriggle out of here. And I know Mr. Goodnight won't have a cow or calf that will get out of this brush corral."

Pa and Will walked to the lake, wet their bandanas, and swiped the dust and grit from their faces.

"I believe you're right, Will. What happened to your hand?"

"A wasp. I wonder how many cows will make the drive up from Texas? If he has a lot of cows, I don't think we have enough money to buy them all. I've heard about ranchers buying cattle on shares. Do you think Mr. Goodnight would do something like that?"

Pa stood for a minute, watching the big steers in the enclosure.

"He's a good businessman. I think we can come to an arrangement."

Will and Pa mounted and rode out of the corral. Will started to dismount to shut the gate.

"Sit tight, son. Your hand is swollen. I'll get the gate."

He pulled it shut, slipped its loop over the corner post, and tied it again with an extra piece of an old lariat rope he pulled from his saddle bag. Heading back to the house, they met Two Feathers coming up out of the creek bed. The clouds looked like burning yellow, red-orange, and dark-purple cushions as the sun slipped below the tops of the sandstone bluffs along the Pecos. Tired, dirty, and dusty, they rode into the ranch yard to discover two horses tied to the hitching rail and smoke drifting from the chimney.

A trail-worn Charlie Goodnight leaned against the door frame, sipping coffee. The steam from the hot brew drifted in little puffs as he blew into the cup and took a tiny sip.

"Coffee's on, boys. Step down and come into this fine hacienda."

"Hello, Mr. Goodnight. We've been wondering when you'd show up."

Will swung his leg over the saddle and dropped to the ground.

"Boys," said Pa, "bed the horses down for the night. I'll start supper." He walked over to Charlie, beating the dust off his pants with his hat. "Good to see you."

The old friends shook hands and walked into the house.

The boys hurried through their chores with the horses and ran to the house. Two Feathers yipped with delight when he saw Smokey. The scout wrapped his arms around the Indian and squeezed till he hollered. The embarrassment on Two Feathers's face didn't fool Will. The sparkle in his brother's eyes told how much he missed his family friend, the only friend who had known his parents.

Pa and Smokey had a stew bubbling on the stove and an iron skillet full of biscuits baking in the oven. Cookie had sent a Dutch oven full of his famous dried apple and pecan cobbler from the drovers' camp. Will feared the loud rumble in his stomach might stampede the cattle bedded down across the river. The evening hours slipped past unnoticed, with Goodnight and Smokey telling story after story of their adventures since the last time they had been together.

Goodnight had given Curtis—Will's mentor and sometime antagonizer—Pa's job as ramrod after they had left the herd a year ago. The cattle they had trailed up from Texas sold well in Colorado, and Charlie gave Pa his money for their steers. The price was a bit more than they'd expected, and Will thought maybe they could afford to buy Two Feathers a rifle.

Goodnight and Smokey decided it was too late to head back to the herd, so they climbed the ladder to the sleeping loft above the bunk-lined room Pa, Will, and Two Feathers shared.

Before the eastern sky knew morning was coming, Will crossed the Pecos and slipped into Cookie's camp. He eased around the chuck wagon in time to slip up behind Cookie. He stopped the man before he hollered at the sleeping drovers, who had shared his adventures on last year's drive up from Texas, that their breakfast was ready. With an immense grin, Cookie grabbed Will's hand and shook with gusto.

Will shushed Cookie and hollered out, "Come and get it before I throw it out!"

At the unfamiliar voice, heads popped out from under blankets.

"Will!" rang out from all around the camp. Cowboys plopped hats on their heads, stomped into boots, and reached for a cup. Will poured coffee into each cup when a drover shoved it his way. Twins, Tony and Jake, famous for their expertise at riding drag, stuck their cups toward the fire-blackened pot.

"Bring it to the rim, Will." Tony's grin filled his face.

"Can't get movin' without a shot of Arbuckle's to get my blood boiling." Jake slipped his hat to the back of his head. "Boy, I believe you've growed since we saw you last."

"Me? Look at you two. Eatin' trail dust seems to be just what you boys need. You're taller than a cougar's perch in a cottonwood tree."

With the last cup filled, Will set the pot back on a flat rock at the edge of the fire.

Pa and Charlie Goodnight walked up from the direction of the awakening cattle, and to Will's delight, Curtis followed.

"Yahoo! Curtis!"

Will raced to greet his friend.

"Hello there, Will-boy!" And with a flick of his hand, Will's hat hit the ground.

"Dang it, Curtis! I'm too old for that."

He whacked his hat against his leg to knock off the dirt and tugged it down on his head. His beaming smile canceled the irritation that had slipped into his voice. With both hands on Will's shoulders, Curtis held him at arm's length and looked him up and down.

"I believe you've growed up. I'm not too sure I could throw you up on that big buckskin stallion of yours. You do still have him, don't you?"

"Sure I do. And there ain't no need to boost me up anymore. All I need is a jump-start and I'm ready to go."

After Cookie filled their plates, Will and Curtis settled

themselves on the tongue of the wagon. Between mouthfuls of biscuits and bacon gravy, the friends caught up on the news of the past several months. With their plates sopped clean of any trace of breakfast, they dropped them in the wash bucket, refilled their coffee cups, and headed to where Pa and Charlie sat leaning against a log. Curtis and Will sat on another log across from them.

Will glanced at Pa, and at his nod, Will gave Mr. Goodnight, the trail boss and well-respected cowman, his most serious expression.

"Mr. Goodnight," Will's heart upped its beat a notch, "Pa and I have been making plans for our ranch." He shifted his weight and crossed his feet. "Ummm. We'd like to talk to you about our ideas."

Charlie's eyebrows arched, and he looked from Will to Pa. "Dan, I thought you had steers to send north, like last year."

"We do. Will's a full partner now. We have an idea you'll be interested in."

"What's on your mind?"

Pa nodded toward Will. Charlie's head swung hesitantly toward Will.

"Okay, Mr. Will Whitaker—New Mexico rancher—what's on *your* mind?"

Will took a deep breath and slowly blew it out.

"We want to grow our herd faster than with the cows we have. But we don't have the cash to buy more cattle. So we want to go into a partnership with you by keeping the cows and calves that survive the drive and a bull or two, if you have any. Then, for the next two years when you come through, we'll split their calf crop."

Goodnight pushed himself a little higher against the log and sipped his coffee. "I'm working on cattle interests in

Colorado and Wyoming, so that sounds good to me. It's an easier drive without cows and calves. We can move faster."

With handshakes all around, the deal was done. A big grin threatened to split Will's face. He'd done it. He'd made a cattle deal with the best cattleman in the country.

TRACKS

Later that morning, Will found Curtis walking around Buck, looking him over.

"I see you're still babying this horse. He's in great shape. I swear he's grown taller. Is he any friendlier around strangers? Last year on the drive up here, we all tiptoed around him like you would a rattlesnake."

Will laughed. "No, not one bit. I'm still the only one can ride him. He lets Pa handle him, like he always did, and now he'll let Two Feathers saddle and feed him. That Indian sure has a way with horses."

Curtis took the horse Naldo, the wrangler for the cattle drive, brought him from the remuda. The wiry Mexican's face lit up when he saw Will.

"Señor Will, it is good to see you."

Will grabbed his outstretched hand in both of his and they shook.

"Naldo, it's good to see you too."

He stretched his arm up to reach the top of Will's hat. "Muchacho, you muy big. Taller than Naldo."

Will felt his face flush.

"We've got to go, Naldo. Mr. Goodnight wants me to show Curtis our cattle."

Once mounted, Will and Curtis worked their way through the grazing trail herd and toward the Pecos River.

"Do you think Mr. Goodnight would mind if we took a few minutes for me to show you the ranch?" Will asked. "We've worked hard, and it is shaping up."

"I don't think he'll mind a bit, and if he does, he won't holler too loud."

"Well, let's go then."

Will tapped Buck, and they rode off at a high lope.

When they reached the river, Will led the way up a steep path to the top of the bluffs that bordered the Pecos. He pointed out the area they claimed as the Pecos River Ranch—from the flat grassland dotted with their cattle and split with its arroyos and gullies to the south, all the way to the red sandstone bluffs in the distant north.

"You got a fine ranch, Will-boy. You and your Pa should be proud. Maybe someday I'll come ridin' by and decide to stay in these parts."

"You'd be welcome, Curtis. The Pecos River Ranch could always use another cow-savvy rider."

Following the path back down, they rode upriver a short distance to a crossing where the creek that flowed by their house entered the river. They made their way up that creek toward the ranch headquarters. Near the area where Will and Two Feathers had stopped clearing the underbrush, he pulled Buck up short.

"Stop, Curtis. Look there." In the sandy soil, he pointed to the tracks of several horses. "They stopped here for water. Those aren't any of our horses' tracks."

They dismounted to take a closer look.

"No, Will-boy, they're not. They're all the same. These horseshoes ain't hand forged. They're bought shoes for the army. It's the same type shoe I've seen at Fort Sumner. The tracks have been here several days. You seen any strangers lately?"

"No." Eyes on the ground, Will walked to a cluster of oak trees. "These riders didn't stop here just for water. They tied their horses here for quite a while. The ground is trampled, and they left droppings."

Will walked around the tracks, then stepped closer to the edge of the creek. His eyes on the ground, he slowly made his way upstream.

Curtis splashed through the water to the other side of the creek. "They crossed over and stayed in the taller grass. How far is the house from here?"

"It's a ways yet. Just over the rise where you're standing. We cleared the underbrush upstream a good distance past the house to make it easier to keep an eye on things. The creek cuts through that rise and falls through some ripples before it levels out at the river."

Splashing back through the water, Curtis followed Will along the creek bank.

"If it was soldiers, why didn't they come on up to the house? I never knew a soldier to pass up something to eat and a cup of good coffee."

Will heard Curtis but couldn't answer. There, in the mud at the edge of the water, one of the visitors had stepped across the creek on stones and his foot had slipped, leaving a clear heel print. A print with a notch in it.

The drover walked up. "You find something?"

Will put his foot on the track and wiped it out, knowing Two Feathers wanted to keep it secret. "No, nothing." He smiled at Curtis. "There's no telling what's in a soldier's mind. They probably weren't supposed to be on this side of the river. I bet they were supposed to stay on the road on the other side. It would make for easier travel." He mounted Buck. "Come on. I want you to see our cattle."

Will's mind reeled with what he had seen. That was the same track they saw at the cave where they found the first cache. The same track Two Feathers saw at the fort, but not from an army boot. Who had ridden with the soldiers? Why were they here? Why didn't they come to the house?

Later that afternoon when Curtis returned to the herd, Will told Pa he needed to check some cows and calves down by the creek.

"I want to get a count, to be sure they're all there."

But instead, he headed to the boot tracks.

Back-trailing the soldiers, he followed to where they angled toward the Pecos, upstream from the mouth of the creek. From there, he followed them to the river and along the same path taken by the two wayward heifers he and Two Feathers had been hunting when they found the first cache of supplies. The tracks didn't stop at the bend in the river as the heifers had, and Will followed them around the bend. About a mile farther down, the east bank leveled out, and the tracks led away from the riverbank and onto the desert floor. He followed them about a quarter of a mile until they faded out.

Will noticed his shadow growing tall and thin and realized it was getting late. He tapped Buck into a gallop to head home as fast as possible because Pa planned to go to the trail camp to eat with Goodnight and the drovers.

When they returned to the river, he slowed Buck to a walk so he wouldn't be sweaty when they got home. At the creek below where he had found the track, Will let Buck drink in a shady wooded spot. With a quick glance at the setting sun, he decided to let Buck cool down a bit more. He dismounted and sat on a flat rock at the edge of the tree line near the creek to consider what he'd found. The more he thought about those stolen supplies and the tracks so near his home, the madder he got.

How dare dirty rotten robbers hide their loot on my ranch? My ranch! Mine, Pa's, and Two Feathers's. Who do those varmints think they are?

Will's temper erupted like an avalanche of rocks over a cliff. He picked up a good-sized rock and slung it as hard as he could at a nearby hollow log. The solid thud made the log shudder.

An angry bobcat exploded out the end and leaped at Will. Before he knew what was happening, the cat shredded his shirt, leaving claw marks on his arms and chest. Then it ran over the top of him and used Buck's rump to launch himself across the creek. Buck screamed, hunched his back, and kicked his hind legs behind him.

Will let out a holler, fell off the rock, and into the creek. He sputtered and floundered around until he could get his legs under him and stand up. Buck pranced in circles, eyes wide, ears flat against his head, and ran off a few yards downstream. Both looked around, but the bobcat was gone. Blood mixed with water dripped down Will's arms. His shirt was in shreds, and blood soaked through in several spots. He stood there, looking first at himself and then for Buck. Weak in the knees, he wasn't sure he should move.

"Where'd that cat come from?" he said aloud to no one. His heart slowed its wild stampede, and he took a deep breath and called out, "Buck, come here, boy."

Buck walked up to the edge of the creek. Eyes searching, he pawed the ground. Will grabbed the reins that dangled from the bridle.

"Back, Buck."

The horse pulled him up the bank and out of the water. There was blood smeared down his horse's rump, but a closer look showed the cuts were shallow. He circled Buck but found no more wounds. Will raised his arms and buried his face in the long black mane. Buck's head settled within Will's arms. They stood together until their trembles stopped.

"I don't know about you, but I don't like the present that old bobcat left. Mine's beginning to throb and burn. How about you?" He scratched behind Buck's ears and rubbed his neck. "I think we'd better head for the trail camp. I want Cookie to doctor these claw marks before Pa sees you or me. He's not going to be happy."

He started to mount Buck but dropped his foot back to the ground.

"Oh, Buck. If he finds out the robbers have been on the ranch, a bobcat will be the least of our worries. He won't let me out of his sight. There's no way I can tell him about that boot track. All that talk about being partners won't count for much if we got robbers around. He'll have Two Feathers and me stuck to him like suckling calves to their mommas. It'll have to be our secret. Ours and Two Feathers's."

Darkness arrived before Will and Buck reached camp. The lantern light cast shadows on Cookie's worktable at the back of the chuck wagon and on the men lounging around the cook fire. Cookie cleaned Will's wounds with alcohol. The sting sent shivers all the way to Will's toes, and he ground his teeth to keep from hollering in front of the cowboys. When Cookie finished with him, Will held Buck's head and crooned soothing words while Curtis and Cookie cleaned the claw marks and spread thick salve over the wounds.

Will let Buck into the rope corral with the remuda about the time Pa and Goodnight rode in and left their horses with Naldo. Slipping behind the wagon, Will put on the shirt Tony had given him. He promised to replace it next time they came through with a herd so he could keep the secret and not tell Pa about the bobcat. Curtis and Cookie had agreed to remain silent about the accident as well, sparing Pa some worry.

"Will, there you are. Why didn't you come back to the house before coming over here?"

"Uhhh. I followed those cows to the creek and started thinking about Cookie's cobbler, so I decided to come on. Sorry, Pa. Hope you didn't worry."

Pa took a cup from the chuck wagon, and Curtis poured it full of coffee.

"But that's just it, Will. I did worry. Being partners doesn't mean you can be irresponsible."

Will sat down beside Two Feathers after Smokey got up to join the older men. He blew a sigh of relief when the talk changed from him to their cattle and when they would drive them to the herd for the trip north.

"I found another boot track with the chip out," Will whispered. "Mixed in with soldier's tracks."

Two Feathers head snapped around. "Where?"

"In the creek below where we cleared the underbrush."

"Are you sure it's the same track?"

"Yep. That's three times we've seen that track. Once where we found the first cache, then in the wagon yard at the fort, and now here. Here! Right on our ranch."

"Not good!" Two Feathers rested his head in his hands.

"I think the next time we go to the fort we need to tell the colonel about the track."

Two Feathers didn't move or answer for a long minute. "What if the one we tell is the thief? Then he knows about us. What if he comes after us? I think we need to wait till we know who it is."

Will sat up straight, and his eyes popped wide. "Colonel Dowell? I don't think so."

"Maybe not. But someone sent the soldiers out after the supplies."

Cookie sang out his familiar song. "Come and get it before I throw it out."

The boys headed for the line of cowboys with empty plates. Will pulled on Two Feathers's arm to stop him.

"Maybe you're right. We better wait till we learn more. Na-es-cha prowls around in the dark. Maybe she's learned something new."

The following morning—with Curtis, Jake, and Tony in tow—Charlie rode into the ranch yard, and they all followed Pa to the brush corral. Will and Two Feathers talked to the two young drovers about the Pecos River Ranch. They managed to get close enough to a heifer to show off the Pecos River brand.

"Pa and I are partners on this ranch." Will's pride in his new position gave him a serious, business-like tone. "I wish you boys would consider staying on here and working for us. We've got a deal with Charlie to increase our herd. We'll need good help this winter."

"I'll admit, I'm gettin' tired of sleeping on the hard ground." Tony shifted his position in his saddle, as if to find a softer spot.

"Me too," said Jake.

"I like the idea of staying in one place for a while."

"Me too," said Jake.

"But we signed on with Mr. Goodnight for the drive. I believe in sticking to my word."

"Me too," said Jake.

"We'll talk to Mr. Goodnight. If he needs us, we'll stay with the herd. If he can spare us, we'll stay on the ranch. I'll wait to see what he says."

Will looked around Tony at his twin. "I know. You too, Jake."

By midafternoon, the P~R cattle had crossed the Pecos and settled in with the Goodnight herd. Curtis assigned extra drovers to night patrol, to stop any cattle that might want to return to their cozy spot in the brush corral.

Will, Pa, and Charlie sat on their horses, looking over the herd, each with a leg draped around their saddle horns.

"About how many cow-calf pairs do you think made it this far?" Pa asked Charlie.

"Oh, maybe a couple dozen or so. It's hard for a calf to survive all the way to Horsehead Crossing. We lost several on the alkali flats. I don't like trailing with calves. They're nothing but trouble. I'll be glad for you to take 'em all."

"What about cows and heifers?"

"Maybe a hundred or so. I tried not to bring any on this drive. Just steers. But somehow I always manage to pick up a few. How about we cut them out and move them across the river over the next few days?"

"Sounds good to me." Pa swung his leg back down to the stirrup. "What do you think, Will?"

"I agree. A few days on good grass with fresh, clear water and they won't want to be anywhere else."

Smokey and Two Feathers rode up. The old scout leaned from the saddle to shake Dan's hand.

"Can you do without this Comanche for a couple of days? We've decided to go hunting for fresh meat. The boys pushing this herd are gettin' a little tired of beef. They're clamoring for antelope steak."

"I can do without him, under one condition." Pa pushed his hat to the back of his head. "You bring Will and me a slab or two of that steak. Being a full partner on a cattle ranch is hard work and makes a man hungry."

STOLEN CATTLE

After an hour's ride to the southwest from the Pecos River Ranch toward the Guadalupe Mountains, the sun rose, casting Two Feathers's and Smokey's long shadows ahead of them. Two Feathers's stomach rumbled.

"Is that Comanche for 'I'm hungry'?" Smokey asked.

Two Feathers took off his hat, and the breeze blew a turkey feather from his braids across his face. He brushed it aside.

"I believe that means 'I am hungry' in any language."

He stood in the stirrups and looked around for a place to make a breakfast stop. A cluster of juniper trees off the trail a ways offered fuel for a fire and a break from the bite of the early morning wind. Smokey stepped down from his long-legged brown horse and lifted the tow sack that hung from his saddle horn.

"You start us a fire, and I'll fry up bacon to go with the biscuits Cookie packed."

Two Feathers waited under the twisted branches of a juniper, and its sharp smell mixed with the aroma of coffee brewing and bacon sizzling and popping in the skillet. Smokey dumped flour in the bacon grease, stirred in water from their canteen, and soon thick gravy bubbled in the skillet. He handed Two Feathers a plate of crisp bacon and biscuits covered in gravy.

When he was full and his coffee cup empty, Two Feathers sat cross-legged by the fire. His eyelids got heavy, and the only sound he heard was the horses cropping grass nearby. The sun was not high enough to warm the air, and the fire's heat spread over him like a blanket. Smokey stretched out on the ground and draped one arm over his eyes. Two Feathers waited to hear snoring. It didn't come.

Finally, he heard, "Boy, you been livin' in the white man's world for nearly a year now. Have you decided to stay?"

That thought put a downcast look on his face. When he couldn't let the silence go on any longer, he said, "No."

"No, you ain't decided, or no, you ain't stayin'?"

"No, I have not decided."

Two Feathers leaned over and put a couple of stout sticks in the fire.

"What's the holdup?"

"You do not want to stay here with me. You always leave. And there is Weeping Woman."

Smokey sat up and ran his fingers through his thinning gray hair and over his gray beard.

"What's your aunt got to do with it?"

"I want to be with her, to take care of her as she grows old. All her children are dead."

"Then go back to Yellow Hawk's band."

"I *cannot* do that. My uncle hates me." Two Feathers took the end of a smoldering stick and blew till it flamed. "Weeping Woman said Yellow Hawk shot my father when the soldiers came on the day of death. The day the soldiers killed my mother." He shoved the burning stick into the center of the fire, and its flame joined the others. "He hated my white father. He hates the white in me, and I hate him."

Smokey made no answer.

Because there *was* no answer to make.

On the third day of their hunt, Two Feathers once again steadied himself against a tree. He held himself still. The dark tan of his buckskin shirt and pants blended with the trunk. He held the nocked arrow in his fingertips and pulled the bowstring to his cheek. He didn't move. He didn't breathe. The deer's head snapped up. The arrow flew. He didn't miss.

Why did I make that shot? Two Feathers wondered. *We have enough already.* He and Smokey had spent the last two days hunting, jerking the meat, and curing the deer hides.

Staggering into camp, he dumped the deer carcass on the ground.

"I think we have hunted enough. Pa and Mr. Goodnight will think we ran away if we do not return soon."

He flopped down beside the fire and rubbed his aching shoulders.

"Yep." Smokey rolled the skin he was working on and tied it with strips of leather. "Charlie will be gettin' anxious to head the herd north. We've enough deerskins to make us both a suit of clothes and moccasins to last all winter." He stood, walked away from the fire, and added the skin to the pile of finished hides. "We'll head back in the morning. Besides, we've about et up all our supplies." He poured a cup of coffee and sat next to Two Feathers. "Some of Cookie's dried apple pecan pie sure would go good with this coffee."

Two Feathers licked his lips.

They spent all afternoon and evening drying the meat from Two Feathers's deer on racks over the fire and cleaning the hide. They worked together well and with no wasted movement. Each knew what to do, and the work went smoothly. Two Feathers kept a low, smoldering fire under the jerky. The smoke not only dried the meat strips but kept the insects off. He and Smokey stretched the deer hide tight between stakes driven into the ground, and Smokey scraped it clean. They rubbed deer brains into the hide to cure it. Throughout the night, they kept the fire smoldering and the curing hide wet so it wouldn't dry too quickly and become stiff.

The next morning, after Smokey packed the jerky and skins, he made up the last of the flour into biscuits and settled the Dutch oven in the coals. With fresh venison backstrap sizzling in the skillet, he sat cross-legged next to Two Feathers by the fire.

"Well, when are you going to tell me?"

Two Feathers looked at the old man and cocked one eyebrow. "Tell you what?"

"Curtis told me about the army tracks in the creek bed, about the soldiers not coming on up to the house. Will wasn't looking for any lost heifers when that bobcat jumped him, and I've seen you two whispering to each other. What's goin' on? Do you boys know something about that dead soldier and those missing supplies you ain't telling?"

Two Feathers made up his mind to tell Smokey just enough to keep him from asking too many questions.

"Okay, we have been wondering about it. We know someone at the fort has to be a part of it."

"That makes sense. What else?"

"We have more questions than answers. Where do they get the supplies? I think they came from Fort Sumner. Will thinks it is Captain Stanaway who steals them. But why was

Private Tucker killed? Who killed him? How are the supplies getting moved around? No one sees them."

Smokey refilled his cup. "I've been wonderin' who's gettin' them stolen supplies. Where are they goin'?"

"That is what Will and I want to know."

Two Feathers leaned against a log they had pulled up.

"Is that all you two know?"

He didn't look at Smokey. "Yes, that is all."

"It ain't much."

Two Feathers thought of Na-es-cha, and he thought of the chipped boot track. He drew his knees to his chest and wrapped his arms around them. He lowered his head. *I do not like lying to Smokey.*

They sat in silence for a while.

"That skillet's cooled enough," Smokey finally said. "I'll clean it, and you pack the plates and cups."

Two Feathers and Smokey crossed the Pecos and arrived at the cow camp in time to see Charlie swing his gun belt around his hips and buckle it tight. He pulled his rifle from the boot on his saddle, checked the load, and slammed it back in place.

"Smokey!" His voice cracked like the snap of a whip. "Thank goodness you're back. Rustlers hit the herd. Get a fresh horse. Go after 'em. We'll follow as soon as the boys get their gear together."

Will rode Buck up to Two Feathers, leading two roan horses. "Here's fresh mounts. Swap saddles, and I'll take Gray Wolf to Naldo. They took a bunch of our stock when they hit the herd. We didn't work all last winter keeping 'em alive to let a sorry rustler get 'em."

Two Feathers took Smokey's horse and Gray Wolf to the chuck wagon, stripped their gear, swung the saddles onto the replacement horses, and gave the skins and tow sacks of jerky to Cookie. Then he walked the horses to join the men gathered around the cook fire to get Goodnight's instructions. Smokey got his final orders and rode northeast, toward the Llano Estacado.

Anger built inside Two Feathers, and he worked to hold it there. He wanted to be a warrior and would fight with the skill of a Comanche. The tension in the men charged the atmosphere around the campfire like a brewing thunderstorm. Two Feathers feared the air would crackle if he moved suddenly and eased his way through the gathered men till he stood beside Will.

"Men," Goodnight called out, and all talking stopped. "They got a good hunk of the herd. It took us a while to round up what they left, so they have a head start. We can move faster than the herd, so we should catch them in a few hours. Hank, Gill, Tony, and Jake, stay with the herd. The rest of you, saddle up. We're leaving as soon as you're mounted."

Eager to ride into battle, Two Feathers leaped astride his horse and patted its neck. *You are not Gray Wolf, but you look strong and have the legs of a runner. We will fight well today.*

The posse headed out from camp at a high lope. Goodnight and Dan took the lead. Will, with his rifle in its boot, and Two Feathers, with his bow and quiver strapped to his back, rode alongside. Curtis, Rory, and Russ followed behind. Each drover carried a rifle, a pistol, extra ammunition, and a grim expression.

The horses ate up the miles as the afternoon faded toward evening. Two Feathers spotted a dust cloud in the distance. Goodnight slowed and raised his hand to signal a stop.

"That's them up ahead. We don't want to run over Smokey. We'll slow up a bit and wait for him to let us know what's ahead."

Two Feathers slipped off his horse and walked to let it catch its breath and cool down. Will did the same with Buck. The drovers followed Two Feathers's lead and walked their horses.

Smokey rode up. "They're about a mile ahead. They've run the cattle to the limit, and with no water in sight, those critters are about done in."

"Did you get an idea who they are?" Tendons in Goodnight's neck bulged with his tight, clipped words.

"I sure did. And you ain't gonna like it. They're Comanche, and Comanchero, and maybe a white man. He was on the far side, and with all the dust, I'm not sure. But there was something familiar about him. The Comanche sported war paint. I saw their leader, and he wore yellow paint on one side and black on the other."

"Yellow Hawk!" Two Feathers spoke the dreaded name. He tried to swallow, but his mouth was too dry.

Will's eyes bulged wide, and his head jerked toward his brother. "He's back!"

"Yep!" Smokey spat a stream on the ground. "It's Yellow Hawk all right. Either the army never caught him, or he got away somehow."

"I don't care who it is. We're gettin' those cattle back." Goodnight's voice boomed, full of authority. "Dan, you take Smokey, Curtis, and the boys with you and come up on the left flank. Rory and Russ, come with me and we'll flank 'em on the right. Smokey, let go with that Sharps Fifty, and maybe we'll scare 'em off. Dan, spread your crew out on swing and flank and head for the leaders. I'll do the same. We'll turn the herd around. Boys, let's get 'em."

Will held Buck to a pace slower than the buckskin wanted. The horse tossed his head with impatience, sensing the excitement in Will's body.

"Whoa, Buck. Easy boy. You'll get to run soon enough."

He patted and stroked the stiff neck to help calm the feisty horse. Two Feathers rode beside Buck, but his roan didn't like to be near the bigger stallion and shied away.

When the riders reached their assigned positions, Mr. Goodnight kicked his horse into a gallop. Pa kicked his and veered to the left as the tail end of the herd appeared in the dust. Will loosened Buck's reins and gave him his head. Buck took off and left Two Feathers and his roan behind. Will rode the buckskin to the far outside so cattle couldn't turn away from the main body of the herd.

Then *Boom!* Smokey's Sharps fired, and rifle shots popped up and down the length of the herd. A rider appeared in the thick dust, and Will tapped Buck. The horse leveled out, and they gained on him. The distance between them shortened. A Comanche, covered with paint—one side yellow, one side black.

Yellow Hawk!

Will dropped the reins, gripped with his legs, and yanked the rifle from the boot. The gun jumped in his hands as he fired, but the Indian rode on. Buck leaped with a sudden spurt of speed, and Will fought to keep his seat. He dropped his rifle and grabbed the reins.

For the second time in his life, Buck would not respond to Will's commands and chased his enemy, Yellow Hawk, at top speed. He came even with the Comanche's leg where it gripped his mount. Buck bared his teeth and lunged with a savage thrust of his head. He missed the Comanche and caught the flank of the racing horse. It screamed and shot ahead. Yellow Hawk swung his rifle at Will's head, barely missing. A shock of fear threw Will off balance, and he grabbed the saddle horn to keep from falling off.

Regaining his seat in the saddle, Will caught the loose reins, pulled back with all his strength, and Buck slowed. With his heart racing and his breath coming in gulps, Will rode along the flank of the herd. Terror left room for only one thought: *Yellow Hawk is here.*

Will watched Yellow Hawk veer away from the herd, and two other Comanche followed him. They disappeared into the dusty distance. Buck stopped, his sides sweat-soaked and heaving for air. Will slid off and led the horse back to where he dropped his rifle. The walk helped slow his breathing as well as Buck's. He found the gun in the dust. Looking it over, he ejected the shells, wiped the dust off with his bandana, sighted down the barrel to be sure it was clear, and reloaded.

After Buck cooled down, Will mounted, kicked him into a lope, and joined the men, who had the cattle milling in a circle. Dan and Charlie headed the leaders back the way they had come, and the others fell in behind. Will settled in at drag, but his hands still shook. He didn't want to talk to Pa until he felt better. If Pa hadn't seen his battle with Yellow Hawk, he wouldn't tell him about it. Pa was going to be worried enough already.

Curtis rode up and walked his horse alongside Buck. "You okay?"

"Yes, I'm fine."

"Don't push 'em up too tight. Charlie's up on that rise, counting each head as they pass a twisted old juniper. He wants 'em stretched out."

"Got it. You seen Two Feathers? Is he all right?"

"Yes, he's riding swing with Rory. I'll send him back."

A few minutes later, Two Feathers loped back on the roan. He was dusty, and one braid had come partially loose. He circled behind Buck and came alongside.

"I saw Yellow Hawk. He had a rifle. He shot at me but missed. He is a bad shot with a bow. I guess he is a bad shot with a rifle too."

"He tried to crack my skull with the butt of that rifle." A small smile twitched the corners of Will's mouth. "I guess he's a bad shot with anything."

"Did anyone else see him attack us?"

"I don't know. Buck almost got him. For the first time since I was a little kid, I nearly fell off. We spotted Yellow Hawk about the same time. I shot and missed. Buck took off after him like a hungry fox after a fat rabbit. I dropped my rifle, and Buck tried to bite a chunk from his leg. That's when I nearly got my head caved in. Buck missed his leg and got his horse instead. That horse took off like the devil set fire to his tail."

"Are you going to tell Pa that Yellow Hawk took a swipe at you with his rifle butt and shot at me?"

Will sucked air in through his nose, held it, and blew it out the side of his mouth. "You know what will happen if we do. We'll spend the rest of this fall and all of the winter tied to his tail. And I'm not gonna do that!" He wished he felt as confident as he sounded.

They rode in silence for a few minutes. Will tried to convince himself that not telling wasn't the same as lying.

"What do you think? I don't really want to tell him how close we came to Yellow Hawk getting either one of us. He'd be more than mad at the risk we took."

Two Feathers pulled the roan to a stop. With unhurried but practiced movements, he rebraided his hair and secured the feathers.

"How can we guard what is ours if we have to stay at the house? But I do not like lying to Pa."

"Me neither, but we've got no choice."

He snuck a peek at Two Feathers from the corner of his eye. The look on his brother's face spread another layer over the guilt Will already carried.

The next morning, Charlie and Smokey arrived at the ranch house with the sun. Dan and the boys met them with fresh coffee.

"Curtis has the herd headed north behind Ol' Blue. That ol' longhorn fought a big brindle steer for the lead, but one jab with those enormous horns of his put that upstart in his place."

Charlie took a small sip of coffee.

"Mr. Goodnight, how old is that steer? How many more times do you think he'll lead a herd?" Will nibbled on a biscuit left over from the day before.

"Oh, I don't know. He's a stepper. I expect there's lots of miles left in him." Goodnight's tone changed from friendly to serious. "Dan, did you see what those Comanche carried?"

"I sure did. Rifles! I'd guess they're Enfields, left over from the war. Someone is selling them guns and ammunition. It might be that white man Smokey saw."

Will watched Two Feathers draw circles on the table with his finger. His troubled expression turned first to Goodnight, then Smokey, then Pa. When his gaze reached Will, he lifted one shoulder.

"I've been thinking about that." Goodnight rubbed his black beard. His eyes narrowed, and his face clouded. "My guess is Comancheros." An unhappy silence fell over the group. "Dan, I think you and the boys should go to the fort to let Colonel Dowell know about this."

"You're right. We'll go tomorrow."

Will watched as worry spread over Pa's face and hardened his eyes.

Smokey stood, slid his chair under the table, and cleared his throat. "Uh, Two Feathers, I'll see you next spring. Maybe by then I'll have my wandering days behind me and be ready to settle down here. I thank ya kindly for asking me to stay. If you ain't against it, Dan, I might take Two Feathers up on that offer someday."

Dan smiled. "You're welcome here anytime, Smokey."

Will noticed Two Feathers was drawing circles again and did not lift his eyes.

Goodnight stood and shook hand with Dan. "I want you to do something I think is important. You need to do it before winter sets in."

Puzzlement crinkled Pa's forehead. "What's that?"

"I want you to go to Santa Fe and register your land and your brand. You need to protect what you and the boys are building here."

"You think that's necessary? This is all free range. We can hold what we've got."

"It *is* necessary. Dan, we've ridden many rough trails together, as Texas Rangers and driving cattle. We both know death lurks just around the corner. Protect the Pecos River Ranch for your boys. Register the land along the river and any other water sources you claim. Then you can free graze what you need to support the herd."

Pa studied his friend. "My ranch in Texas wasn't registered. All the ranchers grazed the land."

"What was good yesterday, might not work tomorrow." Goodnight walked to the door and leaned against the doorpost. "I've ridden for miles over this country, and it's a beautiful place to be. People will be moving out here someday. If anything happens to you, who is going to hold the Pecos River Ranch together for your boys?"

BADGER

"Here you go. Your 'home, sweet home' on the Pecos."

Will pushed open the door of the cave house and with a sweep of his hand ushered in Jake and Tony, followed by Two Feathers. The hard-packed dirt floor and stone walls felt chilled without the benefit of the warm fire Will remembered from the frigid days of last winter.

"I can promise you it will be a lot warmer than your blanket on the cold Colorado ground. We lived in here before Mateo and Lupe built the new house with all those adobe bricks we made. It kept us warm through several snowstorms last winter."

Will walked to the fireplace and wiped dust off the plain mantel, now empty. Last year, it was the place of honor for the wooden box he had painstakingly carved to hold his mother's green hair ribbon and the soft deerskin pouch Two Feathers made for the braided hairs from Old Pony's mane. Now they rested on a more ornate, carved mantel, the honored place in the new house.

"If you have something special, this is a good spot for it."

Tony and Jake dropped their gear on the dirt floor. Each picked a bunk and tested the straw-stuffed mattresses. Their skinny rumps settled right through the old straw and onto the tight ropes lashed to the frame.

"I'm so used to sleeping on the ground, I might pass up this excuse for a mattress and settle all nice and comfy on the floor."

Tony bounced up and down on the tightly stretched ropes. They didn't give a bit.

"Me too." Jake gave his bunk a wiggle.

"You haven't even moved in, and you're already complaining." Will pushed Tony off the bunk, grabbed the mattress, shook it, bounced it up and down in his arms, and laid it on the framework. "There you go. Light and fluffy. Like sleeping on puffy clouds. I slept on this bunk all last winter and didn't complain."

Two Feathers snorted, shook his head, and put his hands on his hips.

"Go kill a buffalo. The hide makes a good bed."

"That's a good idea." Jake laughed.

"One of these days, I'm gonna do that very thing," Tony said.

He and Jake headed out the cave door and toward the ranch house. Will rolled his eyes, and they followed the twins out.

The next morning, the air held a brisk snap, and Pa changed his mind about going to the fort.

"We'd better spend the next few days checking the hay fields before we go traipsing off doing the army's job." Pa's irritation surprised Will. "We can go to the fort after we cut the hay and stack it for winter."

They mounted their horses.

"Tony, come with me. Will, take Jake and Two Feathers with you and check all the meadows. Don't skip any. I need to know what we're facing this winter."

"I'll check everything," Will said. "We had good grass last time I checked, and we've had a wet summer." *Pa is worried awful bad about Yellow Hawk. He's all tense and grumpy.*

Pa rode out with Tony close behind.

"Jake, Pa sent you with us because of Yellow Hawk. So, let's all keep a sharp lookout."

Jake nodded and his gaze swept the area around them as they rode away from the house.

By midafternoon, Will's stomach held nothing but a memory of breakfast.

"We've checked all the meadows, and the grass looks good. I think we have more hay than we can cut. Let's go by Mateo's. Maybe Señora Alma baked fresh bread today or even tortillas. She always gives me some when I come by. And I want to see if Pa warned them about Yellow Hawk and the robbers."

He got no argument from his partners.

A pack of barking dogs and a porch full of giggling girls greeted them when they rode into Mateo's yard. They endured Señora Alma's hugs and enjoyed her slices of roasted leg of lamb and goat cheese wrapped in tortillas. The best part was the warm sopapillas dripping with honey.

After eating their late lunch, Will and Jake sat with Mateo at the kitchen table. Somehow, Two Feathers managed to slip outside. They talked of hay meadows and haystacks and feeding through the winter. Before they left, Will told Mateo his worries about Pa and the ranch.

"Do not worry, muchacho, your pa is a man that knows trouble. He is a Western man. Listen to him. He knows when bad men are near. He told me of los ladrones, the thieves, and of the Comanche." His last word dropped to a gruff growl.

With a tow sack full of potatoes, squash, and a large stack of tortillas wrapped in a piece of cloth hanging from Will's saddle horn, they rode away from Mateo's.

"Jake, do you think Mateo is right about Pa? That he's worried about the thievery going on around here?"

"I wouldn't be surprised. That's enough to put anyone in a bad mood."

"I know. But something in Mateo's voice made me think he's worried about Pa too."

Will glanced at Two Feathers. "Do you think Mateo was worried?"

"Yes, and Dulce said she heard her father tell her mother to make the children stay close to the house. There were bad men around."

"I hope they figure out what's going on before long. When Pa gets in a bad mood, it usually means one of two things. Either we get run over with extra work, or he worries we'll get captured again and won't let us leave the house."

Two Feathers twisted his mouth sideways and narrowed his eyes with a look of disgust. "One is as bad as the other."

"Wait a minute. What did you say?" Will cocked his eyebrow and grinned at Two Feathers. "Did you say Dulce? Mateo's daughter?"

Two Feathers slid his hand down the reins till he reached the end of the leather strip.

"How do you always manage to find a girl to talk to? First at the fort, and now at Mateo's."

A tap of his heels, and Two Feathers rode ahead of the rest. He threw a wide grin over his shoulder at Will before he took off at a gallop toward home.

Jake reached over and slapped Will on the knee. "Maybe you should ask him to give you girl talk lessons."

They spent the next week cutting and stacking hay. Swinging the scythe had put blisters on Will's hands, but the hay was almost all stacked. The cool nights left a slight nip in the early morning air. Pa's increasing nervousness seeped into Will, and they both kept a sharp eye on the countryside.

Finally, Pa decided it was time to tell Colonel Dowell about the cattle raid. Jake and Tony stayed to guard the ranch, finish stacking the hay, and bring in several wagonloads to store in the barn for the horses.

"Boys, stay alert. When we get back I want to find you both safe and our horses and cattle still here. Keep a watchful eye."

Pa kept the buckboard moving at a good clip, and after a long day that started in the dark and ended in the dark, Will was happy to see the wagon yard behind Ben Wallace's store.

With stiff, jerky movements, Pa climbed down from the seat of the wagon. As always, he stretched his back till it popped.

"I'll make a fire and boil up coffee to wash down the jerky and tortillas for supper. We'll talk to Colonel Dowell in the morning. I'm done in."

He got no argument. Will took the wagon team, and Two Feathers led Buck and Gray Wolf to the barn. By the time the sliver of moon cast its feeble light over the wagon yard, Will heard the buzzy *peent* of the nighthawk's call and Pa's soft snore from under the wagon.

After reveille the next morning, Will followed Pa and Two Feathers across the compound and stepped onto the wooden porch outside Colonel Dowell's office. Sergeant Baker grabbed Pa's hand and shook it eagerly.

"Hello, Dan. It's good to see you." He looked at both boys. "I don't know which of you is getting taller." Opening the office door, he stepped in. "Colonel Dowell is already in his office. I'll tell him you're here."

"Will," Pa handed him a paper, "here's the list of supplies we'll need for the winter. You and Two Feathers go to the sutler's store and get what you can." He stepped into the office, stopped, and turned back. "I forgot to put salve on that list. Some of the blisters swinging that scythe put on my hands popped from tugging on those reins yesterday."

Walking through the door to the store, Two Feathers made a sudden stop, and Will smacked into him from behind. When he stepped on Two Feathers's foot, they crashed to the floor and Will's foot twisted under him. He sat down hard on his spur.

"Ouch!" he yelped.

Two Feathers rolled away, and Will shifted his weight off his bent leg and snapped at Two Feathers.

"You trying to kill me? Why'd you stop?"

Will threw a quick glance at the counter and spotted Na-es-cha. Her hand covered her smile, and laughter sparkled in her eyes. Mr. Wallace's booming laugh filled the store and bounced around the cavern-like room. Scrambling to their feet, Two Feathers wiggled his foot, and Will rubbed his backside. Bright-red faces looked at Na-es-cha.

Will glared at Two Feathers and, with irritation in every word, mumbled under his breath, "You hauled up short for a pretty face."

"Boys, many people come through that door, but I believe that was the most entertaining entrance ever." Wallace put his hands on his ample hips. "What can I do for you?"

Trying not to limp, Will walked across the worn wood floor and fished the list out of his pocket, trying to be dignified.

"My pa, Dan Whitaker, said to give you this list of stuff we will be needin' for the winter. And to add salve for our blisters."

"Whitaker, ya say? I remember now. You're the kid was in here a few months ago and bought a skinnin' knife."

"Yes, sir. That's me."

"I told you when you bought it, an old trapper named Badger sold it to me. He came in a little while ago and wanted to buy it back. He got ugly when I told him I sold it. Wanted to know who bought it. Said he'd get it back one way or another."

"I never heard of anyone called Badger."

"He's a nasty character. You be careful. Where's your pa? You boys didn't come all the way from that ranch of yours by yourselves, did ya?"

"No, sir."

Will spotted Two Feathers across the room. He and Na-es-cha stood by a side window. She pointed at something outside, screwed up her face, and pinched her nose.

"Pa's in Colonel Dowell's office. Comanche hit Charlie Goodnight's herd and took a bunch of cattle. Some of them were ours. We got 'em back, and Mr. Goodnight said Pa needed to tell the colonel. And about the Comanche having rifles."

"Rifles?" Wallace's face lost its jovial look and turned hard. "You folks need to be careful on that ranch of yours. There's trouble brewing. I'd move closer to the fort. It's too dangerous to ranch in that country. You boys are too young for that kind of trouble. There's Comanche raiders, stolen cattle, missing supplies, and the Navajo are getting mighty restless. They're about to starve to death. Food's in short supply around here." He blew a long hard breath out his mouth and rubbed his broad muscled hands down his not-too-clean apron.

Will took a quick look at the nearly empty shelves that lined the wall behind the counter. He noticed a lot of bare spots that were full the last time he was there.

Wallace scanned the list Will gave him. "This is a hard land. I don't know how much longer things can hold together. I'm thinking about closing this store and heading back East."

Footsteps sounded on the porch, and Pa walked up to the counter beside Will.

"Who's heading back East?"

"Mr. Wallace said he might." Will was glad Pa had showed up. Wallace's sharp words made him nervous.

Pa raised one eyebrow. "Seriously?"

"You never know. I might. Let's get this list filled before winter sets in. Too much talking gets a man in trouble."

Will noticed the smile return to Wallace's face but not to his eyes. They shifted back and forth between him and Pa.

He shouldn't be worried about us. Pa and me been takin' care of ourselves a long time. He glanced around the store. *Where'd Two Feathers get off too?*

Will spotted Two Feathers and Na-es-cha talking together at the far end of the store's porch. He chuckled, then noticed the strain on their faces. They didn't look like two people enjoying each other's company.

Two Feathers motioned for him to come. When he walked over, the girl stepped behind Two Feathers.

"Do not be afraid of Will. He is my brother." He reached for her hand and pulled her back beside him. "Will, this is Na-es-cha. I told you about her. Come to the wagon yard. We can talk there. Na-es-cha told me something you should hear."

They stopped behind a high-sided freight wagon and checked to be sure no one was near. Two Feathers spoke to the girl in Comanche, and she ducked her eyes away from Will.

"What's goin' on?"

Will watched Na-es-cha, but she turned her face away from him. Two Feathers gently gripped her shoulders.

"You can trust him. He will not harm you. Tell him what you told me."

Facing Will, she took a deep breath. "I like the night. I learn much in the night. I move like the owl, silent. No one knows I am near. I hear men talking, and I listen. There is much trouble here. The People, the Navajo, wish to go back to our land." She rubbed a moccasined foot in the dirt. "The Navajo are hungry. There is no food." She glared at Will, as if it was his fault. "I am hungry and cannot sleep."

The empty look in her eyes made Will feel guilty. He cleared his throat and swallowed the lump her look put there.

"What happened? What did you see?"

"I walked upriver a long way because no animals live here. There is nothing left to hunt. The river twists and turns, and I walked far to find a place to set a snare. But instead, I found Comanche. I did not know them. I listened to their words."

Will's heart kicked up a notch at the sound of the word Comanche.

"How did you understand them?"

Two Feathers answered for her. "Remember, I told you the Comanche captured her when she was younger. She lived with them for a time." He turned back to the girl. "Go ahead. Tell Will."

"I saw two Comanche, one man and one not much older than Two Feathers. They tried to take cattle, but got none. Angry words blamed each other. I smelled meat cooking, so

I waited. Riders came. Two men. One evil-faced Comanche. One white man from the fort. I remembered him from the Comanche camp where I lived. He came with the drink that steals the mind."

"We saw him." Two Feathers told Will, lowering his voice to just above a whisper when two soldiers passed the wagon and went into the barn. "A few minutes ago."

"What does he look like?"

"He dresses like a scout or a trapper, but not like Smokey. He is dirty."

Na-es-cha wrinkled up her nose. "And smells like a skunk."

"Mr. Wallace told me about a scout named Badger. I bet that's him." Will pulled his knife from the scabbard. "This is his knife. I bought it, and he wants it back. He's a trapper. His name is Badger, and Mr. Wallace called him a nasty character."

At the thought of more danger, Will's skin burned from the inside. *Now two men are after me—a Comanche and a nasty trapper.*

The soldiers came out of the barn and walked back to the store. Will whispered, "What about the Comanche? What did they look like? Would you know them if you saw them again?"

"It was too dark until the evil one stirred up the fire. He called one of them Running Wolf, and the younger one he called—"

"Barks Like Coyote!" Two Feathers stood rock still, not breathing. He drew a long, slow breath through his nose and let it escape in a low whistle. "Will, Yellow Hawk is around here. Do you think he knew those cattle were ours?"

Na-es-cha looked from Two Feathers to Will and back. "Your cattle?"

"The evil-faced man you saw is Yellow Hawk, my uncle. He stole our cattle. He wants to kill us."

Mr. Wallace stepped out the back of the store. "Na-es-cha!" he hollered. "Where are you, girl?"

"I must go."

She ran to the store and disappeared inside. Will rested his head on the rim of the freight wagon's wheel.

"What're we gonna do? How long can we go without telling Pa what we know?"

Two Feathers didn't answer. He sat on the ground, drawing circles in the dirt with a small stick.

"My father never liked Yellow Hawk and would not listen when mother talked to him about her brother. Father didn't trust my uncle. I don't remember much, except the day of death."

Will said nothing. He sat on the ground beside his brother.

"My father and Yellow Hawk fought that morning because my mother would not go with my grandfather when most of the people moved to a new camp. My grandfather broke up the fight. Yellow Hawk said he would no longer go with my grandfather. He decided to make a raid on the whites that night to get more horses. My father was going to take my mother and me home to our cabin the next morning. But soon after Yellow Hawk returned, the soldiers came. I do not remember what happened after that. Weeping Woman told me the soldiers killed my mother. Last year I learned Yellow Hawk killed my father."

Will and Two Feathers sat for a long time. Neither boy spoke.

Pa and Mr. Wallace came out the back door of the store.

"I don't know where those boys got off to. I guess I'll load the wagon by myself."

The sharp tone of Pa's voice propelled Will to his feet and into the barn to get the wagon team. Two Feathers followed, as close as Will's shadow.

Moments later, they led the horses out the barn door.

"Let's wait a while before we decide what to do," said Two Feathers. "When we get back, we are going to Santa Fe to register the ranch at the land office, like Mr. Goodnight said. We will not be in danger of running into Yellow Hawk there. We have time to decide."

Will dropped his chin to his chest and nodded a quick agreement. Ever since his capture by the Comanche at Horsehead Crossing the year before, thoughts of Yellow Hawk made his stomach feel like a bucket of spiders. Now his uneasiness made the spiders dart around in a frenzy.

SANTA FE

Three days later, Will and Two Feathers led Buck and Gray Wolf out of the cave barn, along with Pa's Rojo and a mule loaded with supplies for the trip to Santa Fe. Mateo and Pa stood on the porch, and Pa held up one hand, ticking off each finger as he went through a long list of things he wanted done while they were gone.

"Finish gathering in the hay. Check the water holes to be sure they're cleaned out. Make any repairs on the brush corral. It's dry, so the garden needs watering. Pull up the boards in the dam to let the water in and—"

Mateo burst out laughing, grabbed Pa's hands, and pushed them down.

"Amigo, I have lived here all my life. I could give you lessons on ranch chores. Do not worry. I know what I'm doing. Tony and Jake will pray for you to come home after working for me for a week."

Pa stuck his foot in the stirrup and swung into the saddle.

"I know I worry too much. Come on, boys. It's a long way to Santa Fe."

Will jumped, slipped his foot in the stirrup, swung into the saddle, and settled himself for a long ride. He turned Buck to follow Pa, but when Two Feathers didn't mount Gray Wolf, he stopped.

"Aren't you comin'?"

"No. I am not going to Santa Fe."

"Not goin'?! Why not?"

"It is not a time for me to go."

"What are you talking about?"

Pa rode back. "What's going on here? I thought we were going to Santa Fe?"

"Two Feathers says he's not going."

"Why not?"

Will felt relieved the sharp bite of Pa's words weren't directed at him. Two Feathers ducked his head. No one spoke. The only sound was the creak of Pa's saddle as he swung to the ground.

"What's wrong, son? Why don't you want to go?" Pa's tone softened, and concern laced his words.

Two Feathers's eyes met Pa's, and his words rushed out.

"Winter is coming soon. I am thirteen summers. It is time for me to be a hunter and a warrior. I have no Comanche father to show me the way. No uncle to help me. No medicine man to guide me into my manhood. So I must figure this out by myself. I need time to prepare for my vision quest." Sucking in enough air to catch up with his words, Two Feathers slowed down. "I will do this while you are gone. When you return, I will have my spirit guide. I will be a hunter and a warrior. I will be a man."

Will jumped off Buck. "Wait, Two Feathers. Wait till we get back and I'll go with you."

"No, Will," said Pa. "That's not the Comanche way. Two Feathers must do this by himself. Come on. We need to get started." Pa put his foot in the stirrup and stood that way for several seconds, looking at Two Feathers, before he swung into the saddle. "Be careful, son. Come back safe. You'll make a fine man." Then he turned to Will. "I forgot to tell Jake and Tony something. I'll catch up."

Pa rode up to Tony and Jake at the barn, spoke to them, patted one on the shoulder, and galloped after Buck.

"Come on, Will. Let's get a move on. It's a long ride to Santa Fe."

After three days in the saddle, Will heaved a sigh of relief to see the adobe buildings of Santa Fe in the distance. He wanted to eat hotel food, soak in a hotel tub, and sleep in a hotel bed. But Pa had a different plan, and it didn't include a hotel.

At dusk, they located a campsite on the outskirts of town along a clear, narrow stream. Will stomped around camp, shot Pa squinty-eyed glances, and muttered under his breath all the wonderful things he could think of about a hotel.

"There's plenty of time in the morning to go to town." Pa cut strips of sowbelly and laid them in the frying pan over the fire. "We're tired, and more important, the horses are tired. The first thing we'll do is go to the land office and register the ranch and our brand. I'm sure that office is closed by now. So morning is soon enough."

"Can we stay in a hotel tomorrow night?" Will's voice came close to a whine. At Pa's sharp glance, he cleared his throat and changed his voice to a more business-like tone. "I've never stayed in one."

"Now wait a minute. We stayed in the Elm Hotel at Buffalo Gap on the drive up from Texas."

"Ha! That was nothing but a big elm tree where people

camp when they come through the Gap. That joke wasn't funny then, and it's not funny now." Spreading his ground sheet out, Will unrolled his blankets on top. "I slept on the ground there, and I guess I'll sleep on the ground here."

He pulled off his hat and boots, rolled up with his back to Pa, and yanked the blanket over his head. But he still heard Pa's chuckle.

Morning found the streets of Santa Fe busy. Will and Pa asked directions to the courthouse. They found the government offices in the Palace of Governors on the Plaza and stood under the long covered porch with its heavy log pillars, watching the people coming and going. Will had never seen so many people at one time. Men rode by on horses. Ladies passed in carriages, some plain and some with fancy trimmings. A huge freight wagon rumbled past, the driver calling out to the mules. A stagecoach with a team of six horses took off from down the street and headed west, and people walked up and down the wood plank sidewalks and even in the streets.

Will's eyes wouldn't stay focused on any one spot. Excitement made his gaze jump from one side of the street to the other. His words skittered across his tongue in short bursts as he strained to see around the people.

"Pa, do you need me to help you with the homestead business?" He stood on his tiptoes. "I see a sign ahead. It says Exchange Hotel. I want to see what it looks like."

"You go ahead," Pa's voice bounced with laughter, "and study every detail of that hotel."

He patted Will on the shoulder, then flipped the back of his hat so it slid over his son's face.

Shooting Pa a quick grin, Will grabbed his hat before it hit the sidewalk and settled it back on his head. He took off toward the hotel across the plaza on the southeast corner of San Francisco Street and the Santa Fe Trail.

Will walked up the sidewalk alongside the building and looked into every window that lined the street side of the hotel. Each revealed things grander than the last one. Glistening lamps hung from the walls and ceiling. Chairs and couches were upholstered with soft velvet in colors he had never seen. The polished wood on their arms and on the tables gleamed in the sunlight from the windows. He tiptoed to the door and peeked in. The room held a large number of people, even that early in the morning. A man dressed in a Sunday suit stood behind a long counter.

The murmur of voices mixed with the clang of dishes followed a fancy-dressed man through a door at one side of the room. He wiped his fingers with a handkerchief before folding it and sliding it into his breast pocket. A cowboy with a dusty hat and spurs followed him. He stopped in the middle of the room and stuffed a last piece of bread dripping with butter into his mouth and wiped his fingers on the seat of his pants.

Will smiled at the difference between the two men and stepped a little farther into the room. WHAM! A blow struck him from behind and he hit the floor. Rough hands flipped him over, grabbed the front of his shirt, and jerked him to his feet.

"It's all right, folks." A gravelly voice laced with rotten breath assaulted his ears and his nose. "He's not hurt. Just standin' in the way."

The rough hands didn't let go. Badger twisted one arm behind Will's back and swept him out the door and down the sidewalk a few blocks to a side street lined with burros loaded with bundles of wood. The ill-smelling man jerked Will around a corner, slammed him against the wall, and pinned him with one soiled buckskin-clad arm. The other arm tried to reach around Will to his knife, but the scabbard slipped on his belt and was pressed between the wall and his back.

Rage surged through Will with the force of water rushing over a cliff. It filled him from his toes to the ends of his hair. He put his hands on the dirty buckskin chest and shoved with all his might. The man staggered but didn't let go.

"Gimme my knife. It ain't yourn. It's mine, and I want it back."

Badger! Will sucked air through his nose. The stench of the man filled his lungs, and he shoved hard. Badger stumbled back, and Will staggered off the wall.

"You stinkin' excuse for a scout. It's my knife. I paid for it, and you're not gettin' it."

The man lunged at him again, and Will slipped under his arm. When Badger turned, Will swung a right fist that connected with a cactus-bristled jaw. He followed with a hard left. The scout ducked under it, throwing Will off balance, and caught him in a bear hug. Badger's rotten breath exploded in Will's face, and his feet left the ground. Air whooshed out his mouth as the strong arms squeezed his ribs tight . . . tighter . . . tighter. Pain racked his ribs and back. He tried to call out, but his lungs held no air. The light faded and blackness took its place.

"Will." Pats on each cheek brought the light back. "Will? Are you all right?"

Will opened his eyes. His vision cleared enough to see Captain Stanaway kneeling beside him.

"Can you hear me, boy?"

"Yes, sir. I can hear you."

With Stanaway's help, Will sat up and looked around. He rubbed his aching ribs and dropped his hands to his belt.

"My knife? Where's my knife?" He felt for the scabbard behind his back where it had slipped. The knife was still there. He winced when he sucked in air. "He didn't get it."

Stanaway helped Will to his feet. "What happened? I walked by and saw you on the ground with that old scout, Badger, leaning over you. I hollered, and he ran off. What's going on? Where's your father?"

"Pa's at the courthouse, registering our ranch and brand. Badger's after my knife. He sold it to Mr. Wallace a few months ago when he needed money. By the time he came to buy it back, Mr. Wallace had sold it. To me." Will straightened the scabbard on his belt and twisted his pants to a more comfortable position. "Thank you, sir, for stopping to help me."

"I'm glad I came along when I did. Let's find your father."

They met Pa at the front door of the Exchange Hotel as he walked out.

"Where have you been, Will? I've looked everywhere for you." His tone was hard, like his eyes.

"Mr. Whitaker," Stanaway spoke before Will could explain, "Badger, a scout we sometimes see at Fort Sumner, attacked Will and tried to steal his knife."

The hard in Pa's eyes melted to concern. "You all right, son? Did he hurt you?"

"I'm fine. My ribs are a little sore, but I've still got my knife. Captain Stanaway came along just in time."

Pa put his arm around Will's shoulders and pulled the boy against him. He stood with a firm grasp on Will while Stanaway explained what happened.

"Thank you, Captain, for what you did for Will. Even though it's a bit early for lunch, I planned to take Will inside and treat him to a hotel meal." His grin matched Will's. "I'd be pleased if you'd join us."

"Thank you, Mr. Whitaker, I certainly will."

When the waiter put a heavy white plate in front of Will with a thick T-bone steak, roasted potatoes, and a fat slice of hot bread dripping with butter and honey, Will didn't know where to stick his fork first. A bite of steak convinced him he was dreaming. Nothing in real life tasted that good. Even the water was a treat. Their waiter brought a pitcher and filled their glasses. It was cool and sweet, not the alkali-laced water back home.

"Why are you in Santa Fe?" Will asked Stanaway before he stuffed his mouth again.

"As you know, the Navajo are starving. We've tried to make the reservation at Bosque Redondo work . . ."

Will tried to listen, even commented now and then, but the juicy, smoky taste of the steak, the salty crunch of the roasted potatoes, and the sticky sweetness of the honey-drenched bread offered too much temptation. He lost himself in all that delicious goodness.

A hotel's about the grandest place ever, he decided. *Someday I'm gonna make Two Feathers come here. He won't believe me when I tell him.*

To Will's delight, they spent the rest of the day walking around town, looking in store windows, and eating cookies in a bakery. By late afternoon, Pa headed to the store for a few supplies not available back home. As they walked around Seligman's Store, across the street from the Exchange Hotel, Will decided that only rich people lived in Santa Fe. He found every kind of goods he imagined anyone would ever want. The sutler's stores back in Texas at Fort Belknap and at Fort Sumner didn't begin to compare with all the stuff in Seligman's.

The store bustled with customers, and Pa waited at the counter to tell the clerk what he needed. Will wandered around, looking for something to talk Pa into buying, when he spotted rifles in a rack on the wall. He found a Spencer carbine like his.

Two Feathers needs a rifle. I wonder if Pa will get him one.

When Pa finished paying for the supplies, Will followed him outside and helped secure the bags on Rojo.

"Pa, I found a Spencer carbine in there like mine. I think Two Feathers needs one."

"He's a mighty fine shot with that bow of his. He keeps meat on our table with it. Why do you think he needs one?"

"Yellow Hawk!"

Pa stood with his hand on Rojo's rump. He looked off down the street and didn't move, just stared, as if he didn't notice the people moving about the plaza. When Pa turned his head toward the open door of the store, for the first time in his life, Will thought he saw fear in his father's eyes.

"Maybe you're right."

Pa walked back into the big store. Will followed.

When they headed back to camp, Will carried the new carbine across the saddle in front of him. He wondered what Two Feathers would say when he saw it.

With the camp chores done and everything packed for the trip home in the morning, Will and Pa rolled in their blankets with their feet near the ring of rocks warming in the glow of their small fire.

"Pa?" Will raised himself up on one elbow. "Thanks for bringing me to Santa Fe. It's the grandest place I've ever been."

Pa grunted. "You're welcome."

"I didn't hear much of what the captain told you. Did he know anything new about the army supplies or Private Tucker?"

"No, he didn't say much. But two things bother me. He said Tucker had been playing a lot of cards lately. He played against Sergeant Masters."

"What's wrong with that?"

"Sergeant Masters works in the quartermaster's office, under Captain Stanaway."

"Hum. That doesn't sound good." Will wiggled his toes, enjoying the fire's warmth. "What's the other thing bothering you?"

"If Stanaway was looking for food for the Navajo, what was he doing in Burro Alley? That's not a good part of town."

Will slid one arm behind his head and watched the few remaining leaves of the cottonwood tree twist and dance with the cold breeze in the faint light of the moon. The stars winked at him.

As soon as I decide Stanaway isn't so bad, Pa ruins it. Are the captain and Masters faking the records so no one knows about the stolen supplies? Will thought about the conversation between Pa and Stanaway at lunch. *He told Pa he came here to see about extra supplies from Fort Marcy for the Navajo.* The cold finally left Will's feet, and he rolled onto his left side to ease the pain in his back and chest. Pa's soft snores lulled Will toward sleep. But as tired as he was, his mind still whirled. *I need to talk to Two Feathers.*

VISION QUEST

Two Feathers watched Will and Pa ride off toward Santa Fe. He stood for a long time after they disappeared across the creek. The laughter between the two of them lingered in his head—laughter he used to share with his white father, his ahpu, whose quick smile would flash across his face when he saw Two Feathers. Memories of strong arms that scooped him up and sat him on the back of Old Pony. Memories of long, strong fingers that cupped over his short stubby ones and gripped the stringy mane.

He lifted his eyes to the mountains of white clouds and inhaled long, deep breaths. His muscles let go of the tension the memories wrapped around him, and he exhaled. A red-tailed hawk soared high above him, making lazy circles as he hunted.

A vision quest. His vision quest. What would he do? Where would he go? How would he find his puha—his source of power? His guardian spirit. Who would teach him? The hawk broke from his lazy circle, and with the powerful beat of its wings and a high-pitched scream—*keeear, keeear, keeear—*

he shot in a straight line to the northeast. Unwavering in his direction, the hawk soon disappeared.

"Two Feathers?" Jake said, his tone puzzled.

"You all right, boy?" Tony, with Jake behind him, walked up.

"Why didn't you go with Dan and Will?" asked Jake.

Concern for him spread from one twin to the other. The feelings of aloneness faded. He knew he could do this himself. He had seen other Comanche boys prepare for their vision quest. He remembered what to do.

"It is my time."

Excitement flowed through him and filled the empty places. The clouds drifting northeast blew like buffalo before the wind. He knew the direction to go. He would follow the hawk.

"It is my time to find my medicine. My time to seek my puha. My time to become a warrior, a man."

"What are you talking about?" Tony's confusion brought a smile to Two Feathers.

"I am talking about my vision quest. I will find my spirit. I will find my medicine that will make me a strong Comanche warrior."

"Are you leaving us?" Jake's voice held a hint of sadness. "Are you going back to Yellow Hawk?"

Two Feathers laid his hand on Jake's shoulder. "No. I will never go back to Yellow Hawk. He is my enemy. I am still half white. I am still John Randall. That will not change. But I am also Comanche, and Two Feathers will be a man."

He walked away from the two cowhands to his cot in the house. He went to make himself worthy to meet the spirits.

For two days, Two Feathers focused on clearing his mind of negative thoughts. He often went to the bluffs overlooking the Pecos River and prayed for peace in his heart. His hatred of Yellow Hawk was a living being that filled him, leaving no room for peace. For now, he imagined a lasso, like the one Cesar used when branding cattle. He swirled it inside his mind and let it settle over his thoughts of Yellow Hawk. The rope jerked tight. He pulled his hatred into a corner of his mind and left it there, tied tight.

Midmorning on the third day after Will and Pa left found Two Feathers in the deepest pool in the creek. The cold water made him shiver, but he soaked in it anyway and scrubbed himself with fine sand until he was clean. His body needed to be purified before the spirits would visit him. He felt strong and knew he had grown a lot in the past year. Most Comanche boys his age were at least a head shorter, especially Barks Like Coyote. He knew he could outwrestle him. Maybe, someday, the chance would come.

On the bank lay his new breechclout and moccasins that reached to his hips. He'd made them last winter in preparation for his vision quest. How many times since he had run away from the village of his uncle, Yellow Hawk, had he used the skills Weeping Woman taught him? Yellow Hawk tormented him about doing women's work, but he had put his trust in his aunt, and she had not failed him.

Two Feathers lay in the water and thought about his quest. Was he strong enough to go four days without food or water? Would he have the patience to wait for his spirit to visit him? What would it ask of him? Would he have strength enough to get home? These questions had no answers. Only time had answers. His body shook, and he wondered if it was a shiver from the cold water or a shudder of fear.

He swam to the bank and stretched out to dry. Last night had been long and restless as he struggled with his decision to go on the vision quest. He knew most Comanche boys were older when they went on theirs, but he had been on his own for a long time, and he needed the guidance of his spirit. Morning had appeared over the horizon before he had made his choice. Now, with his tension released and the last of his doubts gone, he fell asleep.

The sound of horses walking alongside the creek nudged him into awareness. The hoof beats stopped, and he heard the rip of grass from a horse taking a mouthful. Two Feathers opened his eyes. The twins stared down at him. He shivered in the cold breeze.

"Is this how the Comanche do a vision quest?" Jake's attempt at sternness failed, and he and Tony burst out laughing.

Tony stepped down off his horse. "I don't believe I ever saw such a sight. A Comanche, stretched out on a creek bank, sound asleep and buck naked."

Embarrassed, Two Feathers scrambled into his breech-clout, pulled on the high moccasins, and tried to brush the leaves and sticks out of his long hair. He did not say a word.

Tony stepped back into the stirrup and swung into the saddle. With laughter in his eyes, he reached his hand down. Scowling, Two Feathers grabbed the outstretched hand, and Tony pulled him aboard. All three rode back to the house in silence, except for Jake whistling a merry tune.

When they arrived, the twins dismounted, and Two Feather shoved himself off the rump of Tony's horse and stomped into the house. Tony and Jake tied their horses to the hitching rail and followed their disgruntled friend inside to fix lunch.

"You know what I think?" Jake set a cast iron skillet on the stove, then ladled water into the coffee pot.

Two Feathers watched the twins from the sleeping room. He rolled the buffalo hide from his bed and tied it with long leather strings.

"I didn't know you could think," Tony said. He unwrapped

a slab of beef and cut slices. They sizzled as the fat on the edges hit the hot skillet.

"I think that boy needs to find one heck of a vision to make him a man."

Jake said his words in fun, but they stung. Two Feathers sat on the edge of his bunk and wished Smokey was there. He hoped someday the empty spot in his heart would fill again with the love of his own family.

A soft deerskin bag from under his bed held a bone pipe and a pouch of tobacco Smokey had given him in preparation for his quest. He tied it to the belt around his waist. Then he added a second pouch, this one larger, filled with tinder, matches, and his skinning knife.

I am ready.

"You think we ought to follow him? To make sure nothing bad happens." Tony layered strips of hot meat inside a tortilla, rolled it up, and handed it to Jake.

"Do not follow me." Two Feathers walked into the kitchen, his hair freshly braided with his turkey feathers securely bound by their quills and hanging beside his face. He carried his rolled buffalo hide. "I must do this alone."

Jake handed him a beef-stuffed tortilla. "Eat this before you go. You're going to get hungry."

His face serious, Two Feathers took the food and sat at the table.

"Don't you think you should at least tell us where you're goin'?" Jake squinted at Tony and jerked his head toward the boy.

Tony's face held a serious expression, all teasing stopped. "You're gonna be plumb wore out after no food or water for four days. There ain't nothin' wrong with a man needin' help when he's down. We need to know where to search if you don't come home."

Two Feathers studied their faces. He saw only friendship in their eyes.

"You will not follow me?"

"No," Tony said.

Jake shook his head.

"I am going northeast, across the Pecos. I will find a high place to be closer to the spirits."

Two Feathers finished the meat and tortilla, walked to the water bucket, and drank. Starting to hang the dipper back on the hook, he decided to load up and drank again. He picked up his buffalo hide, slung it over his shoulder, and walked outside. Stopping, he looked at the ranch hands. The concern on their faces pulled at his determination to go.

"Take care of Gray Wolf." He could not make his feet move. They seemed stuck in the dirt like stout tree roots. He looked at them, shifted his weight, and took a step. "I will find a place today. I will stay four days, seeking the wisdom of my puha. Then I will return."

With no food and no water, dressed only in breechclout and moccasins, he headed northeast toward the Pecos River and beyond.

He did not look back.

Two Feathers had been alone before. For many moons, he lived on his own, without the help of any man, and lived well. Even though he had eaten the midday meal, the thought of four days without food made him hungry already. The miles stretched before him. He crossed the Pecos, where the sweet water of the creek that runs past the house joined the slow alkaline-laced water. Even though he was not thirsty, knowing he could not drink made him yearn for it.

The hours passed. Two Feathers kept his lengthening shadow off his right shoulder. The left shoulder ached from the weight of the buffalo hide. He spotted a hawk flying northeast, and he felt an ever-increasing desire to follow its path. Were the spirits guiding him already?

A sense of panic flashed over him, and he dropped the buffalo hide, sending up a puff of dust.

My prayers. I forgot the most important part. I must send my prayers to the North, South, East, and West and ask for the blessings of the spirits.

Flexing his sore shoulder, he looked around for anything to start a fire. Rabbitbrush provided plenty of dried twigs and leaves. He saved the tinder in his bag for the place of his vision quest. Soon a tiny fire burned, and he packed his spirit pipe with Smokey's tobacco. Sitting near the small flame, he took a burning twig and lit the pipe. The hot smoke filled his mouth and burned slightly. He faced the East and blew, sending his prayers for guidance on the smoke to the spirits.

After his prayers drifted away with the wind, he carefully tamped out the pipe, smothered the fire with dirt, and continued his northeasterly route. Three more times he stopped and sent his prayers on the wisp of smoke from his pipe. Once to the West. Once to the North. And once to the South. After smothering the fourth fire, he climbed out of a dry creek bed so choked with scrub brush only a lizard could pick its way through. In the near distance, a red mesa pushed up from the flatness of the desert floor. Two Feathers smiled. He knew the spirits had answered his prayers and sent him to this place. He followed a trail made by antelope to the top of the mesa.

The twisted, gnarled gray trunks of juniper trees mixed with scattered rocks of various sizes, shapes, and colors covered the mesa's flat top.

This is a good place. Here, I will find my puha. Here, I will become a man.

The sun sat low in the west, and his shadow stretched tall on the ground. Two Feathers prepare a place to wait for his vision. Tired and footsore, he smoothed away rocks from an area under one of the wind-twisted juniper trees and spread the buffalo hide. Once more he built a small fire and lit the pipe. He blew the smoke from his lips and sent his prayers to the spirits.

Thank you for showing me the way to this place. Here, I will learn the lessons my puha will teach me. Help me to understand the power of my puha, that I may use it for good.

Two Feathers smothered the tiny fire and arranged the buffalo hide so when he woke the next morning he would be facing east and receive the power that comes from the rising sun. He lay down and rolled himself inside the hide. Wiggling one arm loose, he pulled the remaining flap over his head and turned over, so the edges were under him. He knew to stay covered throughout the night, to keep his body pure.

He lay there, wrapped in the buffalo-hide cocoon. For the first time since he left the ranch, he felt warm and waited for sleep.

His throat felt dry and raspy. He waited.

His stomach rumbled. He waited.

He thought about Pa's good biscuits. He waited.

He rolled his tongue around until spit collected, and he swallowed. And he waited.

Time lost all meaning, and he was surprised when light filtered around the edges of the buffalo hide. It had slipped during the night. He unrolled himself and sat up to face the morning sun. The air was brisk, and he wrapped the hide around his shoulders. He stood, stretched, walked east to the edge of the mesa, and sent prayers of thanksgiving for the blessings of the spirits.

The second day stretched long before him. During the afternoon, the wind shifted to the north and brought a cold bite to Two Feathers's bare chest and back. He wrapped the hide tighter around him and watched the clouds race across the sky. Throughout the long day, Two Feathers prayed and sent requests for his guardian spirit.

He watched the sky, but there was no sign of life.

He studied the ground on the mesa top, but there was no sign of life.

He watched below, far out on the desert floor, but there was no sign of life.

By evening, he had a parched throat, a bone-dry mouth, a loud, rumbling hunger, and a pounding headache.

Two Feathers woke the morning of the third day to a cloud-covered sun. He lifted his eyes to the gray sky, rolled out of the buffalo cocoon, and sat up.

His head spun. His sight faded. He fell over.

Splat. A cold drop, followed by several more, hit his face. He opened his eyes. Not wanting to faint again, he pushed himself up with his hands and sat up—slow and easy. The few cold drops reached his dry, cracked lips, and he licked them. He stuck his tongue out to catch another drop, but no more fell. The brief shower passed. Soon the clouds scurried on their way, and the sun greeted him. He sat on the buffalo hide and sent prayers to the spirits, offering thanks for the raindrops. He decided they were a good sign that today his puha would show itself.

The night had been long. Pain from leg cramps had jerked him from sleep many times throughout the night. Knowing he needed to stay within the buffalo cocoon, he had struggled to reach his spasm-racked calves to massage the cramped muscles.

The morning sunlight worked its warmth into Two Feathers. He stood, took a deep breath, risked a cautious step.

Then another.

And another.

He walked to the edge of the mesa top and scanned the sky above and the ground below but saw nothing moving. Raising his arms over his head, he faced the morning sun and soaked up its warmth. He sent prayers out on the wind.

Thank you for your warm greeting. Please send me the power to face this day. Give me strength and courage.

The long hours of the third day wavered with the smoke from the small fire he kept burning, to be ready when his guardian spirit brought food. If he did not have food and water soon, he would not make it back to the ranch. He no longer sweat, nor peed, nor swallowed. The grit in his eyes made it hard to find fuel for the fire. Weakening energy and the pain in his joints made moving difficult. The hours passed as he rose only to add fuel to the fire and send prayers to the spirits.

Great Spirit, I grow weak. I need the power of my puha to . . .

Two Feathers sank to his buffalo hide bed, and darkness swallowed him.

Late that afternoon, Two Feathers opened his eyes and watched the clouds build mountains in the sky. The lead gray bottoms were heavy with water, and the white tops billowed into peaks. A black fleck moving below the clouds caught his attention. He blinked and shook his head to clear his sight. What was it? It came closer and changed its flight from a straight line toward him to soaring circles over the mesa. Then, it folded its wings and shot toward Two Feathers.

A red-tailed hawk!

Two Feathers froze on the buffalo hide. Was this his puha?

He watched the hunter strike with its mighty talons and sharp beak and lift a fat rabbit into the air from the ground about halfway between him and the edge of the mesa. The unfortunate animal wriggled and squirmed, but the sharp talons and fierce beak held, and the beat of the hawk's powerful wings carried its prey into the air.

A dark flash streaked across the sky from behind Two Feathers, and an eagle hit the hawk a glancing blow. The force knocked the rabbit from the red-tail's talons, and it landed in a crumpled heap not far from the buffalo-hide bed. Two Feathers scrambled on hands and knees to the spot and grabbed up the rabbit. He stood and watched the aerial battle until the hawk drove the eagle away.

The red-tail circled the mesa top and landed in a juniper tree not far from Two Feathers. Its screeching—*keeear*—washed over him, and he sank to the ground. He watched the bird on its perch in the top of the tree. Its mottled brown and gray wing feathers folded over its back. The red tail feathers glinted in the evening sun. The hawk looked down, and its sharp dark eyes ringed in gold stared—unblinking.

"Thank you for this gift of much-needed food." Two Feathers waved his arm at his puha. "I wish you well on your hunt."

The hawk opened its long wings, spread its tail feathers to flash red, and took off. It flew into the gray haze that hovered over the mesa, its piercing *keeear* lingering after it.

Thunder rumbled. Two Feathers grabbed dry fuel and returned to his camping spot. With the buffalo hide and long branches he found under the tree, Two Feathers made a lean-to before the rain fell. Soon, a small fire blazed, and he skinned and cleaned the rabbit. While it roasted, he stood in the pouring rain, head back and mouth open, and let his parched body soak up the water. He slipped into the lean-to, warmed himself at the fire, and enjoyed the few small bites he was able to eat. He put the rest of the rabbit into the bag with the tinder he had brought from the ranch. After the rain, he searched for small puddles, and even though they were muddy, he eagerly drank before the water soaked into the ground.

That night he slept better. His puha flew through his dreams, and its piercing *keeear, keeear, keeear* sent messages meant only for the heart and mind of a man called Two Feathers.

DOUBLE TRAGEDY

The morning sun crept under Two Feathers's closed eyes and brought the desert grit with it. He rubbed them with dirty hands, rolled away from the bright light, and buried his head in the crook of his elbow.

I want to go home. I am tired, and I hurt.

He took two deep breaths and pushed up to his knees. His head ached, and a cramp grabbed the calf of his leg. Frustration fired his temper. He kicked his leg to stretch the cramped muscles and hit a support pole of the lean-to. The wet buffalo hide collapsed on top of him and mashed his face into the dirt, pushing more grit into his eyes.

Stop! I have had enough.

Minutes passed before he shoved himself up and threw off the hide. He sat facing the morning sun.

Guardian spirit, are you there? I want to go home.

The cramp now gone, he stood, and the world swirled around him. He took several shaky steps, stretched his arms over his head, bent to touch the ground, and the dizziness drained away. He looked to the sky, hoping to see his puha, hoping it would lead him to water. The sky was clear, no red-tailed hawk circled on the wind. Disappointment dropped him to his knees, and he sat in a dazed stupor. Where was his guardian spirit? Where was his puha?

Am I going to die?

Yesterday, the hawk provided him with the food he needed. Today, nothing.

Yesterday, his puha came to him. Today, it was gone.

Yesterday, he became a man. Today, what was he? He didn't feel any different.

He searched the sky again, but it remained empty. Soaking up warmth from the morning sun, Two Feathers crawled to the wet buffalo hide and sat for several minutes.

Yellow Hawk's voice invaded his thoughts. He remembered one of the few times the war chief showed him any patience and care during his childhood. They were hunting for dogwood trees, to harvest the young shoots to make arrows.

"A good arrow must be straight," Yellow Hawk had said. "It takes time to hunt for the right tree and find the right branch. Go slow. Look hard. Learn to take the time to find what you need to finish the work."

Two Feathers stood, and shame flushed over him for his weakness of spirit. He looked to the rising sun and its colors of red and purple, fading from the clouds as it climbed over the mesa.

Does a hawk sit in a tree and wait for food and drink to come to him? No, he watches for his prey. He hunts for what he needs. Yesterday, I was a boy that waits. Today, I am a man that hunts.

"Thank you, Guardian Spirit. Lessons can be learned, even from an enemy."

The buffalo hide was wet and heavy from the rain. In the middle was a small hump. He wriggled an arm far enough under the hide to pull the bag out and tore off a bite of last night's rabbit big enough it nearly choked him. The bite filled his dry mouth, and the more he chewed, the bigger it got. He spit it into his hands and pinched off a small tidbit, chewed that, and swallowed several times before it finally went down his dry throat.

He must have water today—and soon.

Two Feathers rolled the hide and bent to pick it up, but he was too weak to carry it. He slumped to the ground and ate a few more bites of the rabbit. Chewing each one into tiny bits, he hunted for a place to stow the hide so he could return for it when he was stronger. He found nothing.

Nothing to protect the hide he had skinned from the buffalo that killed Old Pony, the last gift his father gave him. Then he spotted the lean-to poles. *A travois.* He draped the hide over the poles to pull it home. Keeping his back to the sun and his shadow slightly to the left, he headed down off the mesa and turned southwest toward the Pecos River Ranch.

The hours dragged behind Two Feathers like the heavy load he pulled. Finally, the sun stopped pushing him and started leading him. His stopped to rest more often. The poles slipped in his dry hands and tore his skin. Walking turned into stumbling, and he fell over a circle of rocks. He lay still, his face once again in the dirt.

Rolling onto his side, he curled into a ball and lay still. Way off, the *keeear, keeear, keeear* of a red-tailed hawk called to him. His lips dry and cracked, he muttered to his puha, "I am dying. I need my father to help me." The shadow of the hawk swept over him, and sleep slid him into a dark nothingness.

His three-year-old feet beat the packed dirt of their yard as he ran to his father's arms, away from the buzz of bees. "Don't be afraid." His father's words chased away the memory of past stings. "They're our friends. They help the plants grow. Watch him to see where he lives." Giggles and laughter replaced his fear as he followed the zigzag path of the bee. "Always remember, bees need water. Where you see bees, water will be close by."

Sleep brought him through the afternoon to the stillness of dusk. Bees buzzed in the silence, pulling him from his sleep. He lay still and listened. No breeze blew to cover the sound of the busy insects.

He sat up, sent a prayer of thanks to his puha for sending his father, and stood on shaky legs. A bee flew past. He followed it to the edge of a dry creek, where he found several wide, shallow holes lined with tight-fitting flat rocks to create catch basins for water. They were about half full from last night's rain. He bellied down, scooped up mouthfuls of water with cupped hands, and drank. After several swallows, he sloshed water over his face and neck. Then, reluctantly, he backed away to give his shriveled stomach time to absorb the water. He didn't want to waste any by throwing up what he had greedily drunk. Anyway, the thirsty bees needed their turn.

Throughout the night, Two Feathers drank from the catch basins and nibbled on the rabbit, and by morning he felt stronger. But the buffalo hide was still slightly damp, leaving him chilled. He climbed out of the dry creek bed into the warm sun and discovered the blackened fire ring of rocks that had caused him to stumble the day before.

Searching for fuel to make a fire, he found the tracks of four men. One had a chip out of the heel. He studied it until he was sure. Yes, it was the same chip he had seen before.

Soldiers! The man with the chipped heel rides with soldiers.

Fear pounded in his chest and weakened his knees. He scanned the area around him, but saw no dust of anything moving.

I am Comanche, he reminded himself and collected his courage. *I can hide from soldiers in the open desert.* His pounding heart eased, and his breathing returned to normal.

Not far from the fire ring, he found wagon ruts caused by a heavily loaded wagon.

More stolen army supplies?

His breathing quickened, and anger built as he followed the tracks. They came from the north and continued to the west. He moved back toward the rocks, studying the ground in widening circles. He could see that two men came on the wagon and two rode in from the west on horseback. The man with the chipped boot was one of the riders.

What did they do here? They didn't unload the wagon. Two Feathers frowned and studied the tracks again. Confused, his thoughts made no sense. *If the supplies are stolen from Fort Sumner, why is the wagon coming from the north?* He shook his confused aching head. *Thieves. This place is only hours by horse from the ranch. Thieves are everywhere.*

Two Feathers moved away from the wagon tracks and stopped near a cluster of sagebrush. He found a depression in the dirt where a saddle was dropped and used for a backrest. Scuff marks from boot heels and a generous sprinkling of small wood chips and shavings lay scattered on the ground. Puzzled, he picked them up. They had been cut from a clean block of wood, not anything like tinder for a fire. Whoever made them had worked for a while. Two Feathers found shavings scattered on both sides of where the man sat with his legs outstretched and where he brushed off the chips as he walked toward the fire. Gathering as many chips and shavings as he could find, Two Feathers put them in the deerskin pouch.

To take his mind off his hunger, he sat next to a sage bush to rest and wondered about the tracks. *The thieves must be soldiers. Who else could get army supplies?* Two Feathers pulled his knees up and laid his head on his folded arms. He wished he was anyplace but there.

I do not know what to do. Smokey will not stay with me. If I go back to the Comanche, Yellow Hawk will kill me. He rubbed his aching head. The rabbit he put in his bag the day before was long gone, and he wished he had eaten more sparingly.

I live near soldiers. Bad soldiers. Soldiers that let the Navajo starve.

He grabbed both sides of his head and squeezed as hard as he could. He wanted to squeeze out all thoughts of soldiers.

Thoughts of his puha slipped between his hands, and he let go of his throbbing head. What would his guardian spirit tell him to do? Anger and frustration gnawed at him. He picked up a rock and threw it at the bush. It clinked. Curious, he took a stick and poked under the bush, then slid it back and forth to scare off any biting or stinging critters. It banged into something with a clunk. He pulled the object out.

Beans. A can of beans!

It must have rolled out of the man's saddlebags. He scrambled to his feet. After several hard whacks with his sharp knife, he pried the lid open and scooped up beans with gritty fingers. He could not remember when he had tasted anything so good.

Two Feathers went one last time to drink, and he emptied two catch basins. The third one held only a small amount of water, so he drank several swallows but left the rest for the bees. After a quick search of the empty sky for his puha, he draped his buffalo hide over the poles once again, picked up their ends, and started walking to the southwest—and home. But his mind would not let go of the boot track and the shavings.

Who were these men? Where were they taking the wagons? Was it full of stolen army supplies? What did they do with the supplies?

The morning passed, and he still had no answers. With the sun overhead, he stopped under a shady overhang on the side of a small outcropping of rocks. The hide was dry, and he stretched out on it to rest. But sleep would not come. The beans he ate that morning no longer held the growling monster in his belly. Hunger pushed at him till, once again, he draped the buffalo hide over the poles and started toward home. By late afternoon, and with many stops to rest, his shadow dragged after him, and he often stumbled and fell.

A black spot appeared in the distance. Two Feathers watched it waver in and out of the glare of the setting sun. He sat down and sent his thoughts to his puha.

Hunter of the skies, send me strength. You came to me in my need with the gift of a rabbit. Do not let me die.

He watched the spot grow bigger and change its shape from round to tall. Part of it pulled away and flew toward him. Its *keeear, keeear, keeear* called to him, and it passed overhead.

Two Feathers sent it a prayer of thanks. He knew someone was coming to save him. The black spots grew into tall silhouettes of riders on horses. They rode as white men, not Comanche—not Yellow Hawk. Two Feathers waited.

Will and Pa rode up and stepped off their horses. Will handed Pa Buck's reins along with Gray Wolf's, took his canteen, and sat on the hide beside his brother. With a grin wide as a buffalo wallow, he handed Two Feathers the water.

"You look like you've been dragged through a knothole backward." He crinkled his nose. "And I don't know which smells worse, you or rotten eggs."

Two Feathers wiped the water dripping from his mouth with the back of his dirty hand. He blinked his dry, gritty eyes, surprised the tears he felt on the inside didn't spill down his face.

"It is good to see you too." His raspy voice quivered and cracked. He took another small sip.

"Go slow. Too much will make you sick." Pa held his canteen and knelt in front of the boys. "You okay?" He pulled his bandana off and wet it. "Here, wipe your face. Will, wet your bandana and wrap it around his neck."

"You brought Gray Wolf." Two Feathers tried to smile but dry, cracked lips would not let him. "I am glad to see him."

Will tipped the canteen to Two Feathers's lips. "We started to leave him at home. Thought maybe you liked walking, but he insisted on comin'."

"Will, get a fire started and heat some water. Drop jerky in it. Broth will do him good." Pa wet the bandana again and wiped the grit from Two Feathers's hands. He held each hand longer than it took to clean the dirt off.

Two Feathers coughed to make his scratchy voice work. "I am glad to see you too."

Pa sat back on his heels. "You gave us a scare." He had to clear his throat before his husky voice would work. "Jake and Tony lost your trail in the rain. When we got back and you weren't home, we started hunting." He pulled his hat off and ran his hand through his hair. "You went too far."

"I know. I had to find the right place."

"Did you?" Will asked. He shaved thin strips of jerky into a cup, poured in water, and set it at the edge of the small fire to heat. He sat beside Two Feathers. "Did you find the right place? Did you find your spirit guide?"

"Yes."

"Is it a red-tailed hawk?"

Startled, Two Feathers swallowed before the words came out in a hoarse rasp. "How did you know?"

"I told you, Pa," Will said with a satisfied smile. "That hawk that kept flying ahead of us. I told you he waited till we caught up before he'd fly off again."

"There's all kinds of things we don't understand in this world," Pa admitted. "Maybe you're right. The important thing is we found him before . . ." Pa's voice faded. Clearing his throat again, he handed Two Feathers the cup of warm broth. "Sip this slow, son. You'll feel better soon."

Will unsaddled the horses and emptied the contents of a tow sack onto the buffalo hide.

Two Feathers reached for a biscuit and dipped it into the broth. He would be home tomorrow. A hot bath would feel good. He took another biscuit and watched as Pa and Will spread out their bedrolls. And his. They had come for him. And brought him water, food, blankets, and Gray Wolf. That was more than his uncle had done for him in his life. His eyes filled. One tear dribbled down.

No! Comanche men do not cry.

A drink of water from the canteen helped clear his throat. He finished the last of the biscuit and broth and stretched out on the bedroll. He was now a man. That thought stuck in his head. What did it mean? Why did he still feel the same? Before his vision quest, Pa said he was only thirteen, a boy. But he found his puha. His spirit guide spoke to him. Why did he not feel different?

All the next day, Will rode beside Two Feathers as they headed toward the ranch. By the time they reached the creek and turned away from the river, Will held him in the saddle.

Pa pulled his horse up and stepped down. He knelt on one knee and studied the ground.

"What is it, Pa?" Will dismounted and joined Pa.

At the edge of the creek were tracks. Unshod horse tracks.

"We had visitors." Pa's face hardened into chiseled stone.

Two Feathers followed Will. "See those." He pointed to a set of tracks in the damp dirt at the creek's edge. "Barks Like Coyote watered his horse here." He looked at Will. "This is Yellow Hawk's men."

The color faded from Will's face.

"How do you know that for sure?" Pa walked over to see the tracks.

"He stood here while his horse drank." Two Feathers pointed to the ground. "Weeping Woman told me he was born with twisted feet. She and his mother bound them to straighten them out, but they never straightened all the way. They always turned in. I could run faster than him, and it made him mad that he never beat me."

Will shook himself and drew in a deep breath. "Those tracks do turn in, Pa."

They mounted their horses and rode the rest of the way to the house. Two Feathers inhaled the smells of fried ham and cornbread coming from the kitchen. The front door flew open, and Tony burst out.

"Boy, you gave us a scare. We started tracking you on the third day till that gully washer came along and wiped out all your tracks. I sure hated to tell Dan we lost you. Where you been all this time? Did you find what you wanted?"

Two Feathers smiled, closed his eyes, and slid sideways into Tony's arms.

Startled, the cowboy looked at Dan.

"Tony, bring him in the house. Will, take the horses to the barn."

Pa held the door, and Tony carried Two Feathers to bed.

"Jake," Pa hollered. "Bring water. This boy smells like he's been to a skunk fest."

He pulled off the tall moccasins. Pa faced the twins, his face as serious as a hanging judge.

"Be careful, and keep your eyes open. We saw fresh Indian sign about half a mile down the creek. Tony, go with him and keep watch."

Will woke when the sun peeked in the window, and he found Pa in a chair beside Two Feathers's bed, asleep. Determined not to make a sound, he tiptoed over to check on Two Feathers. His color was better, and he slept easy. The pitcher beside the bed was nearly empty. Pa must have stayed up all night giving him sips of water every hour or so.

Will dressed and went to the barn to take care of the horses. Tony and Jake met him at the barn door, buttoning their coats. The November morning wind was brisk, and the air was crisp.

"Have you talked to him yet?"

Jake went inside and forked hay into the troughs.

"Did you find out anything? What happened on this quest thing he did?" Tony asked as he poured water into the buckets tied to the side of each stall.

Will dumped grain in each bin.

"No, not yet." Buck nudged him, spilling the grain. "Hey, you want to eat yours off the ground? Stop hurrying me."

They each picked up a brush and started working on the horses.

"Pa will keep all of us close to the house today because of the tracks we saw. I'll try to get Two Feathers alone. He won't talk about it in front of people. He's good at keeping secrets."

After breakfast, Pa assigned chores around the house that promised to keep all of them busy for the day. In the afternoon, Will was cleaning out the horse stalls when he saw Pa go to the corral behind the barn. Will slipped into the house and peeked into the bedroom.

"You awake?"

Two Feathers sat up. "Getting all those chores done without me?"

"You ain't faking just to make me do all the work, are you?"

Two Feathers shrugged. "Sit down. I found more chipped boot tracks and wagon tracks."

"Where?"

Will sat on the edge of the bed. He noticed the new carbine hanging on a set of antlers above the bed. Will smiled. It looked good there.

"I'm not sure. I did find something different."

Two Feathers opened the little pouch and poured the chips and shavings into his hand.

"These are carving chips," Will said, "and from good wood. Not from a stick found lying around. Where'd you find them?"

"In the camp with the chipped boot and wagon tracks."

Two Feathers poured them back into the pouch.

"Hang onto them. They might be important. You're not gonna believe what happened in Santa Fe." Will didn't wait for Two Feathers to answer and rushed on. "We saw Stanaway. I ran into that trapper, Badger. He tried to get my knife, and when I wouldn't give it to him, he jumped me. Stanaway came along and pulled him off."

Two Feathers leaned back against the wall. "Do you think Stanaway is in this?"

Will nodded. "In Santa Fe, I didn't. Now, I don't know. But who else could it be?"

"I think you are right. He is a soldier. They cannot be trusted."

Will cocked one eyebrow. "I don't know about that. I like Sergeant Baker."

"Do not tell Pa what I found. Not yet. He will tell the soldiers, and we do not know for sure who is doing these things."

"Okay, but we need to tell him about the camp and the wagon tracks. We can hold off on the chipped track and wood shavings."

Two Feathers studied Will's face. He closed his eyes and lay back on the bed.

"I will tell him at supper."

While Will did his chores, his mind stewed over keeping information from Pa. Not telling seemed like a lie. Not a full-out lie, but just around the corner from one. The afternoon dragged on, and a small blister swelled up on his lip where his teeth helped his mind fret.

Will thought about the stolen goods. Stanaway had to be involved. Maybe he was one of the men at the camp Two Feathers found. Maybe he was on his way to Santa Fe and stopped there for the night. Maybe he was the one with the chip out of his boot. Will wished he'd thought to check Stanaway's boot tracks in Santa Fe. Maybe he . . . Maybe . . . There were too many maybes.

For weeks after Two Feathers found the soldiers' camp, Will continued to fret over the stolen supplies. Pa said it could be anyone's camp. "It's army business, so let the army take care of it," he'd told them. But Will's mind wouldn't let it go. And besides, Pa didn't know about the boot tracks or the wood chips.

During those weeks, Will, Two Feathers, and Pa drove the hay wagon throughout the ranch, feeding the cattle hay.

Finally, for the first time, on a bright sunny day, he agreed to let them go alone. Will pulled up the collar of his coat to stop the cold wind from finding its way down his back.

"It gets cold earlier in New Mexico than it did in Texas. Christmas is over a month away."

The wagon bumped over the hard ground, and Will tightened the reins on the team of horses, slowing them down. He didn't want the hay in the wagon bed to bounce out. They finished forking hay to several bunches of cattle and came to their noon camping spot.

Will stopped the team on the leeward side of a cluster of cedar trees about halfway through their feeding route. The trees blocked the north wind and made it easier to start their fire for coffee. Two Feathers walked the horses to a trickle of water that worked its way down a rise of rocks at the far end of the cedars. Dropping a handful of coffee grounds into the pot, Will set it on a flat rock at the edge of the fire. They kept a supply of tinder and sticks ready each time they stopped there while feeding hay to the cattle.

A rock pinged off the coffee pot and landed in the fire, sending up a shower of sparks. Will looked up to see Two Feathers motioning with his new carbine for Will to come. He grabbed his own gun from the wagon and ran to meet him.

Two Feathers climbed up the rise of rocks and down the other side, and Will followed. The trampled ground showed unshod horse tracks and the prints of moccasins. Will spotted Barks Like Coyote's tracks.

"Yellow Hawk!" Two Feathers said the name out loud, his eyes searching the distance around them. He picked up a stick, scraped away the ashes of a small fire, and felt the ground beneath them. "The ground is warm. The tracks are fresh. They made camp here early this morning."

"Yellow Hawk." Will whispered the name and sharp needles of fear exploded within him.

A faint *pop–pop–pop* sounded in the distance.

The boys stood frozen. They looked at each other, then in the direction of the shots—in the direction of the ranch.

They ran up and over the rise of rocks. Each stripped the harness from a horse and leaped astride bareback. With the long reins in one hand and their carbines in the other, they raced for home.

Close to the house, the shots grew louder and more frequent. Two Feathers motioned Will to circle behind the house and come into the yard between it and the cave barn. Will could hear Pa's shots from near the house, and he spotted Jake and Tony shooting from the woodpile near the garden. Two Feathers's carbine blasted twice.

When he reached the yard, two Indians were driving Gray Wolf, Pa's extra horse, and Tony's and Jake's horses from the barn, through busted corral bars, and toward the creek. Caught between them with ropes stretched tight around his neck was Buck. Will yelled and raced after them through the broken corral bars. The riders drove their stolen herd at full gallop across the creek—where a third Comanche, his bow and a fist full of arrows raised high, met them—and raced out of sight. Will knew those riders. They had captured him and Buck before. One wore red and black war paint. The other was covered in paint—one side yellow, one side black.

Fury swarmed over Will like a raging prairie fire. He aimed his carbine at the fleeing Indians but didn't shoot. He feared he'd hit Buck. The warriors slid to the far side of their horses and rode with only a foot in sight. The horse Will rode would never catch them. When out of rifle range, they appeared like ghosts atop their mounts again and rode off, taking Buck with them. Even knowing he was out of range, Will aimed his carbine and shot until it was empty.

Silence. The only sound was the ringing in his ears.

Emptiness.

Gone!

He raced toward the barn, hoping to find one saddle horse, but slammed to a stop when Two Feathers screamed his name. He whirled around. Two Feathers knelt on the ground beside a bloody man with an arrow in his chest.

OH, BURY ME NOT

"Tony!" Will screamed. "Bring bandages! Pa's hit!"

Will flung himself on the ground at Pa's side. Panic swept over him and brought paralyzing fear.

"Will." Pa's voice came weak and breathy. He sucked in air and coughed. Pink froth bubbled around the arrow sticking from his chest.

"Don't talk." Will's hand fluttered over the wound, wanting to stop the flow of blood but afraid he might hurt Pa.

Tony slid to a stop next to Two Feathers, spilling rolled bandages over Pa's legs.

"The arrow has to come out so we can close the wound."

"No." Pa gasped. "No use . . . Arrow went through . . ." He sucked in a small gulp of air. The wound wheezed. Red blood welled up around the arrow and spread across his chest. "Give me . . . your knife." His words came raspy and in short spurts.

Will fumbled with the scabbard, his movements awkward and wooden. He jerked the knife out and gave it to him. Pa held Will's hand and made a shallow cut in his palm. He did the same to Two Feathers. He wrapped both boys' hands in his, their palms together. Their blood mixed.

"You are brothers, in blood, in spirit." He fought to breathe and forced the words out. "The ranch . . . is both . . ." He dropped their hands.

"Pa?"

Will's scream echoed in his ears, faint and distant.

Time stopped.

His heart splintered.

He leaned over and pressed his hands to Pa's ashen face, searching for the strength that had always been there. The blood from his cut palm smeared into the prickly stubble of Pa's cheeks.

"Don't leave, Pa!" His voice cracked. "Don't leave me."

The knife fell in the dirt.

Two Feathers did not let go of Pa's hand. "Ahpu. Father." He squeezed hard. "Do not let him take you too." His last word faded into a whisper that held no hope.

Pa closed his eyes.

Will's body shook with sobs. "Don't go! No! Pa?"

Tears and saliva dripped from his chin. His ears roared. His head spun. He collapsed, his cheek pressed against Pa's.

One faint word slipped from Pa's lips into Will's ear. "Jo-anna."

Will struggled to whisper past the knot in his throat, "Ma, take care of him."

Two Feathers rocked back and forth on his knees. "Kee. No. Kee." Tears dripped from his cheeks and mixed with the blood that no longer bubbled.

The next morning, Will woke up in Buck's stall. He had gone to the barn after he and Two Feathers finished preparing Pa's body for burial. He brushed hay from his clothes and hair, surprised he had slept. The night had stretched hour by slow hour while thoughts of Pa and of Buck, now in Yellow Hawk's hands, tormented him. Now that Pa was gone, Buck was all he had left, and the possibility of losing him too was unbearable. He shook the hay off the saddle blanket he'd used for a pillow and hung it on the stall wall. He latched the barn door and walked to the house.

Two Feathers sat at the kitchen table, a half empty cup and a plate of untouched biscuits in front of him. Will sat and stared at Two Feathers, but didn't see him. The light of the rising sun slanted across the tabletop, but he didn't see it. Horses' footsteps sounded in the yard, but he didn't hear them. He was lost in an empty place of no thought.

The door opened, and a blast of cold air shocked Will back into the present. Two Feathers shivered. Jake and Tony shut the door, shucked their coats, grabbed cups from the shelf over the stove, and poured coffee.

"That wind is blowing straight out of the north. It's gonna be a cold one today," Tony said and flipped a chair around backward, sat, and rested his hot cup on the top of the chair back.

Two Feathers pushed his plate away. "That was a cold ride from here to the brush corral."

Jake sat across from his brother and took a tiny sip of the hot brew. "Yep. And last night was plenty windy. Dan's Rojo must have heard us coming because he was standing next to the gate. The bruise on his shinbone healed. He's good to go. There was no more heat or swelling in that foreleg." He blew on his coffee and took a bigger sip.

"We brought Dan's horse and three more to the barn and then rode for Mateo's. He said he'd be here before noon. He asked that you wait to . . . to . . . bury Dan till he gets here." Tony took a couple of biscuits from the plate and dunked one in his coffee. "Will-boy," his voice cracked. He cleared his throat and tried again. "Will-boy, we're torn to pieces about this." Sucking in a shuddering breath, he held it for several seconds before he let it out. "Dan was a fine man and a good boss. We'll do whatever you need us to do."

Two Feathers dropped his gaze to his hands lying idle on the table, then looked at Will.

"Pa left this ranch to Two Feathers and me." Will's voice shook, and he stopped. He pulled a deep breath in through his nose, blew it out his mouth, and tried again, his tone low and husky. "Pa and I were partners. Now Two Feathers is my partner."

Two Feathers stood and walked to their bedroom, where Dan's body lay cleaned of all the blood and dressed in his best clothes. Will followed, and they stood together at their father's bedside. Tony and Jake waited in the doorway.

Two Feathers looked down at Pa. His jaw muscles bulged, and his voice flattened and became as hard as flint.

"I will find Yellow Hawk. I will get Buck and Gray Wolf back. Tomorrow, the hunt begins."

Will walked over to Jake and Tony. Weariness weighed him down. His face sagged, and his eyes felt gritty and burned. The heavy ache in his chest matched the pounding in his head.

"I'm going to Fort Sumner in the morning. I need to tell Colonel Dowell about the raid and about Pa. He will send word to Charlie Goodnight."

"And Smokey," Two Feathers said from across the room.

"Yes, and Smokey. Maybe he'll stay with us now."

Will walked over to Two Feathers. He sat on the edge of the bed and stroked Pa's chest. The shirt he had ironed last night felt smooth and crisp. He straightened a crinkle in the collar.

Will looked up at Two Feathers. "I know your people bury belongings with their dead. What do you want to put with Pa?"

Two Feathers went to the rack of elk antlers hanging on the wall and brought Pa's hat.

"I brushed it clean and steamed out the dents and smashed places." He turned it around and around in his hands. "He always said a good cowboy needs a good hat." The gray in Two Feathers's eyes deepened to dark slate, and his light-coppery skin was ashen. He squeezed his eyes shut. "Pa taught me how to steam a hat when he gave me mine."

"It looks good as new."

Will handed Two Feathers Pa's knife. He had polished the antler handle until it gleamed, and the blade was sharp from the strokes of the whetstone. Will placed Pa's hat on his chest and Two Feathers fastened the scabbard to Pa's belt and slipped the knife inside.

Will went to a chest in the corner of the room, opened it, and took out a blue and green patchwork quilt.

"My mother made this." He took a deep breath and held it. His chest ached, and when he eased his breath out, the pain eased with it. "Let's use it to wrap him in."

Two Feathers nodded. One tear slipped down his face. Will looked away so Two Feathers wouldn't know he'd seen it. Comanche men don't cry.

After laying the folded quilt at the foot of Pa's bed, Will walked to the window and stared out at nothing. In a low, mournful voice, so soft Will strained to hear it, Two Feathers sang a song in Comanche. When the song ended, they stood in silence until Tony called.

"Boys, come in here."

The twins waited at the table, faces solemn. Will and Two Feathers pulled out chairs and sat opposite them.

"We need to talk to you." Jake's tone was serious. "You have us worried."

Tony laid his hand on Will's forearm and squeezed. "Jake and I lost our parents too. We know what a hard time this is. But you both need to think before you take off."

He let go of Will's arm and spoke to Two Feathers. "You want to trail Yellow Hawk alone. A Comanche war chief? To get two horses back? Think about what you're doing. He's already tried to kill you—more than once."

"And you . . ." The no-nonsense look on Tony's face irritated Will. "You're only twelve years old, and you want to take off by yourself to Fort Sumner. That's a long day's ride through Comanche country."

"You boys can't do this," said Jake. "Dan would never allow it."

"And we won't either." Tony laid his hands on the tabletop and pushed himself up from his chair.

Will studied the leathery skin and work-hardened callouses on Tony's hands, and the rest of the cowboy's words drifted away. Anger sparked and flared through his body until he felt the heat on his face. He jumped to his feet, and his chair slammed to the floor.

"No!" The sharp bark of his word pushed Tony back into his chair. "This ranch is mine. Mine and Two Feathers. We decide what we do. I WILL get Buck back."

Jake walked around the table to Will and picked up his chair. "We're not trying to take the ranch or boss you around, Will-boy. We want you to be safe. That's what Dan would want."

"Sit down, Will." Two Feathers's gentle voice brought Will and Jake back to their chairs. "Anger will not help. Tell them what we decided last night."

Will scrubbed his face hard with his hands, ignoring the pain from the knife cut on his palm, and ran them around to the back of his neck. He looked at Tony.

"I'm sorry. I shouldn't have lost my temper."

Tony wrapped his hands around his cup, looked at Will for a minute, then nodded. Will walked to the stove and added hot coffee to the cold brew still in his cup.

"When we went to Santa Fe, Pa made sure the ranch would be left to Two Feathers and me. Charlie Goodnight is our guardian until we reach eighteen. He and Charlie made that decision when the cattle drive headed north last fall.

"I never wanted to listen when Pa talked about this, but now I'm glad he made me. He told me to notify Charlie first thing, and that's what I'll do. I need you two here to feed through the winter, watch over the cattle, and guard the ranch. Maybe you're partly right. Maybe yesterday I was not grown. Today I am." A sharp tingle of fear crept up his spine. "I have to be."

Two Feathers stared at the biscuit on his plate. "We need you to stay here. We need to know the stock is cared for while we are gone." He walked to the window over the sink and stared out. "This is a good place. It is a good place to live." Returning to the table, he slid into his chair. "I am no longer a child. I have grown tall." A quick smirk twitched the corners of his mouth. "Taller than my uncle. Now he will see me as a Comanche warrior. This is not the first time I have traveled alone and not the first time I have trailed a Comanche war chief. Yellow Hawk will take the horses, with Buck and Gray Wolf, northeast to the canyon country. That is where I will go."

Will's hard gaze passed back and forth between the twin cowboys.

"I'll catch up with Two Feathers, and together we'll bring Buck and Gray Wolf home, back to the Pecos River Ranch. And no one will stop us."

Jake and Tony looked at each other. They said nothing for a time. Then, as if each knew the other's thoughts, they nodded.

"Okay," Tony said. "We don't like it, but it wasn't that long ago we made the same decision to go on our own. Sometimes you have to grow up fast."

"We'll look after the ranch," Jake said. "You boys go and do what you have to do."

Will heard the rattle of an approaching wagon, and they all walked outside. Mateo, with his wife on the seat beside him, drove into the yard. Cesar rode alongside the wagon on a striking black gelding. Mateo helped Alma down from the wagon seat, and she grabbed Will and Two Feathers in a smothering hug.

"Oh, muchachos, I am so sad for you. Such a terrible thing happened."

After the boys wriggled free, Will reset his hat on his head, and Two Feathers checked for bent feathers.

Cesar let down the tailgate, and Tony and Jake helped Alma carry baskets of fresh tortillas and pots of something that smelled of peppers into the house. Will refused to let his eyes rest on the long wooden box that filled the wagon bed. He turned his back and sat on the tailgate. Mateo laid his heavy muscled arm on Will's shoulders.

"It is time to dig the grave for your Pappa. Show us where you want him to be."

Two Feathers followed Will to the large cottonwood tree that had drawn them to this spot a little over a year ago. The place where he and Pa decided to make their home. Two Feathers walked away from the large tree and about halfway to the creek. He stopped beside a boulder with broken slabs of rock clustered around its base. Will joined him.

"At times, I found our father sitting here in the evenings. We would talk."

"You did? I didn't know that."

Two Feathers stared off across the creek. "Pa was a good man. He made me feel I belonged here. I had not felt I belonged anywhere since my father and mother were murdered." He faced Will. "When he spoke of your mother, I could see his love for her was great. I told him about Weeping Woman, how she became a mother to me. And about my friend, Red Wing, and my feelings for her. I wanted to bring them here to live. He said they would be welcome. Not many white men would say that about a Comanche."

Will kept his silence for a long time.

"Pa was right," Will finally said, his voice choked. "They will be welcome here if they want to come."

They walked back to the wagon, where Mateo and the others waited with shovels.

"We'll put him next to that boulder," Will said. "It's shady there, and he liked to watch the water tumbling down the creek."

The ground was hard.

The wind was cold.

The afternoon was long.

Alma kept the coffee pot full and the food hot, but she couldn't make the boys eat or drink. They sat on the tailgate and watched the hole in the ground grow deeper and deeper. Will remembered how Rory, one of the drovers on the drive the year before, used to sing a sad song to the cattle. The words spun around and around in his head.

Oh, bury me not on the lone prairie,
Where the coyotes howl and the wind blows free.

In a narrow grave just six by three,
Oh, bury me not on the lone prairie.

He wished he'd never thought of that song because it anchored itself in his head and stayed there.

Stripes of a deep rose, golden orange, and fiery red painted the sky above the cluster of mourners as they lowered the pine box into the grave. The north wind rattled the bare cottonwood branches overhead. Will pulled his hand from the warmth of his coat pocket and picked up a handful of dirt, tossed it onto the coffin, and quoted from Genesis 3:19 in a low, thick voice: "For dust thou art, and to dust thou shalt return."

Jake and Tony stood behind Will and Two Feathers and sang "Amazing Grace," their voices blending in soft harmony. To keep himself from crying, Will drummed his fingers over and over on his pant leg. Forcing deep, slow breaths past the tightness in his throat slowed his racing heart and held his rising panic at bay. Without blinking, he kept his eyes on the fading sunset until the last notes drifted away. Will stood frozen, not daring to move for fear he would crumple in a heap on the ground.

Two Feathers whispered, "Look" and pointed to the sky. Outlined against the last color in the clouds was the circling flight of a red-tailed hawk. "My puha."

Will put his hand on his brother's shoulder and felt eagerness pulse through him at its faint call—eagerness for the hunt. In a voice so soft only Will heard him, Two Feathers sent a prayer to the hunter above: "Guide us to the hiding place of Yellow Hawk."

Will sent his prayer behind his brother's, "And to Buck."

MAKING PLANS

Will lay in the dark and decided he must have fallen asleep. The sliver of moon had risen, giving only a feeble light that flittered between thin clouds. He lay still, aware of the silence, aware that no soft snore comforted him in the darkness. He felt as empty as a dry well with no bottom. A quick deep breath with a slow exhale and eyes shut tight stopped the tears and kept him from sinking into a depth of relentless grief.

He lay still, and his breathing settled. There was no sound of Two Feathers even breathing. *Where is he?* Will sat up and slipped his pants over his long johns, then shook out his boots and pulled them on. Grabbing his coat from the rack by the front door, he stepped outside. Shadows swayed and moved with the wind. A low call brought no response. Will walked farther away from the house and called again.

"I am here." Two Feathers answered from the direction of Pa's grave.

Will found him sitting on the boulder, wrapped in a blanket, and climbed up beside him.

"Can't sleep?"

"No. I have been thinking about tomorrow and what we are doing."

"I know." Will shifted his seat to see Two Feathers's face in the dim moonlight. "So have I. How am I going to follow you? What if I lose your tracks?"

The wind picked up, and his shivers weren't all from the cold.

"I was worried about that, but I have a plan."

"Good, because I don't."

He hoped it wouldn't take long to find Two Feathers because the idea of being far from home and alone out in that giant nothingness left a deep ache in his chest and a hollow feeling down to the tips of his toes.

"When you leave the fort, come back here. Get a fresh horse and one for supplies. Bring enough for at least fourteen nights. We don't know how long this will take. I will be two nights ahead of you, so come as fast as you can."

"I can do that." *I hope.*

"Jake said he trailed our horses after the attack. They crossed the river past where we found the first army supplies. You know where the east bank flattens out past that bend in the river?"

"Yes, I know the place."

"He said they left the river there and headed northeast."

Will nodded. "There should still be tracks. There's been no rain or wind."

"The tracks will be harder to follow as they cross the Llano Estacado. I will leave markers."

"You told me about that. A small pile of rocks with one at the side. That rock points the direction to go."

"Yes. Watch for other signs. A bent twig. A broken branch. Even scratches on a rock. Watch for anything odd that should not be there. Anytime I change direction, I will leave a marker."

"What happens if you lose his trail?"

Two Feathers slid off the boulder. "That could happen. If it does, I will wait for you. Then we will go the canyon country, to Yellow Hawk's winter camp."

"I don't think we'll have to go that far. I think Buck will get loose and bring Gray Wolf with him." Will jumped off the boulder. "Let's go in. I'm cold."

"Will." Two Feathers's voice was a harsh low growl that sent sharp prickles up Will's spine. "Yellow Hawk killed both my fathers. I am sorry for what my uncle did to you. He will answer to me for what he did." His last words faded into the cold, sharp wind.

Will placed his hand on his brother's shoulder. "He took everything from me, my father and Buck. Everything but you." He strained to see his brother's face in the faint moonlight. "We . . . Two Feathers *and* Will. We will make him answer for what he has done."

The next morning at first light, Two Feathers left the Pecos River Ranch, heading northeast. The rolled buffalo skin behind his saddle held blankets and four days' worth of jerky. Two canteens of water hung from the saddle horn. In his saddlebags was a day's supply of jerky and ammunition for the carbine in his saddle boot.

Will watched him until he was out of sight. In the house, he pulled up the loose stone from under Pa's bed and pocketed what he hoped was enough money for the supplies he needed to buy and for any emergency. He gave a small amount to Tony and Jake, in case they needed it. Tony tied Will's blanket roll, wrapped in a ground cloth, behind the saddle, and Jake filled his canteen. Will strapped on his knife, picked up his rifle, and collected his courage. When mounted, he headed southeast toward Fort Sumner. Rojo held a smooth, even gait, and the pull of the extra horse with an empty packsaddle didn't break his stride.

The sun was slow to poke its head over the horizon, as if it didn't want to face the cold wind. Will was a good distance from the ranch when it finally appeared. He thought about how uncomfortable Two Feathers must be riding into the wind. At least he had his back to it. The morning stretched long and empty, the silence broken by the plodding of the horses' hooves. The coffee Will had drunk for breakfast had long since left him, and his stomach felt queasy. Was it hunger or nerves? He jumped at every sound he thought he heard. His eyes studied each shadow he thought he saw.

Fortunately, traffic to and from the fort had worn a road into the desert floor. Before, Will simply followed Pa and didn't pay attention to landmarks, but he remembered what Pa had taught him.

Pay attention to what you see around you.

Look ahead of you and behind you. Things look different coming back then they did going forward.

Study the land close in and study it farther and farther out. Look for anything out of the ordinary. Be aware of anything that is not in its natural place.

Pa had been a good teacher. Will wished he had been a better student.

The shadow of Will on Rojo stretched tall on the ground by the time he reached Fort Sumner. He stumbled when he stepped down and stomped his feet to get the circulation going in his legs once again.

Sergeant Baker stepped out from behind his desk in Colonel Dowell's office when Will walked in.

"Will Whitaker! This is a surprise. Don't tell me you found more supplies."

He stuck out his hand, and Will gripped it in a firm shake.

"No, we haven't found any supplies. I need to see Colonel Dowell. It's important."

"He's gone to his quarters for the day. Can it wait till tomorrow?" He looked out the door. "Where's Dan?"

Will froze. He thought his heart would stop beating. "He's . . ." He cleared his throat. "He's . . ."

"What's the matter, son? Are you sick?" Sergeant Baker pulled out a chair. "Sit down. You're white as a sheet." He poured water in a cup. "Here, drink this."

Will drank the water, and his head cleared a little.

"I only want to say this once. Can you please get the colonel?"

Sergeant Baker stepped out to the porch and called to a trooper to get the colonel. He returned to the commander's office and lit a lamp.

"Come in here. Have you eaten?"

Will moved into the larger office and dropped into the chair.

"Just jerky."

Baker called to another trooper to go to the mess hall and bring food, on the double. Will had finished the plate of beans and fried salt pork by the time the colonel walked into the office.

"What's going on, Sergeant? My wife and I just sat down to dinner?" Irritation peppered his words.

"I'm sorry, sir. But Will Whitaker is here and insisted on seeing you."

The colonel snapped at Will. "What is it, boy? What's so important it can't wait till morning?" The last words rose in pitch, rose in volume, and shot like arrows at Sergeant Baker. The sergeant stood at silent attention and said nothing. Colonel Dowel leaned his hands on his desk, sucked in a calming breath, and spoke to Will. "Where's your father?"

"Yellow Hawk killed him." The words fell from Will's mouth and landed with a crash on the colonel's desktop. He grabbed his cup and drank the remaining water before his dinner followed his words. "And took Buck."

The colonel frowned. "Buck?"

"The boy's buckskin stallion." Sergeant Baker's words held a glint of reproach.

Colonel Dowell sat down and leaned his forehead on one hand. A tight sigh slid through his lips, and he ran his hand over his head to the back of his neck, then folded his hands and looked up at Will. Shame turned down the corners of his mouth and sadness softened his eyes.

"I'm sorry this happened to you. You and your Pa chose to live in a hard place. Bad things happen out here, even to tough men. Your Pa was a fine man. When was the attack?"

Will felt his body sink, as though his weariness was a heavy weight pressing him through the chair into the ground.

"Day before yesterday." The words came out in a husky whisper. "Yellow Hawk raided the ranch, killed Pa, and stole all the horses we had at the house."

The colonel's eyes hardened and took on a steely glint. He stood, clasped his hands behind his back, and paced back and forth.

"Are you sure it was Yellow Hawk?" His words had the rapid bark of bullets. "I figured that Comanche had settled in for the winter."

"Yes, sir. It was Yellow Hawk. Two Feathers saw him, and one of the hands followed the raiding party till they crossed the Pecos."

"Two Feathers?"

"The half Comanche boy Dan Whitaker adopted," Sergeant Baker said. "You know him as John Randall."

"Where is he?"

"He's following Yellow Hawk," said Will. "I'll catch up with him when I leave here."

The colonel walked around to the front of his desk and leaned against it, facing Will.

"I know you think you can take care of yourself. But alone on the Llano Estacado is dangerous for grown men and impossible for a boy. It's a hard, bitter, brutal land. Everything out there, from the smallest ant to the biggest buffalo, will kill if disturbed." He glanced at the sergeant.

"He's right, Will." The sergeant gripped Will's shoulder. "You can't go out there alone. It's far too dangerous."

"I can't spare any troopers to help you find this Yellow Hawk." The colonel returned to his desk and sat in his chair. "We have our hands full trying to keep the Navajo on the reservation. We can't feed them enough, and they won't stand for it much longer. There's no telling what's going to happen come spring." A heavy sigh burst from the colonel, followed by a sad smile. "You don't need to hear my problems. You have enough of your own."

Will pushed himself up from his chair and faced the colonel. He stretched tall, picked up his hat from where he'd slid it under his chair, and swallowed the lump in his throat to speak in a firm voice that hid his weariness and fear. He put out his hand and gripped the colonel's.

"Thank you, sir, but I'm not asking for soldiers. I will go wherever it takes to get my horse. Yellow Hawk killed Two Feathers's father and mine and stole the most important thing I own. I'll find him, and I'll get Buck back, and I'll report that Comanche's location to the nearest fort."

The Colonel frowned at Will. "I can't stop you, but I will pray for your safety."

Sergeant Baker followed him to the porch. "There's an extra cot in my quarters, if you want to sleep in a warm place tonight. The ground in the wagon yard where you usually sleep will be cold and hard."

"Sounds good." Will tried to smile. "Thank you."

They stepped off the porch and walked across the compound—first to a barn where Will unsaddled and fed Rojo, then to Sergeant Baker's quarters. The room was warm from the iron stove against the back wall. Two bunks with army issue wool blankets covering straw mattresses flanked the stove. A chest stood beside each bunk, and a trunk anchored the foot of Sergeant Baker's bed.

Will dropped his saddlebags and bedroll next to his bunk and sat down.

"Sergeant?" His voice sounded flat and dull to him. A sense of hopelessness threatened to wash away his remaining courage. *Maybe the colonel is right. How am I going to find Buck? I wish Charlie Goodnight was here. He'd know what to do.* "Can you send a message to Mr. Goodnight? Tell him Pa was killed and ask him to send Smokey to the ranch. We need him now."

"Yes, I'll send it out with the next dispatch rider." The sergeant sat on his bunk, across from Will's. "Everyone knows Charlie Goodnight. The message will get to him 'fore too long." He pulled his suspenders off his shoulders and let them hang down to his hips. "Will, the colonel is right. You and Two Feathers have no business going alone into such wild country. Even troops of soldiers get lost out there. Let the army take care of it. Eventually, we'll find Yellow Hawk, and the army will take care of him in one way or another or get him settled down in the Nations."

Will pulled off his boots and sat, rubbing his left foot.

"I don't think the army is going to be worried about my difficulties, and I certainly don't think they'll be concerned about finding two horses." He put his left foot down and picked up his right. "Two Feathers and I have to learn to take care of our own problems." He stopped rubbing when Pa thrust painfully into his thoughts. It took a few seconds before he could push him away enough to speak. "I didn't expect to start learning with such a big one."

He shucked his pants, stretched out on the bunk, and snuggled under the warm blankets.

"Thanks for the bed. It's been a long day, and I have nothing but long days ahead."

"Goodnight, Will."

Will answered with the slow, steady breath of sleep.

The sound of the bugler blowing reveille found Will waiting outside the store for Ben Wallace to open up so he could get his supplies.

"Will," Sergeant Baker called from the center of the compound, "come have breakfast with me."

Will jumped off the porch and followed him into the mess hall for breakfast. Long rows of tables filled the room, and the serving line was even longer. Will frowned at the wasted time waiting would cause, but once the soldier's plates were filled, they ate and were out the door in a matter of minutes. The sergeant found empty chairs next to Captain Stanaway, and before Will could say he didn't want to sit there, the sergeant sat.

"What are you doing here?" The captain's irritated tone matched the snarl on his lip.

"Will brought us sad news." The sergeant answered before Will spoke. "His father has—"

"Has he found more stolen supplies?" Stanaway's voice rose in anger and grew louder. "This is getting more and more suspicious, that Dan Whitaker is the only one who manages to *find* stolen supplies."

The extra burst of volume the captain put on the word "find" sent Will bolting out of his chair. With flailing fists, he launched himself at the captain, knocking the man's chair backward and spilling both of them on the floor. Will straddled him, and before the sergeant pulled him off, he bloodied the man's nose and raked a spur down one leg, ripping his pants and leaving a bloody trail. Through the roar in his ears, Will heard someone calling his name. Sergeant Baker pulled him off Captain Stanaway, pinned his arms to his sides, and suspended him in the air. Will sucked in a deep breath and stopped thrashing before his spurs cut the sergeant's legs.

"Put me down, Sergeant. I'm okay now."

Around the mess hall, the soldiers' forks hung in midair and jaws stopped in mid-chew. Silence spread from corner to corner. Will sucked in another long breath, stood with his head down and hands on his hips until his heart slowed its raging pace.

"Captain Stanaway." Lifting his head, Will hooked—then held—the soldier's gaze. "The Comanche war chief Yellow Hawk killed my father. His band raided our ranch three days ago. They stole my horse, Buck." Will's words dropped like lead bullets into the silence of the room. "If you even hint that my father was anything but an honest man, a man of honor, you will get more than a bloody nose. And if you're wondering if that's a threat, it is!"

Every soldier in the mess hall heard Will's words.

Stanaway jumped to his feet, holding a bandana to his streaming nose. In a voice brittle with rage, he spat his words at Will.

"Only the evidence will prove me right or wrong. Not you." His quick glance around the room revealed nothing but averted eyes or smirks. He stepped close to Sergeant Baker and snarled, "You better get this boy off the fort grounds before I have him arrested for assault and maybe for being a thief." He limped out the door.

Will and Sergeant Baker walked out onto the porch. They watched as Captain Stanaway entered the hospital.

"Be careful what you say, Will. Sometimes words can get you in trouble."

"Thank you, Sergeant Baker. Soon as I load up the supplies I need, I'm going home."

"That's good, Will. Go home, and *stay* there. The army will take care of Yellow Hawk, sooner or later."

Will headed down the wooden walkway that led from the mess hall to the sutler's store. The furious thump-clunk of his boot steps pounded like a hammer driving nails. Ben Wallace stood behind the counter, and a welcoming smile lit his face when Will entered.

"Hello, Will Whitaker. How are things on that Pecos River Ranch of yours? Hope you and your Pa cut enough hay. Looks like we're in for a cold winter."

"Yes, sir. We cut enough. I have a list of supplies I need. Can you fill it quick? I need to head for home."

"If I remember right, you and Dan got your winter supplies several weeks back." His laughter filled the store. "Don't tell me Dan forgot something important."

Will handed him a scrap of paper, and Wallace read the short list. Frown lines replaced the laugh lines in the storekeeper's forehead.

"This is a traveling list, boy, not ranch supplies. And this is a tough time of year to be doin' much traveling. Maybe your Pa forgot to finish the list. Where is he?"

Will kicked at the scuffed wood floor. *I hate that question. I don't ever want to hear it again.*

"He's dead, Mr. Wallace. The Comanche killed him when they raided our ranch and stole our horses three days ago.

They took my stallion." The last word came out as a squeak, and Will cleared his throat.

Mr. Wallace dropped his heavy chin and with slow even movements shook his head from side to side. His hands resting on the counter clenched.

"I hate to hear that. Your Pa was a fine fellow. I hope you got someone to help with your ranch, or maybe you should sell out and move. This country is way too much for a young'un to handle alone."

"Yes, sir. Charlie Goodnight is Pa's partner." Will blinked in surprise at Wallace's startled face.

"I didn't know that." His usual friendly smile reappeared. "He's a good man, and he certainly knows the cow business."

Wallace spent the next several minutes finding the items on the list and stacking them on the counter. When he was done, Will called out the items as the storekeeper tallied up the bill.

"Two blankets, two canteens, coffee, flour, baking powder, bacon, jerky, ten cans of beans, matches, and lard."

Will counted out the money into Mr. Wallace's big hand and glanced at the candy jar at the end of the counter. Dropping his change into his pocket, he decided candy wasn't so important anymore.

"Will?" Mr. Wallace helped pack the supplies in the pouches on the packsaddle.

Will saw the concern on the man's face, pulled the reins loose from the hitching rail, then faced him. "Yes, sir?"

"These supplies are for you and that Comanche boy. You're going to try to get that big stallion of yours back, aren't you?"

Will put on his most determined face. "Yes, sir. There's no one else to do it."

"Your life is not worth any horse. Even that big buckskin."

Will didn't answer. Wallace laid his thick arm across Will's shoulders.

"This is not a good idea. But if you're determined to do it, you need to know that Badger, the trapper that sold me your knife, is around. He was here at the fort last week. Be careful. He's not a good man. I think he deals with the Comanche."

"Thanks for telling me."

Will mounted Rojo, and with the packhorse in tow, rode out the fort gates.

Badger, thieves, the Comanche. And alone on the endless high desert of the Llano Estacado.

One fear piled on top of another—and another—until his heavy heart felt like a lifeless lump in his chest.

THE HUNT

When Will rode up from the creek by the house, a feeble glow from the sliver of moon lit the trail. A quiet voice from behind a willow spoke out. "Pull up your horse and state your name."

"It's me. Will."

Jake stepped out of the trees. "About time you got back. Tony started frettin' when the sun went down and you hadn't showed."

The cowhand walked alongside Rojo to the house and tied the packhorse to the hitching post at the front door.

"Tony," he called out. "Will's back. Come get these supplies."

"No use unpacking. I'm leaving at first light. Set 'em inside by the door."

After Jake and Tony unloaded the supplies, Jake took the horses to the barn.

"Give Rojo a good-sized bit of oats," Will called after him. "Fill a grain sack and put it with the supplies. He's going to need it, and so will Buck and Gray Wolf."

He flopped into a chair at the kitchen table. Tony handed him a plate of beef and potatoes and a cup of coffee. He sat across from Will.

"You ain't changed your mind about going?"

Breakfast had long abandoned Will, and it took hefty mouthfuls to soothe the growling in his belly. He made no effort to speak for several minutes while he ate. When his belt began to squeeze, he pushed back from the table and answered Tony.

"No, I ain't changed my mind. I have to get my horse."

But his mind wouldn't focus on how to get Buck from Yellow Hawk. During the long ride home, he'd buried that same thought over and over. Each time he let his guard down, the worry threatened to turn into panic, so he'd shove it away. The time to think about freeing Buck was when he found him. He drained his cup and set it with his plate in the dishpan in the sink.

"I'm give out. I'm goin' to bed."

The sky was black. Only an occasional star winked in the dark expanse overhead. Will had waited for morning as long as he could through the sleepless night. He sat on the front steps, warming his hands on the hot cup and taking careful sips of his coffee. The only light was the low glow from the stove keeping the coffee pot hot. The need to be on Two Feathers's trail crawled up and down his impatient legs like ants in a sugar bowl. His eyes never strayed from the east, and he sighed with relief when a faint pink glow eased its way up to show the horizon.

Tony and Jake led the horses up from the barn and secured the supplies on the packhorse. Tony gave Will a leg up, and the saddle made a faint creak when he settled himself into the smooth, well-worn seat. Jake handed him the lead rope for the packhorse and patted Will's knee.

"Keep your eyes and ears open. Stay alert."

"Come back to us, Will-boy." Even in the pale light, Tony's eyes shimmered a bit.

The knot in Will's throat wouldn't let him answer, so he nodded. Doubts sprang into his thoughts, and he dreaded facing the long ride on the open desert alone. What if he couldn't find Two Feathers? What if he couldn't find Buck? What if he got lost? He'd never traveled without Pa. He shoved the "what-ifs" to the back of his mind and hoped they'd stay there. He clucked to Rojo and didn't look back. Even when he crossed the creek, he didn't look back.

The sun had faded the color from the sky by the time Will reached the spot on the Pecos where they had found the first cache. He followed the river around the sweeping bend, studying the sandy riverbank for Two Feathers's tracks. He was beginning to think he'd missed them when he found the churned ground where the stolen horses had left the riverbed. At the edge of the water, a small cairn of rocks with an extra one on the northeast side caught his eye. If he hadn't been searching for it, he'd have missed it. The tracks led him across the desert for several hours. Twice during the morning, he spotted signs of Two Feathers on the trail. Once a bent twig, and once a broken prickly pear cactus pad—both pointing to the northeast. Each time he found a trail marker, his worry eased a little, and he'd relax his tight, nervous grip on the reins.

Several strips of jerky, eaten in the saddle and washed down with water from his canteen, made up his lunch. The sun crossed over his head and started its slow descent. By late afternoon, the tracks of the stolen horses began to fade when the cold wind picked up. Will pulled his coat collar up around his ears and wiggled his toes inside his boots. After a while, that wasn't enough to keep him warm, so he rode into a shallow gully and built a small fire. He filled his cup with water and chunks of jerky. After steeping for a few minutes, the broth was tasty, and the jerky was soft and easy to chew. He pulled off his boots, leaned against the wall of the gully, and toasted his cold toes in the warmth of his small fire.

Clink! Will sat up, his heart stuttered in his chest, and he choked on the small piece of jerky still in his mouth. The sound of a hoof on a rock had snatched him from his exhausted sleep. The sun was barely above the western horizon, casting its last streaks of color. Rojo, with the pack-horse still tied to the saddle horn, walked up and nudged Will with his nose. Will stood and stretched his back.

"I'm not a good cowboy, am I, Rojo?" Reaching his fingers under the horse's forelock, he scratched from there to behind the pricked ears. "Falling asleep before taking care of you and your partner is not fair."

He decided to camp there for the night since he'd slept too long and it was dusk. Besides, the floor of the gully was out of the wind.

That night, wrapped in blankets and with his feet resting against fire-warmed rocks, Will lay awake. His nap had taken the edge off his sleepiness, and thoughts of Pa slipped inside his mind. All day he had kept them boxed away in a corner of his heart, but now the lid blew off, and they spilled out all over him. He felt as though his heart had slipped from his body and into a deep hole in the ground beneath him. He wished he'd listened more when Pa talked about the ranch. He wished he'd listened more when Pa and Charlie talked late into the nights about buying and selling cattle. He wished he'd listened more.

Now he was alone. Pa wasn't there to ask. Pa wasn't there for anything. He had to run the ranch alone, make decisions alone. The word swept over him and sank into the marrow of his bones.

Alone.

Late the next afternoon, a black spot appeared in the distance. Will rode toward it, watching it grow bigger and form into the shape of a Comanche on a horse. Will's head filled with rage. *Yellow Hawk? You killed Pa! You took Buck!* He jerked his carbine from its boot and aimed.

No! Never shoot unless you're sure of your target. Pa's words rang in his head like the blast of a train's whistle.

He lowered the carbine and squeezed his eyes shut. *I will not let Yellow Hawk do this to me. I won't let hate decide. I won't let him win.*

He opened his eyes and spotted another cairn on the trail. This one pointed directly toward the rider, who raised his arm in a wave. *Two Feathers!* Relief that he hadn't shot his brother made his muscles tremble and his grip on the saddle horn strong enough to crush rocks. He kicked his horse to a faster gait and rushed to meet his brother.

"Did you find them?" Will asked as soon as he was within range.

Two Feathers shook his head. "They are gone. Let us make camp. Then I will tell you everything."

Shortly Will and Two Feathers sat by their fire, eating bacon and biscuits.

"You know what Pa called biscuits like these?" Will cocked one eyebrow at his brother.

Two Feathers nibbled on the edge of his hard lump of flour and shook his head.

"Sinkers. That's what these are. Hard, flat biscuits are called sinkers."

"Why 'sinkers'?"

"Because they sink to the bottom of your stomach and sit there." Will soaked the edge of his in the bacon grease and took a bite. "I guess I need to use more baking powder." He sopped up more grease. "That's one thing Pa didn't teach me."

Together, Will and Two Feathers cleaned up the supper dishes and made their beds for the night. They slipped the feed bags, heavy with grain, on the horses and hobbled them so they wouldn't stray. The night was cold, but they couldn't risk a fire being seen, so they settled into their blankets. The remaining coals cast a weak light, and they talked into the night.

"I found Yellow Hawk's camp, but he was gone," Two Feathers said. "Only Running Wolf and Barks Like Coyote were there. My uncle took everything from me and only gave me blame." His words hissed out between clenched teeth. "He blamed me for my mother's death because my father was white." Will heard a sharp intake of breath, and after a few minutes, Two Feathers spoke again. "I remember Running Wolf teaching me to ride. It was he who taught me our ways, not Yellow Hawk. He is my uncle's friend. Why?—I do not know."

For several moments, neither spoke.

"I talked to Running Wolf." Two Feathers's voice was mournful. "He told me to stay away from Yellow Hawk. Any feelings my uncle had for me are dead, except hate."

"I remember Running Wolf." Memories of his captivity in Yellow Hawk's camp stiffened Will's muscles and made breathing difficult. "He kept Yellow Hawk from killing me." His voice shook. "Twice."

A slight breeze fanned the few remaining coals into a brighter red. Will listened to the sound of the horses munching on their grain. He knew he'd have to leave his warm blankets to remove the feed bags for the night.

Two Feathers started talking again. "Barks Like Coyote told me the dunnia escaped and took the grullo with him. Yellow Hawk thinks the spirits turned the horse loose, and he believes he will get him when the spirits give their blessing. I do not believe that will happen. The spirits know the dunnia is yours. The spirits know that Gray Wolf is mine."

"Where is Yellow Hawk now?"

"He was hunting when I came into their camp. Running Wolf said they were going to the Nations. Yellow Hawk wants to return to Weeping Woman."

"He's leaving! That's a relief." The tightness between Will's eyes eased, and the night sky wasn't so dark. He tucked his blanket tighter under his chin. "How did Buck get loose?"

"Barks Like Coyote said the spirits untied his rope."

"Humm. You think so?" Will's chuckle came close to being a giggle. "It took me weeks to teach him to untie a knot."

Two Feathers propped himself up on one elbow. "I wish the spirits had been the ones to suffer Pa's scolding when he had to catch Buck three times in one day."

Will's laughter rippled through the night. "Me too. There was no way I was going to tell him what I'd taught Buck."

The coals in the fire shifted, and tiny sparks flashed in the dark.

"Do you think we can track Buck and Gray Wolf?"

Two Feathers's answer was slow in coming. "No. We cannot. It's been too many days." Will heard a long yawn before Two Feathers spoke again. "We must find them another way."

"Fort Bascom must be northeast of here. Maybe if we go

there, someone will have seen them. We can tell them about Yellow Hawk."

The only answer he got from Two Feathers was the even breathing of sleep. Will slipped from his blankets and removed the horses' feed bags.

Two days later, Will and Two Feathers decided to camp in a grove of cottonwoods on the south bank of the Canadian River, about an hour's ride from Fort Bascom. Will's eagerness to find any news about Buck hurried him to the river, where the horses got only a quick drink. Back at camp, he handed Two Feathers his and the packhorse's reins.

"This place is far enough from the fort to be out of sight of soldiers coming or going. The last thing we need is for the army to decide we're too young to be on the Llano Estacado alone and hold us at the fort." Will tightened the cinch on Rojo. "Are you coming?"

"No. I will wait for you here. I do not like soldiers." Two Feathers put his hand on Will's shoulder, stopping him from mounting. "What will you tell the soldiers if they ask why you are alone?"

Will scowled, and his forehead creased in thought. "I'll say I'm camped upriver with my Pa and brother. They sent me to buy supplies while they hunted."

"That is almost the truth. I am going hunting. We need meat for dinner." A small, tight smile followed Two Feathers's words.

He handed Will an empty tow sack for the supplies. Mounting, Will looped the drawstring over the saddle horn.

"I'm going to talk to the storekeeper at the sutler's store. Maybe he knows something. I'll pick up supplies and get more baking powder. Maybe before we get home, I'll learn to make good biscuits."

The smile on Two Feathers's face broadened. Grabbing his stomach, he shook his head. "Sinkers."

Will rode through the gate in the fort's adobe walls and past the sandstone officers quarters to the store. Fort Bascom was smaller than Fort Sumner, and so was the sutler's store. Though smaller in size, it was much better stocked. It reminded Will of how the store at Fort Sumner looked the first time he was there. After finding the baking powder, he decided he had enough money in his pocket to get a few cans of beans and peaches. Three large glass candy jars on the other end of the long counter tempted him, and he walked over. He nodded to the storekeeper, who nodded back.

"I'll be with you in a minute. Help yourself to what you need."

Will stood, studying the candy in the jars while the man took care of his customer.

"Corporal, you didn't lose all your money to that horse trader, did you?"

"No sir, I did not. I took one look at that big buckskin and shoved my money deep in my pocket."

"Smart man. I don't know how many tried to ride that devil, but the major is lucky he has any soldiers left to run this fort. I watched for a while, and the air was full of flying soldiers."

Excitement made Will's hands shake, and he dropped his stick candy back into the jar. In the other hand, he held a handful of Two Feathers's favorite flavors but left his in the jar. The corporal finished his business, and Will pushed his supplies down the counter to the clerk.

"Sir, did I hear you talking about a big buckskin horse? Was it a tall stallion?"

"Yes. Do you know that horse?" He didn't wait for Will to answer. "You stay away from him. He's a devil of a horse. He'll buck you off and then try to stomp you to death."

Will shoved his supplies in the tow sack and paid the man. "Was there a gray horse with him?"

"Yes. Pairing him with that gray was the only way the trader could handle that big monster."

"Do you know where the horse trader went?"

"I do. He won all the soldiers' money and headed for Las Vegas on the Gallinas River. Hey, what do you know about those horses?"

Will didn't answer. He was out the door and through the fort gate before the store clerk finished scratching his head.

LAS VEGAS

At the Gallinas River, Will stepped off Rojo at the riverbank. He dropped his head to the water and drank. Two Feathers followed with his mount and the packhorse and knelt to fill his canteen with the cold water. Will grabbed his canteen and joined his brother.

"We've pushed these horses hard. Let's find a camping spot and stop. We can't be too far from Las Vegas."

Crossing the river, Will followed it downstream, weaving Rojo between cottonwood trees and willows that lined the banks. Their bare winter branches swayed like stiff pokers in the wind. The boys found a spot where large slabs of rock layered in steps down to a deep pool in the river. Caught between two low-growing willows was a deadfall of driftwood from a past flood. The chunks of dried bark, dead limbs, and logs offered a good supply of fuel for several days.

"This place is good for hunting." Two Feathers tied his horse to a heavy branch in the deadfall.

Will dismounted and rubbed the small of his back. "We can stay here long enough to let Buck and Gray Wolf rest up for the trip home. I don't know what shape they'll be in."

Will stretched his arms over his head, trying to get the kinks out of his shoulders. *Or what shape I'm in.* Every muscle in his body ached, every bone throbbed, and every piece of clothing stunk. But the best he could hope for was to dream about a hot bath.

Two Feathers fed and hobbled the horses while Will started a fire. The dry wood burned with little smoke, and the heat felt good on his cold hands. Will's misery tumbled his thoughts around and around in his head. *I've been cold for days. Winter's not a good time to travel. I hope I find Buck in Las Vegas. I hope we can go home soon. I hope it doesn't snow.*

With the camp chores done, Two Feathers went hunting and shot two squirrels. After he skinned and cleaned them, he cut them up into a cast iron pot with some dried onion he'd brought in his saddlebag and covered the meat with water. Will threw in a little salt and jerky for flavor, set the lid on top, and nestled the pot in the small bed of coals. His stomach decided to sing its hungry song, and Will added more sticks to the fire to hurry up dinner.

After about an hour, he lifted the lid and the aroma rising with the steam added another verse to his growling hunger. He added flour to thicken the gravy.

"As many times as I watched Cookie fix meat this way, you'd think I'd be an expert. I know I dribble the flour in as slow as he did and stir as fast, but I still get lumpy gravy."

"Cookie's biscuits instead of your sinkers might make up for the lumps."

Two Feathers dodged the chunk of wood Will threw at him.

During the night, the air grew colder, and Will got up several times to add fuel to the fire. When the sun cast its first flame of color, he stuck one arm out of his blankets and stirred the coals with a stout stick. Sitting up, he wrapped a blanket around his shoulders and fed wood to the hungry flames. He dropped coffee grounds in the pot he'd filled with water the night before, set it by the fire, and waited for the aroma to wake Two Feathers.

An hour later, Will rode out of camp with three sinkers in one pocket and a handful of jerky in the other. He chewed first on a biscuit and then on the jerky, unable to decide which was tougher.

Riding into Las Vegas, Will spotted Grzelachowski's Mercantile store next to the tallest building he'd ever seen. It towered three stories into the air.

A man in a buckboard wagon hollered, "Hey, boy, move out of the middle of the street to do yer gawkin'."

Will nudged his horse to the front of the store and sat there staring up at the rows of bricks rising straight up into the sun. *I've got to bring Two Feathers to see this.* He dismounted and walked across the sidewalk.

Inside the store, rows and rows of goods greeted Will. The sound of his boots on the wood plank floor rang through the store. The room stretched so far and was so full he couldn't see where it ended. *Anything on earth a person needs must be in this store!* The size of the room reminded Will of Seligman's in Santa Fe, where he and Pa had bought Two Feathers's rifle. Part of the room held men's clothing and another part held women's. Boots lined one side of a row, and ladies shoes lined the other. A long counter ran along the middle of the back wall. To the right, shelves held canned food and household goods. To the left, they held farm and ranch supplies and tools. Onions, peppers, and garlic hung in bundles from the ceiling. On the floor, lumpy sacks of potatoes leaned against the counter, and barrels of who-knows-what lined one wall. The prettiest girl he'd ever seen walked up and smiled at him.

"Can I help you find something?"

The row of freckles that seemed to dance across her nose trapped him and led his eyes right up to her deep-blue ones.

"Uh . . . I uh . . ." *Why won't my words come?* "I need to talk to the storekeeper," he finally squeaked out, and he felt his face burn.

"That's him." She pointed to the man behind the counter.

Will wished those freckles would stop dancing before he got completely lost in her eyes. A horse blew outside, and his thoughts snapped back to Buck. He pulled himself away from the pretty face and walked to the back of the store. A bearded, reddish-haired man stood behind the counter, talking to a soldier with sergeant stripes on his sleeves.

"Tell Captain Inman the army continued my freighting contract to supply the forts. The supplies are ready?" The soldier nodded and paid for his goods. "I will send the wagons."

Will decided he'd come back to town to talk to this storekeeper before they headed home. Maybe he'd know about the stolen supplies. But that would have to wait. Right now, he only wanted to know about Buck and Gray Wolf. When the sergeant left, Will stepped to the counter.

"Sir, I need information, and I thought this might be the place to get it."

"What do you need, son?" The man spoke with an accent Will did not recognize.

"Have you heard anything about a horse trader with a big buckskin stallion? He'd be taking bets that no one can ride him." *Say yes, say yes, say yes.* The words spun around and around in his head like a whirlpool in the Colorado River, and he gripped the edge of the counter to keep from crumbling to the floor.

"You will ride that horse?" The words rose and turned into a question, and his bushy eyebrows shot up with them. "He is killer."

"No, sir. He isn't. I'm taking him home. He's mine."

The storekeeper stared at Will for a long time. "I am Grzelachowski." A strong, long-fingered hand gripped Will's in a firm shake.

The man's name blew right past Will. *I'll never remember that.*

"You are serious? He is yours?"

Will wondered if he always spoke in questions.

"Please tell me where he is."

"You will get men to help you." This time there was no question. His words held the firm tone of orders. "You be too small to handle a wild horse."

Will shifted his feet and put his hands on his hips. "I've been handling him since the day he was born. Please tell me where he is." Then he added, "Sir."

The storekeeper came out from behind the counter and motioned for Will to follow him. He stopped on the store's porch.

"You tell the truth?"

At the uptick in his voice, Will nodded. "The horse is mine. His name is Buck. The grullo is Gray Wolf."

"At end of street."

Mr. Grzelachowski pointed down Main Street and cocked his eyebrows at Will.

"On the right, is old barn with corrals in front."

"Thank you, sir."

A quick jump off the porch landed Will astride Rojo, and he headed down the street. He found the barn and spotted Buck in a sizable rectangular corral against the barn. Cowboys, soldiers, vaqueros, and townsmen either hung on the corral rails or tried to shove their way close enough to see the action inside.

Even through the roar of the men, Will heard the snorts and grunts of Buck's fear and solid thuds of his hooves landing on the hard ground. Anger rose within him to the point of explosion. His hands fisted, his teeth bit down till the pressure threatened to split them, but he managed to contain his fury.

Several men, money clutched in their hands, gathered around a fat-bellied man in baggy pants and a bright-red vest standing by the open door of the stable. They all talked at once, waving their money to make bets. Will pushed and shoved his way through the group and stopped in front of the man.

"I want to ride that horse." He yelled over the loud men. "I'll bet you anything you want I can ride him."

When he finished, all the men stood silent, and the horse trader stared at him.

"What did you say?"

"I said I want to ride that horse."

The noise of the crowd rose again with mocking snickers and laughter.

"Boy, that horse will kill you."

"No. He won't. He's mine."

"Yours? I don't believe so. I caught him out on the high plains. I have witnesses."

"I know. You also caught a grullo."

"That don't prove nothin'. Everyone around here knows that. If you want that horse, you'll have to buy him. And I ain't in a generous mood."

Taking a shaky deep breath, Will said the only thing that came to mind. "I can't buy him. I don't have any money to bet. But I can win him. I own a ranch near Fort Sumner. It has water rights. I'll bet my ranch I can ride that horse."

"You? Own a ranch? You're a boy."

An older man, dressed finer than a dollar-a-day cowboy, with a bright star pinned to his shirt pocket, stepped up next to Will.

"Hold on here, young fella. What's goin' on?" He looked from Will to the portly man holding a handful of money. "Porter, you got this boy's horse?"

"No, Sheriff, I do not. I caught him southwest of Fort Bascom. You can ask my wrangler, Peterson. He helped me catch him. I caught several more with him. Ask anyone at Fort Bascom. I brought the herd in there. Sold all but the buckskin and one other."

"My pa left our ranch to me. The Comanche that stole Buck killed my Pa. That horse is all I have left." Will looked back and forth between the sheriff and Porter. "The ranch is mine. The deed is in the land office in Santa Fe. But there's one more thing."

"What's that?" asked Porter.

"I want the grullo too."

"I suppose he's yours as well."

"No, he's my brother's. A gift from Charlie Goodnight."

At the mention of the famous cowman, the horse trader's attitude changed from mocking to frustration. Once again the murmur from the crowd rose. Porter took off his well-worn hat and slapped it against his leg, ran his fingers through his already scattered hair, and jerked his hat down tight. Will choked at the familiar mannerism.

Oh Pa, he does the same thing you do when you're upset with me. Are you telling me this is a bad deal? I had to bet the ranch. I don't have enough money for him to let me ride him. Trust me, Pa. Just trust me.

"There's no brand on either horse. How do I know he's yours?"

"I never put hot iron on him. A Comanche war chief named Yellow Hawk stole him."

"Yellow Hawk?" The sheriff interrupted before Porter could answer. "Do you know where that Comanche is?"

"No, sir!" Will's voice bit down hard on his answer. "If I did, I'd have my horse!"

The sheriff gripped Will's arm and walked away from the crowd. His eyes bored into Will's.

"Boy, is that horse yours? I can't let you ride him unless you convince me he's yours."

"Sir, my pa couldn't tolerate a liar, so I'm not one. He is mine. I slept in the stall with him the night he was born. I fed him from a bottle when his ma died. Please let me prove it. That's the only way I can get him back. I'll be fine. I promise. Let me get my horse."

A smile twitched the corners of the man's mouth. "That red-vested, hard-lined horse trader brags about how he never got took in a trade. If you can get one over on him, I'll laugh about it for a month."

They walked back to the waiting crowd.

Mr. Porter folded his hands on his round belly and stared at Will for a long time. Will stood his ground and stayed fixed on the man's coal-dark eyes. He was afraid to blink.

"Okay, boy. I'll take your bet." He looked around at the men watching the deal. "You all heard him. Sheriff, you heard. He made a man's bet, and he'll pay a man's price."

He stuck out his hand, and Will shook it.

Will tried to keep the smile off his face, but it seemed to have a will of its own. He thought back to the boy he had met on the cattle drive last year and how he and Buck won his sack of candy. Then his smile faded.

This was no sack of candy.

Will ran to the corral, made a jump for the rails, and scrambled to the top in time to see the rider fly high into the air. Buck circled to the far side of the corral and backed into the corner by the barn wall. He pawed the ground and tossed his head, his long black mane flying. His nostrils flared, and he snorted. With his ears laid back, tail whipping in a circle, front legs braced, Buck's eyes never strayed from the men on the rails.

Will stood on the top rail, braced himself against a tall corner post, and whistled loud and long.

Buck stopped. His head lifted. His ears shot forward. The men on the rails froze. The sudden silence was deafening.

Will climbed down the rails into the pen, and two cowboys joined him, ready to save him if that "devil of a horse" charged.

Will walked toward his best friend. Buck trotted to him, his ears forward and his head held high. Will raised his arms, and Buck settled his head between them. Boy and horse stood hugging each other for a long time. Will whispered soothing sounds in his ear. Before he let go, Will took a handful of mane and wiped his eyes. He hoped none of the cowboys saw it.

"Hey, ole boy. I'm glad to see you." He scratched behind Buck's ears and pulled at the knots in his forelock. "You're a mess. Every time I get you back from trouble, I spend a week brushing out tangles."

Will walked around the horse, checking for any serious injuries. Satisfied that Buck was okay, he pulled his head down and whispered in his ear.

"I have bad news. Yellow Hawk killed Pa when he took you." Will's throat choked off his voice. He leaned his head against Buck's neck, opened his mouth wide, and took several slow deep breaths to relax his clenched throat. "But don't worry," he said when his voice worked again. "We're gonna find that Comanche." The deep anger growing in Will's heart swelled with a heat that burned his face. "Two Feathers and I will bring him to justice. The army will make him pay for what he's done."

He led Buck to the center of the corral, undid the cinch, and pulled the saddle off. No saddle blanket protected Buck's back. A sharp rock dropped to the ground. Will picked it up. Fury made him speechless. A generous number of sores from earlier rocks peppered Buck's back. Will walked to the rails where the horse trader stood and slapped the stone in his hand.

"Here's your rock!" The fury in his words sprayed spittle across the man's red vest. "You bet me to ride him."

Will walked to his horse. He held the reins below the chin and tapped Buck's knee. The horse went down on both knees. Rumblings and murmurings came from the men lining the corral rails. Will smoothed the sweat-soaked hair on Buck's back, his hand finding too many sores from the rock.

Will stepped on one knee and scrambled onto his back. Buck never moved until Will gave the reins a gentle pull.

"Up, Buck."

Buck rose to his feet again, and Will walked him in a slow circle around the center of the pen. Several cowboys and vaqueros tipped their hats to him as he passed. Then he slid off and led Buck a few steps toward the gate. The men jumped down and gave Buck wide space when he stopped, tossed his head, and flared his nostrils. Will spoke to him, and he followed him out the gate and up to the horse trader, who stepped back about three paces.

"You're right, boy. He's yours." The horse trader's eyes showed grudging respect. "I've been in the horse business a long time, and I've never seen anything like that."

"Thank you, sir. I need the grullo, and I'll need salve for the sores on Buck's back."

The anger in Will's eyes made the trader's face redden.

The trip back to camp took twice as long as the trip in that morning. Will took his time and rode at a slow pace. He stopped often to rest the horses. Buck stayed at Will's knee, and Gray Wolf hung next to Buck.

The sun perched high overhead when they rode into camp. Will smelled something cooking when he dismounted from Rojo. Two Feathers left the deer hide he was working on and met Gray Wolf with a broad grin and a good scratching behind the ears. Gray Wolf lowered his head and rubbed it up and down on Two Feathers's chest. Laughter, something Will seldom heard from Two Feathers, bubbled up and lit his face. Will's hearty laugh joined his. Releasing the tension of these last days lifted their spirits, and life looked better.

Two Feathers scooped a generous portion of grain in the feedbags and slipped them over the twisting ears. Both horses munched their lunch. Will warmed his cold, stiff hands by the fire, where the aroma from the pot set his hunger rumbling. He sat on a rock near the fire, enjoying the warmth that soaked through his coat.

"I see you killed a deer this morning."

Two Feathers poured Will a cup of hot coffee.

"I got two deer this morning. I am working on the skins and will jerk the meat for the trip home."

Will blew on his hot coffee and sipped a drop.

"We need more supplies. We're about out of coffee and flour. The horses need grain. Buck and Gray Wolf are thin." He dug to the bottom of his pockets and pulled out his money. It wasn't much. "I'll get the grain, flour, and coffee. We have meat, so we can do without bacon. If there's any money left over, I'll get beans."

Will and Two Feathers the spent afternoon slicing deer meat into strips and draping them on a drying rack over the fire. While Two Feathers worked the deer brains into the deer hide to cure it, Will gathered driftwood both upstream and downstream. He grew tired, so he decided to use wood from the deadfall at the edge of their camp.

"Leave that." Two Feathers pointed to the clouds building up in the north. "We will need wood close by for the fire. It will get colder."

That night the cold wind picked up and did its best to sting their toes. Will snuggled under the extra blankets from Mr. Wallace's store at Fort Sumner. He and Two Feathers took turns keeping the fire going under the jerky and warming rocks for their cold feet.

Morning made its dull-gray appearance. With a breakfast of biscuits and jerky, Will headed for town. He studied one of the biscuits. It was taller and not as hard and flat as the others. Maybe he'd learn to make them as good as Cookie's yet.

A busy hubbub met Will when he stepped inside Grzela-chowski's Mercantile. The wind caught the door, slamming it into the wall. It took a minute to pull it shut, and one of the men sitting around the potbellied stove hollered, "Close the door!" Will walked over and spread his hands toward the welcome heat. Several men sat in chairs circling the stove. Some leaned toward it, and some sat on tilted chairs away from it. Will didn't stand there long enough for the men to start asking him questions about who he was or where he was going. After the storekeeper finished helping a customer, Will walked to the counter. He hoped to see the freckle-faced girl but didn't.

"Hello, sir. I need a few things—flour, beans, coffee, and grain for our horses."

"You found horse?"

"Yes, sir." Will liked the uptick at the end of the man's sentences. It gave him a happy sound. "I did. I heard you tell the soldier yesterday that you have the contract to deliver army supplies to the forts around here. Do you deliver to Fort Sumner?"

"Yes. Why?"

"My pa and I found stolen supplies a few months back and took them to Fort Sumner. I wondered if they came from Fort Union."

"Captain Stanaway from Fort Sumner come. He ask same question. He went to Fort Union." He shrugged his shoulders. "Nothing missing there, nothing missing here. All shipments good. Fort good. My store good. Your name is Whitaker? Captain told about you finding stolen supplies." The uptick at the end of Mr. Grzelachowski's sentences gave his words a singsong rhythm.

Will nodded and watched the man's face but saw no accusation. Maybe Stanaway hadn't shared his suspicions. Anger that threatened to jump to Pa's defense settled down.

Mr. Grzelachowski stacked Will's goods on the counter and figured the bill. The money in Will's pocket covered it, with enough left over in case they needed it on the way home. Will collected his purchases from the counter.

"Sir, can I ask you one more question?"

The storekeeper cocked one eyebrow. "Question?"

"Do you know a scout named Badger?"

"Thief. Sells guns to Comanche. He is bad." The man's voice was flat and serious. Will wondered what happened to his uptick. "Stay away from this man, yes?"

Will grinned. *There it is.*

"Yes, sir. I will."

Leaving the store, Will juggled supplies to open the door. A blast of wind slammed it against the wall and a chorus of "Close the door!" boomed from the crowd around the pot-bellied stove.

ANGRY BROTHERS

The welcome light spilling from the open door of the adobe house lifted Will's spirits. He and Two Feathers stepped off their weary horses in its glow.

"We're glad to see the two of you!" Jake took the pack-horse's reins. "See you found Buck and Gray Wolf."

Tony lifted the almost empty packs from the weary animal.

"We got plumb worried. Thought maybe Yellow Hawk found you. Did he still have your horses?" He patted Will on the shoulder. "You was gone about two weeks, and that's too long."

Jake handed the packhorse's reins to Two Feathers, giving one of his braids a slight tug.

"December got here while you were gone. Thought we'd have to come huntin' you."

"I was beginning to think we'd never get home. We'll tell you everything at supper." Will's voice drooped along with his sagging shoulders to a depth of tiredness he had never felt before. "We can take the horses. How about fixin' us some food? We're tired of eatin' our own cookin'." He and Buck followed Gray Wolf and Two Feathers toward the barn.

Tony reached out to pat Buck, and the big horse shied away, snorted, and laid his ears flat against his head.

"Easy, Buck. Easy." Will motioned Tony away, patted the stiff neck, and kept a firm grip on the reins. "Step away, Tony. He's skittish. He's had pretty rough treatment and won't let anyone but me near him. He's pretty beat up, and he's sore all over. We traveled slow. That's why it took so long to get home."

The grullo nickered to the agitated buckskin.

Will spoke in a low singsong voice and headed toward the barn. "We're home, big boy. You're safe now."

At the barn, he held all the reins, and Two Feathers forked a thick layer of hay on the floor of their stalls and filled their hay troughs, water buckets, and feed bins. Will handed Gray Wolf's, Rojo's, and the packhorse's reins to Two Feathers and walked Buck into his stall. The solid sound of the wood bar sliding to lock Buck's stall lifted the worry from Will's mind.

"I'll be back in a bit."

He scratched under the tangled forelock and followed Two Feathers to the house. A bowl of thick venison stew with onions and potatoes, a cup of fresh hot coffee, and flaky biscuits filled Will and relaxed the tight muscles that had squeezed into thick cords. His eyes swept the faces of the men around the table, and he enjoyed the relief that showed in the grin-crinkled eyes and happy spirits of all on the Pecos River Ranch. Tony and Jake asked questions, and Will and Two Feathers told where they had gone and how they found their horses.

"You didn't bet the ranch?" Jake scratched the back of his neck.

Will grinned at the uptick in Jake's words. *He sounds like Mr. Grzelachowski.*

"Not seriously?" Tony's face looked like his stomach had done flip-flops.

"Yes, I did." Will sat tall in the chair. "That trader told me I'd made a man's bet and I'd have to pay a man's price."

The twins shook their heads.

"What if you'd lost?" asked Tony.

"There was no way I was going to lose."

Two Feathers took the last biscuit off the plate.

"I think it was the trader that paid the price." He held the biscuit up to the light, studied it, and then broke off a piece. "Who made these?"

"I did," Tony said. "Why? What's the matter with it?"

"Nothing. They are good." He popped the piece in his mouth. "You need to teach Will. He makes sinkers."

That night, Will piled hay and spread his blankets in the corner of Buck's stall.

"I'm stayin' here all night. Sing out if you need me."

Buck snorted and swished his tail back and forth. Will sat on the edge of the hay trough and stroked the muscled neck.

"Easy, boy. I'm not going anywhere." Keeping his voice low and slow, Will talked. "I'll stay with you till you feel better." He picked up a handful of grain and fed it to Buck. "Do you remember the night you were born?" A smile wrinkled Will's eyes. "That's silly. No one remembers when they were born." He fed him more grain. "Your ma died, and I stayed with you all night. I was little. Like you. We've been together every day since then. Except for Yellow Hawk. You've got to watch better. You need to stay away from him."

He settled on his blankets with his head cradled on his arm, like he had so many times when danger was near. Buck lay down on the bed of hay, and before long, Will heard his soft snoring.

The next morning, Will and Two Feathers started cleaning their horses. It took all day to work the tangles, grass, dirt, and grit out of their manes, tails, and coats. Jake brought medicines and clean cloths to Will and left them at the barn door. Will spread salve on the wounds on Buck's back and patted a poultice on his forelegs, sore from all the bucking, and wrapped them in strips of clean cloth. Will brushed his golden coat until it shined in the sunlight.

Then Will gave Rojo some needed attention and Two Feathers worked on the packhorse. With some serious brushing, Will finally removed the dust that had accumulated in Rojo's dark-red coat. The long head with the white blaze pushed against Will's chest and the ears twitched.

"You need your ears scratched? Pa scratched them for you many times, didn't he, ol' boy?" Rojo was his horse now, and he knew the horse missed Pa as much as he did.

Buck's improvement came one day at a time. Gradually, Buck's nervousness eased away. He and Gray Wolf gained back the weight they lost and grew sleek and strong. One day in mid-December Will, Two Feathers, Jake, and Tony watched from the corral bars as Buck and Gray Wolf chased each other.

"You'd never know anything happened to them." Tony leaned over the bars to see Will. "Buck's doing fine. Jake and I been goin' in and out of the barn for a while now without upsetting Buck."

Will nodded. "He's the best." Pride put strength in his words.

"That's what Jake and me been talking about. You need to find good mares and raise horses. You'd have good ones from a fine stallion like Buck."

"That's what Pa said."

Sudden thoughts of Pa always made his heart feel too

heavy for his chest. He climbed down from the rails and went into the house.

Over the next week, the weather grew colder, and snow fell, hiding the ranch under a clean, crisp layer of uncertainty. Will enjoyed the beauty of the fresh snow, but worried about the trouble it caused on young and old stock, including frozen water holes, snow-covered grass, and subfreezing temperatures.

He remembered the fun snow had brought on their ranch in Texas—the snowball fights with Ma and Pa, building a snowman, sliding down hills on the bobsled Pa had made, and making snow angels. Pa's laughter always joined his and Ma's, but sometimes he would stop, study the clouds, even sniff the wind, and his forehead would crease with worry lines. Now Will understood.

Christmas Day arrived, and they all rode to Mateo's for dinner. Will rode Buck for the first time since they had come home from Las Vegas. Two Feathers rode Gray Wolf alongside the big stallion. Tony and Jake followed behind to keep an eye on Buck. Will kept one hand on Buck's neck, patting and rubbing it to reassure him. He talked to him, and the horse's ears turned back to listen.

"Good boy, Buck. Good boy." He and Two Feathers rode side by side for a few miles, both horses moving along with an easy gait. "What do you think, Two Feathers? I think they're gonna be okay."

"I think Buck will be fine." Two Feathers smiled at Will. "And Gray Wolf."

Jake's laughter rang out behind them. "You boys need to quit frettin' over them horses. They're young and strong, and with all the care and lovin' they get, they're right as rain."

Relief at Buck's steady gate relaxed Will in the saddle, and he enjoyed the ride in the brisk cold air.

Mateo's broad smiling face greeted their arrival, and Señora Alma fussed over them, giving smothering hugs and smacking kisses on each jaw. Two Feathers managed to duck inside the house before she grabbed him in her chubby arms.

"Buenos días, muchachos. Welcome. Feliz Navidad."

The delicious aroma coming from the long, narrow, low-roofed hacienda drew the four visitors inside. A wide fireplace in the middle of the back wall crackled with a warm, cheery blaze. Dutch ovens hanging from hooks on one end above the bed of glowing coals held fragrant delights that teased their noses and made their mouths water. Slices of lamb and ham left over from Mateo's family feast after midnight mass in Puerto de Luna filled platters on the long table. Señora Alma and her daughters busied themselves making mountains of tortillas and puffy sopapillas dripping with honey.

After dinner, Will persuaded Cesar to show him how to swing a rope into a wide loop. Twirling his long lariat, Cesar built a loop that danced and sailed into the air as though it were an extension of the vaquero's arm. Mateo's daughters lined up on the front porch to watch the show. Will slid out his loop and swung the lariat over his head, but it wouldn't behave. It tangled, twisted, and turned inside out. The more the girls on the porch giggled, the more Will couldn't make his lariat cooperate. His face burned hot each time the loop collapsed around him. Finally, Will gave up in disgust.

"Here, Two Feathers, you give it a try. The harder I work, the worse it gets."

When Two Feathers settled the loop of rope in his hand and swung it into the air over his head, the loop stayed up, spinning in perfect circles. The girls' giggles didn't seem to affect his efforts at all. Will threw his head back and laughed out loud at the spinning rope. Laughter felt good. It had been a long time since he'd had anything to laugh about. A quick flick of Two Feathers's wrist, and the spinning rope flew through the air. When it settled around Will's shoulders, he pulled it tight with a gentle tug.

"Hey." Will let the loop drop to his feet. "Do I look like a wayward maverick to you?" He picked up the rope and coiled it as he walked to Two Feathers. "That was a good toss. Since we're partners on the ranch and you're good with a rope, you can be the roping partner, and I'll be the thinking one."

"That will work, but when did you learn to think?"

Two Feathers flashed Will one of his rare smiles and beat him into the house for another sweet sopapilla.

The warmth of the long main room surrounded Will with comfort. Comfort of a house filled with love. Comfort of colorful rugs, cowhide chairs, and heavy tables covered with bright embroidered cloths. Comfort of knowing he would always be welcome.

"Señora Alma, thank you for the dinner." Will's words eased around the lump in his throat. "You made this day easier for Two Feathers and me. We made a gift for you."

Two Feathers handed her a braided bracelet made of thin strips of deer hide with a smooth black stone from the creek secured in the middle. One of her daughters fastened it around her chubby wrist, and it fit.

"Gracias, muchachos." Tears pooled in her wide black eyes. "Ustedes son bueno chicos. You are good boys."

Tony and Jake led the four horses to the front porch, and Señora Alma hustled the girls inside to clean up the dishes. Will and Two Feathers mounted their horses, but Señora Alma caught Tony and Jake in her chubby arms and planted her sloppy kisses on each cheek.

"Adios, muchachos. Feliz Navidad. Vuelve pronto."

Señora Alma released the red-faced twins, and they mounted their horses.

"Sí, come back soon," Mateo said and patted Will's and Two Feathers's knees.

The boys rode off with bags stuffed with food hanging from each saddle horn.

After the arrival of the new year, the boring sameness of winter chores began to get on Will's nerves. Tony and Jake rode the rounds, busting ice in water holes and creeks so the animals could drink. Will and Two Feathers rode on the hay wagon to feed cattle. Since his brother's words were few and far between, Will had plenty of time to think. Thoughts of Pa and running the ranch. Thoughts of Captain Stanaway and stolen supplies. And worst of all, thoughts of Yellow Hawk, which set his insides quivering and made his heart feel like a thick lump in his chest. The thoughts followed him wherever he went and tormented him no matter what he was doing. He needed to trust that he could make the ranch work. He needed the mystery of the stolen supplies solved. He needed Stanaway and Yellow Hawk to go away. But he didn't know how to make it happen.

On a cold mid-February morning, Will and Two Feathers headed to the barn, hitched the mules to the wagon, and drove to a haystack. They tossed forks of hay into the wagon until the pile threatened to topple over. Will clucked to the mules, and they started on their rounds. The cold north wind worked its way through Will's heavy coat, through his pants, past his long johns, and through his boots to grab him in its freezing grip.

"I been thinking." Will glanced at his partner on the wagon seat. "We need to go to Fort Sumner."

"Why?" Two Feathers shifted his place on the seat to turn his back more to the wind.

"We should tell Colonel Dowell about the chipped boot track and the wood shavings and everything else that's happened."

"No!" The sharp tone in Two Feathers's voice bit the word off short.

"That's what you always say." Will's tone matched his brother's. He took a deep breath. "Maybe what we know will help the army figure this out. Not all soldiers are like the ones that raided your village."

"No!" Same sharp tone. Same tight word. Same stubborn expression.

Will's back stiffened, and he slapped the reins on the mules' rumps.

"Giddyup. It's too cold out here."

An awkward silence settled between the brothers.

Will pulled up to their first feeding spot. Cattle lowed their welcome and gathered around the wagon, pushing and shoving each other to reach the hay that Will and Two Feathers forked onto the ground. Will clucked to the mules, and they stepped up several paces till Will called "Whoa." The cows that didn't grab a bite followed after the wagon. The boys tossed out more forkfuls, then climbed back onto the wagon seat and headed to their second spot.

Two Feathers's stubborn refusal to talk to the army frustrated Will until he couldn't think of anything else. Every time he brought up the subject, the only response was the same clipped, sharp "No!"

At the noon camping spot, with a warm fire going and hot coffee cups warming their cold hands, Will brought up going to the fort again.

"We know someone at the fort is stealing the supplies and killed Private Tucker."

Two Feathers sipped his coffee and dunked a cold, hard biscuit in it. He nodded his head.

"We think Badger is working for the person at the fort. And we think he got rifles for Yellow Hawk."

Two Feathers dunked his biscuit again and nodded.

"We know he trades with the Comanche."

"Na-es-cha told us that," Two Feathers said as he refilled their cups.

"Yes, she did, and we need to tell the colonel."

"No!"

He poured the remaining coffee over their small fire and packed the pot in the wooden box under the seat. Without speaking, they climbed into the wagon. Picking up the reins, Will could no longer hold his temper.

"We've seen tracks all over this part of the country, and that's all you have to say?" His pitch rose with each word, and the last one exploded with a shout.

He slapped the reins hard on the mules' rumps, and when they lunged into their harness, he and Two Feathers slammed against the seat back. Two Feathers grabbed the reins from Will and hauled back hard, slowing the mules.

In clipped, slow words, Two Feathers said, "I told you before. We do not know who at the fort is the thief or murderer. If we tell what we know, they will come after US!" He leaned close to Will and yelled the last word in his face.

Will stood in the wagon and dipped his words in sarcasm. "So the great Comanche warrior is scared."

The tendons in Two Feathers's neck corded. His eyes bulged. His face darkened to a deep purple, and he threw himself at Will. They tumbled out of the wagon and hit the ground—hard. Will's lungs emptied in a loud whoosh.

Gasping for air, he scrambled to his feet, grabbed Two Feathers's coat, pulled him up, and socked him in the eye. Staggering from the blow, Two Feathers stepped back, sucked in air, and charged, taking Will to the ground. They rolled over the lip of a shallow embankment onto the sandy floor. Two Feathers landed on Will and smacked a solid punch to his mouth, busting Will's lip open. Blood spurted, ran off his chin, and onto his coat. Two Feathers rolled off, and they lay gasping in the dirt for several minutes.

Will's body felt numb, except for his throbbing lip. He sat up, spat out the salty blood, and wiped his mouth. Glaring at Two Feathers, he staggered to his feet and scrambled up the embankment. Two Feathers followed. The team hadn't wandered far and left only a small trail of scattered hay, which the cattle cleaned up.

Climbing to their places on the wagon seat, Will snuck a quick glance at his brother's face. His left eye was nearly swollen shut and red as a fox. Neither boy moved. Silence stretched between them as rigid as a stone wall. An apology pushed against Will's lips, but Two Feathers's mouth was clamped into a tight thin line, and he turned his head away. Will swallowed the apology and shifted farther to his side of the seat. The silent pair began the second half of their day.

Shadows stretched long on the ground by the time they unhitched the team at the barn and got them fed and watered. Will ached all over from bouncing on the frozen ground, and his split lip throbbed. Before he blew the lantern out, he stole a quick glance at Two Feathers. The sight of the swollen purple eye slumped Will's shoulders and dropped his head.

What have I done? Thoughts tumbled through his head. *But it's not just me.* He picked up his head, and his breathing quickened. *Two Feathers won't listen. We have to do something.* He blew out the lantern and shut the door.

They left the barn—walking side by side, but not together. A strange horse stood tied to the hitching rail in front of the house. They exchanged a questioning glance, but neither spoke.

Will stopped the moment he stepped into the room. Two Feathers bumped into Will and gave him a push out of his way. A step around Will and Two Feathers stopped too. Sitting at their table, drinking their coffee, sat Captain Stanaway.

The boys stared at the soldier. Jake and Tony stared at the boys. The captain sipped his coffee.

"What in tarnation happened to you two?" Tony said and jumped up from the table. He grabbed a bowl and poured warm water from the stove.

Jake poured cold water into another bowl. "Did you fall off a cliff? Sit down. You boys need tendin' to."

Will and Two Feathers sat across from Stanaway and let the twins treat their wounds. After Jake threw the bloody water out the back door, Will faced their visitor.

"Captain Stanaway, what do you want here?" His words sounded brittle with a strained politeness.

"I'm returning to the fort and decided, since your place was near, I'd rather stay here than camp out in the cold."

Will decided the captain's smile could chip ice, but he knew Pa would never turn a man out in the cold.

"Of course you are welcome to stay the night."

The conversation at supper was stilted and awkward. With his lip split and his jaw sore, Will nibbled at his food, while Two Feathers stirred his in circles on his plate. Will thought about their fight that afternoon. One minute he felt sorry for what he said, but the next minute he was mad all over again at Two Feathers's stubbornness. They avoided speaking to each other through supper.

After breakfast the next morning, before Captain Stanaway left for Fort Sumner, he stood with Will and Two Feathers on the porch.

"Boys, I have bad news for you. I couldn't bring myself to say it last night, but you need to know what I think about the stolen supplies. I have been investigating, and I plan to report to Colonel Dowell that I believe Dan Whitaker was the mastermind behind the thefts and that he was killed because of a disagreement between him and his partners. They enlisted the aid of a Comanche war chief, probably for rifles, and that's how your ranch was attacked and your father killed. There is no evidence that any army personnel were involved, and you and your father are the only ones who found any stolen supplies. And there was no indication of any thefts before you came here."

No one moved or spoke. Even the wind stopped.

Will stared at the man, and his blood froze in his veins. Legs too stiff to move kept him rooted in one spot. Disbelief forced his head toward Two Feathers, whose mouth stood open in a perfect O. Tony and Jake stood on the porch like statues. A slow red burned away the stark white Stanaway's words put on their faces. Tony stepped between Will and Two Feathers.

"Captain Stanaway, you need to think this through. You can't find the real thieves, so you're taking the easy trail and blaming it on Will and Dan. Look harder. You are wrong!"

Jake pushed Tony over to step beside him. United, the four young ranchers stood facing their enemy.

Will snapped out of his shock and stepped off the porch. Anger pounded through his veins and lit his heart on fire.

"Get on your horse and get out of here! You have no *proof* of what you say because there is no proof. I think *you* sold the guns to Yellow Hawk so he would kill my father. We know *you* are behind the robberies. We have—"

Two Feathers put his hand on Will's shoulder and squeezed. Will's words died.

"If we stole those supplies, why would we bring them to the fort? Leave—this—ranch!" Two Feathers's voice held the sharp threat of a nocked arrow. His braids blew in a sudden gust of wind, and the turkey feathers fluttered like feathers on a war lance.

Captain Stanaway shifted his gaze from one angry face to another, mounted his horse, and rode away from the Pecos River Ranch.

SMOKEY

Will stood by the hitching rail in front of the house, watching Stanaway ride out of sight. *How could anyone think that about Pa?* His knees threatened to collapse, and his breakfast didn't seem to want to stay put.

"Now what do we do?" Will's words squeezed out in a choking cough.

No one answered.

Will faced the others. Two Feathers's face was a sick, pale orange. Will watched him try to swallow. It took a long time for whatever he swallowed to go down.

"What do we do?" Two Feathers repeated Will's words.

They lacked the forceful tone he had used on Captain Stanaway. All he had left was weak and scratchy—almost a whisper.

Tony put his arms on their shoulders and guided them back into the house.

"I'll tell you what we are going to do. Nothing. We are going to do nothing about the army's business. We are going to do a lot about our business. It's winter, and that means our business is feeding and keeping our herd safe through cold weather. Will sent word to Mr. Goodnight, and either he will come or he will send Smokey. They can deal with the army."

February passed into March with the speed of a turtle crossing a dusty road. During those weeks, they heard nothing from the army. The haystacks shrank to more than half their size, and the cattle drifted with their backs to the cold wind. Will dreaded the sameness of each day. Working on the ranch one day—fork hay, turn cattle back toward home, and check for sickness. Then the next day—mend tack, repair tools, and chop wood.

One morning, Will and Jake worked together cleaning the barn. Jake's mood was somber and had been since Will's and Two Feathers's fight. Will felt as if a low-hanging dark cloud had settled over the ranch and everyone on it. After dumping the handcart of old straw from the stalls, Jake confronted Will.

"What happened between you and Two Feathers? Tony and I are tired of nothing but long faces around here."

"We had a fight." Will forked clean straw into Buck's stall.

"We know that. What was it about? You two are brothers. You're not supposed to fight with each other."

"I can't tell you. Maybe someday I will, but not now."

After spreading clean straw in all the stalls, Will headed out to clear water holes. He rode up the creek alone, without Two Feathers. The idea of the army thinking Pa was a thief and murderer intensified his anger at Two Feathers for not agreeing to tell Colonel Dowell what they knew. It simmered in his heart like soup on the stove. He tried to understand Two Feathers, but all he could think about was Pa.

Most of the waterholes were clear or nearly clear, except the one farthest from the house. It was in a curve of the creek, shaded by bluffs that hung over the water and sheltered from the wind. This waterhole held onto its ice. Swinging the heavy ax to break the ice started his shoulders aching. His fingers stung from dipping his hands into the water to clear chunks of ice so the water could flow, and he stuck his fingers into his armpits, hoping to find a little warmth.

Mid-March brought a snowstorm that lasted for two days. When the last snowflake fell, Will and Two Feathers bundled up in layers of coats and saddled Buck and Gray Wolf. Jake and Tony led a not-too-happy team out of the warmth of the barn and hitched them to the hay wagon. The mules shook their heads and blew blasts of steam from their noses in protest.

"Tony, keep a lookout for heavy heifers," said Will, leading Buck out of the barn. "I want to move as many first-calf heifers to the brush corral as we can find. Those high canyon walls block the wind, and the calves will have a better chance to survive."

"Good plan." Jake nodded and climbed aboard the tall hay wagon with Tony. "We'll keep our eyes peeled. Tomorrow we'll round 'em up. Won't hurt to put a few older momma cows with them. Keeps 'em settled. We'll be later than usual tonight. The haystacks we have left are farther out. See you boys at supper."

The wheels rumbled over the snow-covered road the hay wagon had worn between the house and barn over many trips.

Will watched Two Feathers ride off without saying a word. One minute, Will wished he'd spoken to him, and the next minute, he was mad because Two Feathers didn't say anything either. Will rode with his heart sitting like a lump on top of his stomach. The silence between them since the day of their fight, the same day Stanaway showed up, saddened him. His nerves felt ragged. The only time he had spoken to Two Feathers since then was when the four of them had sat around the table making plans for the division of the winter work. They spread out the map of the ranch and divided it into four parts. Each day the hay wagon covered two, and the other two riders took an area apiece to move cattle closer to the ranch and to check for sick calves. Will missed their shared times. He missed sharing ideas.

He missed his brother.

The snowstorm had taken the clouds with it and left a white blanket over the high desert. As far as Will could see, snow sparkled in the sunlight. With not a living thing in sight, the layer of snow hushed all sound except the crunch of Buck's hooves. Will stopped. He and Buck sat still. The trails lay hidden under the snow. The landmarks lost their shape. The pale-blue sky stretched forever. A sense of complete aloneness settled on Will, and he felt as though he and Buck had shrunk to the size of ants.

How can I make this ranch work? I wish Pa was here. Am I doing enough to keep the ranch going? I have questions, Pa. He searched the vast land for an answer, but there was none. *I'm tired.*

A black speck appeared in the never-ending sky. Then another. And another. They grew wings and circled, slow and lazy.

"Buzzards!"

Will tapped Buck, and they headed in the direction of what Will knew could only mean bad news.

And bad news is what he found. One of Charlie Goodnight's old cows had made the trip from Texas with them but couldn't make it through the winter. The storm had brought the birth of her calf and left her too weak to survive. Now the calf shivered in the cold and nudged his dead momma. Will swung his lariat, and it settled around the dark-red neck. Buck held the rope taut, and Will ran his hand down it to the calf, picked him up, and laid him on his side. With a few quick flicks of his hands, he tied the calf's legs. He coiled his rope and looped it over the saddle horn, then led Buck to the downed calf. A tap on the horse's knee, and Buck dropped low enough for Will to settle the calf across the saddle.

All the way back to the barn, Will grabbed either an ear or the tail to keep the wiggling, bawling calf from falling off Buck. The calf landed with a plop when Will dumped him in the hay pile in the back of the barn. He found a length of rope and tied him in the stall next to old Nellie, the milk cow they had bought from Mateo.

"Okay, Little Red, if you behave yourself, she might let you have supper."

Will mounted Buck and headed back out.

The cold March wind slowed and warmed, melting the snow. But one sunny day, the winds held a stiff blustery bite and blew in Smokey. When Will and Two Feathers drove the hay wagon into the ranch yard, tied to the rail at the front porch was Smokey's tall brown horse.

"Smokey!" Two Feathers hollered.

Will laughed at Two Feathers's wild yip and his flying leap off the wagon. Will drove the team to the barn, unhitched them, brushed them down, and filled their troughs with hay. He decided a little time alone with Smokey would be good for Two Feathers. When he finally ambled up to the house, Smokey greeted him with a firm handshake and an even firmer hug. Will had never been so grateful to see someone. He knew once Charlie Goodnight had heard the news about Pa, he wouldn't let him down.

With a good supper under their belts and time spent swapping stories, Jake and Tony headed to the cave house to bed. Will noticed the fire in the cook stove had burned down to ashes and coals.

"I'm headed to bed," he said. "We have chores tomorrow."

Will stood and pushed his chair under the table.

"Will." Sadness widened Two Feathers's eyes, and forgiveness shimmered in their dark depths. "You were right. We need to tell Smokey what we know."

Will's long-held anger slipped away and took the guilty heaviness he had carried since their fight away with it.

"Yes, we do."

"Come on, boys." Smokey stood and walked into the living room. "Let's sit in here in front of the fire. The kitchen is getting a little cold for my old bones."

Two Feathers stirred the coals from the starved fire, and Will handed him kindling and then a few small logs. The boys pulled their chairs close and shared the fire's warmth. Smokey pulled off his boots and slid a rope and cowhide chair close enough to the fire so his cold feet could reach the hearth.

"I've known for a long time you boys were keeping secrets," Smokey said. "You're not very good at hiding things. Too much whispering and sneaking around for an old scout like me." He shifted his rump in the chair and rubbed his feet together. Nodding at Two Feathers, he used his boss-like tone that left no room for misunderstanding. "You didn't tell me much on that huntin' trip. I figured you left out a goodly bit. But it's time to open that corral and let all you know run loose."

Smokey laid his head on the chair back, closed his eyes, and waited.

Two Feathers started at the beginning.

"I found a boot track with a chip out of the heel at the first stash of goods. We didn't know what it meant. So we didn't tell anyone."

His tone was hesitant, but as the story came out, the boys' words tumbled over each other in their haste to finally tell all they knew.

When they finished, Smokey was no longer in his chair. He was pacing back and forth in front of the fireplace, and thunderclouds replaced the relaxed look on his face. That look silenced Will, and he motioned for Two Feathers to hush. They waited for the pacing to stop. When it did, Smokey stood, his hands on his hips, staring at both boys with eyes hard as black slate.

"You should have told the army about that track when you first found it." The pacing started up again. "Why didn't you tell Dan about all this?"

"We knew he'd tell Colonel Dowell," said Will, standing to make their reasoning stronger.

Two Feathers picked up the story. "We think the man planning the thefts is in the army, and we do not know who it is." He stood in front of Smokey. "I hate soldiers. I do not trust them."

Smokey studied their faces. He put his arms around their shoulders and pulled them to him. The woodsy smell of the soft buckskin shirt against Will's face and the strong arms holding onto him felt good. For the first time in many months, he felt safe.

A moment later, Smokey and the boys settled back into their chairs. The scout rubbed his shaggy gray beard and stretched his cold feet toward the fire.

"The time for secrets is over." His scowling face and bushy beard made Will think of a grizzly bear he'd heard about once. "Whether you like soldiers or not, it's past time to tell them all you know. We'll make a trip to Fort Sumner tomorrow and talk to Colonel Dowell."

Smokey's stern face kept Two Feathers silent.

Will woke in the night and lay still under his warm blankets, listening to the gurgling snore of Smokey. Even though the sound brought memories of Pa and caused tears to prick the back of his eyelids, it was good to hear snoring in the house again.

Will sat up on one elbow and whispered, "Two Feathers? Are you awake?"

The blankets on the bunk beside his wiggled, and a tangled mass of black hair poked out. "I am now. What do you want?"

"I'm sorry I got so mad at you for not telling what we know. That was wrong."

More wiggling and squirming brought long strands of hair out from under the covers.

"We were both wrong."

A hand slid from the blankets. Will stuck his hand into the cold air, and the boys shook.

A sleepy voice rumbled from across the room. "Since that's settled, go to sleep."

Sunset the following day found three cold and weary travelers stepping off their horses at the barn behind Wallace's store at Fort Sumner. After feeding the animals, Smokey led the way into the store to ask about a warm place to spend the night.

Mr. Wallace wiped his hands on his apron and shook Smokey's then the boy's hands.

"I don't have any beds, but you're welcome to pick a spot on the floor. You'll find the stove a mite warmer than the wagon yard. There's plenty of wood outside the back door. Help yourself."

He went into his living quarters off the back room and shut the door.

Will stacked a pile of stove wood within reach so he wouldn't need to leave his warm cocoon to feed the fire during the night.

The next morning, sizzling bacon drew the boys out of their blankets and to the breakfast table in the back of the store. Mrs. Wallace filled their plates, and Na-es-cha set a bowl of gravy on the table. Two Feathers picked up a biscuit and waved it in front of Will's face.

"Maybe this is where you need to take biscuit-making lessons."

He took a big bite, and a happy smile spread between his bulging cheeks.

"I make good biscuits." Will spread a thick layer of gravy over his and stuffed a large bite in his mouth. "But not as good as these," he mumbled as he chewed.

Na-es-cha leaned over Two Feathers's shoulder and filled his coffee cup. She whispered, and his fork froze in midair for a second. His head dropped in a tiny nod, and Will wondered what she'd said. Two Feathers continued eating as though nothing had happened. Will glanced at Smokey. The old scout was focused on his plate. When the last spot of gravy disappeared from his plate, Will stood.

"Come on, Two Feathers. Let's go feed the horses."

"Hurry up, boys. We need to see the colonel and head back to the ranch," Smokey said, brushing the biscuit crumbs from his beard.

As soon as they were out of hearing range, Will grabbed his brother's arm and hurried him into the barn.

"What did Na-es-cha say?"

Before he could answer, the barn door opened a little, and she slipped inside. She and Two Feathers spoke in Comanche for several minutes while Will fed and watered the horses. Then she pulled her wrap around her shoulders and hurried back to the store.

The minute she left, Will asked, "What's going on?"

Two Feathers talked as they gave the three horses a quick brushing.

"She heard about the raid on the ranch. A few days before the raid, Badger came to the fort. He tried to trade Mr. Wallace worn bad skins for a knife. They had what she called a 'word fight.' Mr. Wallace said no, he would not buy bad skins. Then about a week after the raid, Badger came back with money to buy a knife."

"Where did he get the money?"

"She does not know. But when Badger left, she was scrubbing the porch in front of the store and threw her dirty water on the ground by the hitching rail where his horse was tied. After he rode off, she looked at his boot tracks, and there was a chip out of the heel. She said it was like the picture I drew of the boot track."

Will's hand stopped brushing, but his words rushed with excitement. "Badger! He's the connection to the Comanche. Do you think he's in with Yellow Hawk?"

"I do not think so. I lived with Yellow Hawk and Weeping Woman for seven years. I never saw a trapper like Badger. Weeping Woman would not allow a dirty, smelly white man around." Two Feathers gaze drifted away from Will, as though lost in memory. "She would complain to Yellow Hawk until he ran him off."

"But what about now?" Will's nerves prickled his skin from the inside. "Do you think he might be working with Badger?"

"No. Yellow Hawk hates the whites. His hate is too strong. He would never make plans with a white man."

After they finished grooming the horses, the boys headed out the barn door. Will made a sudden stop.

"I just thought of something. Stanaway said no one found stolen goods until we came here. We found all the supplies on our ranch." His head went swimmy, and he inhaled several deep breaths to clear his head. "When we settled on the Pecos River Ranch, we interrupted someone's dirty business." He felt unable to move, as though made of stone. "And that decision killed Pa."

Will watched the color fade from Two Feathers's face.

Both boys leaned against the barn door. Will's mind raced in every direction, trying to figure out why this was happening. Who stole the supplies? Why was Corporal Tucker murdered? How was Yellow Hawk involved?

After several minutes, Will cleared his throat and sucked in a deep breath. He pushed himself away from the barn door.

"The only person it could be is Captain Stanaway."

Two Feathers's face flushed dark. "He's trying to put it on Pa, so no one will know it is him."

"Will? John? Where are you?"

Will jerked around to see Smokey walking across the wagon yard toward the barn.

"Come on, boys. We need to see Colonel Dowell and start back home."

Two Feathers's face showed the same panic that Will felt. How much should they tell Smokey? Will needed time to think.

"Smokey, we should get our supplies first," Will said. "Then we won't have to wait after we talk to the colonel."

"Yes." Two Feathers shuffled his feet. "I want to talk to Na-es-cha."

"Who's that?" Suspicion lay heavy on Smokey's words.

"That's his girlfriend." Will shot a guilty look at his brother that said, *I couldn't think of anything else.*

"Well, girlfriend, is it? I haven't heard about this." The old scout's eyes sparkled, and he slapped Two Feathers on the back. "A little time spent with a girlfriend ain't a bad thing."

Will pulled a scrap of paper from his pocket and handed it to Smokey. "Here's the list. You get the stuff, and I'll go with Two Feathers. Okay?"

He didn't wait for an answer but raced off after the disappearing Two Feathers. They ran behind the barracks building and stopped.

Gasping, Will stuttered, "What should we tell Smokey and Colonel Dowell about what we've figured out?"

Two Feathers bent over with his hands on his knees, gasping. When his breathing eased, he slid his back down the barracks wall and sat on the ground. Will plopped down beside him.

"Smokey is on our side," Will said. "We need to trust him."

They sat still. Neither boy made a move to get up. Will dropped his head to his knees.

"We need to watch out for Captain Stanaway. I don't know how he did it, but he must have made a connection with Yellow Hawk."

Two Feathers twisted the end of one of his braids and narrowed his eyes in thought.

"Maybe Stanaway stole the guns and gave them to Badger to give to Yellow Hawk. Maybe Yellow Hawk *would* deal with a white man if it meant getting guns."

A thought exploded in Will's head, hurling sharp needles of fear through his veins.

"Guns would make it easier to get Buck."

No one spoke for several minutes. Their fear of Yellow Hawk hung thick in the air between them.

Will stood and paced in circles.

Two Feathers twisted a knot in the end of one braid.

"When we tell the colonel Stanaway's behind the thefts," Will said, "it won't be a good thing for us."

Two Feathers cleared his throat and coughed before he spoke. "You are right. Stanaway will be angry. He will send Yellow Hawk to raid our ranch again, and now he has rifles."

"The colonel will believe Stanaway. Not us." Will lifted his head. "Do you think Na-es-cha will tell the colonel what she saw and heard?"

"No. She is more afraid of the soldiers than I am. She will not talk to them."

"Maybe you can talk to her before we head home. Maybe she will help us convince the colonel."

Two Feathers's mouth twisted into a grimace and he stood. "That will not happen."

"Without her, we have no proof of anything. If the colonel doesn't believe us, then we'll have to find proof."

"How are we going to do that?"

Will rubbed his eyes with the heel of his hands, then scrubbed his face up and down, stretching the skin till it burned. In a muffled, weary voice he answered, "I don't know."

CAPTAIN STANAWAY

"Smokey!" Sergeant Baker stepped around his desk and grabbed the scout's rough hand in his and shook it. "What are you doing here? I figured you'd be way up north with Charlie Goodnight."

"Charlie and I figured these here boys might need a little lookin' after, so my ole long-legged horse and I headed south."

"Lookin' after? These boys? They seem to be doing fine to me." He shook hands with Will and spoke to Two Feathers. "I see your feathers are gone, and your hair is under your hat, so you must be John Randell today."

Two Feathers's voice sounded serious, and he didn't offer his hand. "Yes, I want to come and go as I please and not be held here with the Navajo."

"I don't think you need to worry about that much longer." The sergeant leaned against his desk and crossed his arms. "What can I do for you folks today?"

"The boys have information about the missing supplies, and we need to talk to Colonel Dowell." Smokey looked at the closed door to the colonel's office.

"You found more supplies?"

Will's grin tilted a little lopsided. "No. Not this time."

"The colonel's not here. We're expecting him back either this afternoon or tomorrow. He went to Fort Union on army business concerning the Navajo."

The frown on Baker's face made Will wonder if he was not happy with decisions already made concerning the Navajo.

"Captain Stanaway is in charge until the colonel returns. You can talk to him. He's been investigating the thefts and the murder of Private Tucker."

"No!" Will's quick bark caught everyone's attention. "We can wait."

Smokey rubbed his beard and put his hand on Will's shoulder.

"We need to get back to the ranch as soon as possible. Jake and Tony can't handle all the chores by themselves for long."

"I know. But we can wait today. If he isn't back by early afternoon, we'll talk to Stanaway and head home in the morning." Will tried to look determined and held his breath.

The old scout's gaze jumped back and forth between Will and Two Feathers.

"Okay. A few hours won't make much difference. I haven't gone by the store yet anyhow."

Back at the sutler's store, Smokey asked Mr. Wallace if they could stay one more night and handed him the list Will had dug from his pocket. Wallace read through the list with a frown.

"I think I have enough left to fill this."

He barked at Na-es-cha to bring a ten-pound sack of flour. She hurried to the back of the store. His scowl changed to a strained smile when Smokey handed him the money for the supplies and the night's lodging. Will noticed more empty shelves. *What is going on?*

After giving Mr. Wallace the flour, Na-es-cha walked to the end of the counter, where the candy jars stood almost empty. Will motioned Two Feathers to follow him, and he joined her. Will studied the limited choices in the jars while Two Feathers talked to her. Words in hushed Comanche flowed between them until Na-es-cha stepped away from him, her face covered with fear. After his next words, her expression relaxed, but each time he spoke, her head made a firm shake. He continued to talk to her. Her shoulders pulled back, and she raised her chin. The words changed from a stiff Comanche "Kee" to a stubborn English "No!"

Two Feathers had been right, Will realized. Ne-es-cha would not talk to the soldiers about Badger or anything else she knew. It was up to them to convince Smokey and the army of Captain Stanaway's guilt.

Mrs. Wallace stepped into the room and called to Na-es-cha. Her tone snapped, and the girl followed her through the back door.

Will and Two Feathers walked to the circle of men leaning back in chairs around the potbellied stove, their feet stretched to the heat. They found no empty chairs, so they stood outside the circle. Mrs. Wallace sang out that lunch was ready. They heard the pounding of chair legs hitting the floor behind them and beat the men to the table. Na-es-cha stood ready with the ladle and filled both boys' bowls with steaming chicken and dumplings. The rich aroma brought memories of Ma's kitchen. The fluffy dumplings and chunks of chicken in a thick broth spread a happy smile across Will's face. Two Feathers stared at his bowl with a "what-is-this?" look.

"Go ahead. Take a bite. You'll like it." Will blew on his spoonful and took a big bite. He closed his eyes in pure happiness. "Delicious."

Two Feathers stuck out his tongue and licked the tip of his spoon. The rest disappeared into in his mouth, along with everything in his bowl.

After lunch, they found Smokey asleep in his chair at the stove. Will whispered, "We need to talk to him. Should we wake him?"

"Not me!" Two Feathers whispered. His eyes popped, and his lips curled down in surprise. "You can risk it. I am not."

Will decided to let the scout sleep rather than wake him up and try to talk to a grumpy old man. He pulled up a chair on one side of him, and Two Feathers sat on the other side.

It wasn't long before Smokey opened one eye. "If you boys keep staring at me, you're gonna bore holes in my buckskins. What do you want?" His last words held a sharp edge.

"We need to talk to you." Two Feathers's words rose barely above a whisper.

"It's important." Will glanced at the few people in the store. "Not here. Maybe in the barn."

"What's wrong?"

The urgency in their voices made Smokey sit up straight in his chair. Will made a quick nod toward the door. Smokey followed the boys through the store and out the back.

"Okay, boys," said Smokey. "What's up?"

"Na-es-cha told us more about Badger this morning before we went to see the colonel." Two Feathers nodded at Will to continue.

"We know who is behind the murder of Private Tucker and the stolen supplies." Will stopped and studied Smokey's face.

The old man raised his eyebrows. "Go on."

"It's Captain Stanaway."

The bushy eyebrows shot up again, and Smokey's sharp gray eyes bulged. "What? Because you don't like a man doesn't mean he is a murderer and a thief."

Silence filled the barn. Even the horses were quiet—not an ear twitched or a tail switched. Smokey's eyes blinked over and over. He swallowed a big gulp and pulled on his beard.

"Wait a minute, boys. You need proof when you say a man is a thief and a murderer. Do you have proof?"

The boys nodded vigorously, and one of Two Feathers's braids fell out from under his hat.

Smokey sat on an upside down water bucket, staring at nothing. He chewed on his knuckle, then stroked his beard for so long Will and Two Feathers shot each other questioning glances. Neither spoke. At last, Smokey stood.

"Okay. We gotta talk to the colonel. But if he ain't here, then we talk to Stanaway. You can't keep this kind of stuff from the army."

"Not Stanaway," Will said. "We can't talk to him. He's the robber and killer." The last word came out in a high squeak.

"I do not trust him." Two Feathers hammered his words.

"I reckon I know what you think. But I ain't so sure you're thinking straight. If the colonel ain't back, and I don't reckon he is, we'll talk to Stanaway 'cause he's second in command. Mr. Goodnight made deals with the captain for cattle when we were here last year. He dickered with Stanaway a goodly bit before settling on a price. Said he was a fine trader. Goodnight's right talented at reading a man's thinking, and he ain't never said nothin' against the man. But if it will make you feel better, we'll get Sergeant Baker to stay in the room and listen."

Smokey led the way across the compound to Colonel Dowell's office. It was empty, and they followed the sergeant to Captain Stanaway's office, explaining that they wanted him to stay and hear what they had to say. He stopped outside the door.

"Boys," Baker said, "you need to understand that I will stay if I can. But if the captain orders me to leave, I'll go. He is a superior officer, and I'm expected to obey orders."

Both boys nodded. Smokey's encouraging smile eased Will's anxiety.

"Do I have to go in?" Two Feathers's face paled. "Can't you tell them?"

Will took a deep breath. "You are a Comanche warrior, and I am a Texas cowboy. We can do this."

Two Feathers heaved in a big breath and nodded. Together they followed Smokey into Captain Stanaway's office.

"What's going on?" The officer's dark, cold eyes narrowed slightly. "You two again."

Relief eased Will's tension when the captain's gaze shifted away from him and toward the sergeant.

"Sir, this is Smokey, he scouts for Charlie Goodnight, who is the guardian for Will and Two Feathers since Dan Whitaker's death. Mr. Goodnight sent him to check on the boys. Smokey tells me they've discovered information that may lead to the resolution of the mystery surrounding the missing supplies and Private Tucker's death."

At the end of the sergeant's explanation, Stanaway's face changed from irritation to real anger.

"I've heard their so-called information or clues before, and they're nothing." His hard eyes shifted from the soldier to the boys. "I see no reason to speak to them again."

"Captain Stanaway." Will paused to swallow the bitter lump in his throat. "Sir." Will sucked in a sharp breath. "We have new information."

The captain was still, and the angles in his face grew sharp. "Okay." He took a deep breath. "Sergeant, bring chairs, and you are dismissed."

"We'd like him to stay." Smokey's tone left no room for argument. "We want a witness."

The captain's stone-hard stare would have staggered Will, but the old scout matched it and never blinked. Will watched Two Feathers, whose beaming eyes showed his pride in Smokey, his only connection to his long-dead family. Stanaway blinked and rubbed the back of his neck.

"Bring a chair for yourself, Sergeant."

Smokey cocked his eyebrow at Two Feathers, and he started his story by describing their finding the first chipped boot track.

The boys took turns telling how each had found evidence. They told about seeing the chipped boot track in several places and finding the small wood chips with it. As the story progressed, Stanaway's face grew deep purple-red then settled into a stiff mask. Will stood and leaned on the front of the captain's desk.

"Na-es-cha, the Navajo girl that works for Mr. Wallace, saw Badger leave the chipped boot track in front of the sutler's store. So we know for sure that Badger is one of the crooks. I know he works for you because he was with you in Santa Fe when he tried to steal my knife. You fooled me into thinking you were not involved, but then you called Pa a thief and a murderer. I know you put the blame on him to take it off yourself. I know you can't operate with the Pecos River Ranch in the way, so you tried to make us leave by having Yellow Hawk steal our cattle. When that didn't work, you killed Pa or had Badger use Yellow Hawk to do it. Just like you used Badger to kill Corporal Tucker. I don't know why you did that."

Captain Stanaway rose from his chair in jerky movements. His eyes, set like black stones in his white face, bored into

Will and into each person in the room. His words slid through thin, tight lips.

"I see it a different way. I think Mr. Whitaker was involved with the Indians and sold them guns to stir up trouble and keep the army busy and away from your ranch. I think when he had no more guns to sell, they killed him."

Silence filled the room like a thick clinging fog. Will stopped breathing. Shock at the captain's words froze him to his chair. He shuddered and gulped for air. Sergeant Baker jumped to his feet, making his chair skid across the plank floor.

"Captain, that cannot be true. Dan Whitaker—"

"Sergeant! That's enough! Sit down! I'll take this up with Colonel Dowell. See these people out of my office and off the fort. If the colonel needs to speak with them, he will let you know."

They left, and Sergeant Baker motioned them to follow him back to the colonel's office. Once inside, he collapsed into his chair. He studied one face after another and chewed on his lip. His hands moved across his desktop, as though wanting paper to straighten. He started to speak, choked, and pulled at the neck of his uniform.

"Well, boys, I'd say you've stirred up a whirlwind. Captain Stanaway has spent a lot of time and traveled a lot of miles to find out who is behind this business."

Will stepped in front of the desk. "Has he been investigating, or has he been planning and accusing Pa to cover up his part in all this?"

"That is a question the colonel will have to answer. But right now I've been ordered to see that you leave the fort. However, it is too late to leave this afternoon, so I'd appreciate it if you would stay out of sight and leave first thing in the morning."

Smokey shook his hand and nodded. "We will be gone by first light."

At the sutler's store, the boys dropped into chairs around the stove. They slid down in their seats, stretching their legs before them and resting their heads on their chair backs. Will closed his eyes and let his arms drop beside him. The warmth from the stove eased tension from his back and shoulders that Will hadn't realized was there. Now that he'd told everything, he expected to feel relieved, but after what the captain said, all he felt was exhaustion.

Two Feathers's haggard face looked like Will felt.

"What are you thinkin'?" Will asked.

"Nothing. I do not know what to think."

Will let that soak a minute.

"Me neither. I wish we'd talked to the colonel and not Stanaway. I don't know why Smokey had to do this today."

Will's back hurt, so he sat up in the chair. Smokey stood at the counter, talking to Mr. Wallace. The storekeeper's hard face made Will decide to join Smokey. Two Feathers slipped out the back door.

"Hello, Mr. Wallace. If you have any cheese, will you add a few pounds to our list?"

"I'd love to, son, but I don't have any. As you can see, I don't have much of anything."

Neither Smokey nor Will spoke. "The army takes my goods to feed the Navajo and barely pays enough for me to get by. They can't grow enough or buy enough to feed them. So they take it wherever they can get it. If this keeps up, I'll be out of business soon."

The man's anger grew, so Will decided to change the subject.

"Have you seen that scout you told me about?"

"You mean Badger?" Disgust spat out his last word. "What do you want with that sorry piece of crow bait?"

Before Will answered, Smokey interrupted. "Have you seen him around the fort lately?"

"Hmm. Not for a few months. A while back he tried to sell me rotten skins, a fox or two and a few skunks. He wanted to buy his knife. He was still mad that I sold it to Will. I told him no on the skins because they were too sorry to sell."

"Was that the last time?"

"No. He came in a few weeks later and bought a skinning knife a soldier sold me for the money he needed to make it back home after his discharge from the army."

"Did Badger say how he got the money to buy it?" Will asked.

"No. It's none of my business how a man gets his money. I was happy to see some coin."

"Did he ever talk about the Comanche or about one called Yellow Hawk?"

"No! And if he has any sense at all, he will stay far away from them."

"If he ever does, will you tell the colonel?"

"Of course I will. What's going on here? Do you folks know something about the Comanche? There's enough Indian trouble with the Navajo. We don't need any more."

"We've told everything we know to Captain Stanaway," Smokey said, "and I'm sure he'll inform the colonel when he returns."

Smokey headed to the stove and sat in Two Feathers's empty chair. Will walked through the store and out the back door. Standing on the loading dock, he saw the barn door was ajar, so he headed that way. Inside, Two Feathers and Na-es-cha stood talking in a stall in the back corner.

"Will," Two Feathers called in a loud whisper, "come back here. You need to hear what Na-es-cha is telling me."

Will checked on Buck before joining them.

"What's going on? I talked to Mr. Wallace about Badger, and he told me the same story Na-es-cha did about the bad skins. He said Badger hasn't been around for a good while."

Two Feathers spoke to the girl in Comanche, and she started talking to Will in broken English.

"My people starve. Many die. We want to go home to Chaco Canyon. We want our ways, our sheep, our homes. My body cries for food. The Navajo grow weak. At home, our land grows our food. Here, food will not grow. There is not enough rain and too many armyworms that eat our crops. At home, the water is sweet and good. Here the water is bitter and salty. It kills our crops and makes my people sick."

Tears streamed down her face, and Two Feathers slid a strong arm around her bony shoulders.

"But what about Mr. Wallace? Don't you work in his store? Doesn't he feed you?"

Will's heart clenched in his chest while she wiped her tears and took a deep breath.

"I help Mrs. Wallace cook for people who pay for meals. I scrub floors. I wash dishes. I wash and iron clothes. I sweep rooms. I get a little flour with bugs in it and sometimes old bacon."

"That's all?" Shock made Will's voice rise to a squeak. "But he's such a nice man. I like him."

"That is not all. Na-es-cha knows more." Two Feathers nodded to the girl.

"I heard Mr. Wallace tell his woman the Navajo are going back to Chaco Canyon."

"For sure?" Will asked. "How did he know?"

"He said he heard the soldiers tell they will send us home when warm weather comes. The people are afraid to hope this is true."

"That will be good. It's what you want."

"But it is not what Mr. Wallace wants," Two Feathers said. "Tell Will what you heard."

"He is angry the army will not send enough food for us. He said when we leave, the fort will close. His store will close. He will go away."

Will's forehead crinkled in thought. "That's what Mr. Wallace told Smokey and me a little while ago, but he didn't say anything about the Navajo leaving."

A grin spread across Two Feathers's face. "That is good news for the Navajo and the Pecos River Ranch."

"How's that?" Will asked.

"If the Navajo leave, maybe the soldiers will leave too."

Will's face lit up. "No soldiers. No stolen supplies. No Stanaway."

The barn door creaked, and Smokey walked in. "I'd be careful about wishing the soldiers gone."

"They bring nothing but trouble." Will frowned.

"And death," Two Feathers whispered.

"They do bring their own kind of trouble," Smokey said. "Girl you better get back to the store before Mrs. Wallace comes huntin' you. And boys, feed the horses good. We have a long ride tomorrow." He walked toward the barn door, stopped, and turned back. "And remember, when the army is gone, who'll catch Yellow Hawk?"

Early the next morning on the ride home, Captain Stanaway held a tight grip on Will's thoughts. He couldn't let go of why Smokey didn't wait for the colonel. Why tell Captain Stanaway their discoveries? Why not another officer? Smokey said Mr. Goodnight traded cattle with the captain.

And the trail boss was a good judge of men. If Mr. Goodnight trusted Captain Stanaway, maybe Will should too. But no, he couldn't. The battle raged on inside his head like boxers in a fight.

TWO FEATHERS'S MISTAKE

March's cold winds gave up their bluster to April's gentle warm breezes. When they made their rounds to check the cattle, Two Feathers and Will enjoyed seeing calves running and bucking. The sun shined brighter and stayed longer, warming the days. The clouds changed from the dull gray of boulders to white wisps of ribbon trailing in the wind. Thoughts of Stanaway and Yellow Hawk settled in the background.

One unusually warm day in mid-April, Two Feathers was working up the creek a couple of miles, digging three catch basins and lining them with rocks. Throughout the afternoon, he watched clouds blow in and build into dull-gray hills in the sky. The air felt heavy, so he headed for the house in case those clouds decided to dump their load. Riding into the yard, he found a soldier from Fort Sumner sitting on the porch with Smokey.

Two Feathers tied Gray Wolf to the hitching rail and stood near the scout but away from the soldier. The stranger handed Smokey a letter from Mr. Goodnight that said he needed Smokey to scout pasture. Mr. John Chisum would be driving steers north from his Jinglebob Ranch below Fort Sumner at Bosque Grande in early summer. Goodnight told Will to get his calves branded, and Mr. Chisum would pick them up on the way. The deal Pa and Will had made with Mr. Goodnight was for Goodnight to give them all the cows from his drive last year and keep half of the money from the calf crop. Smokey would bring their half when he returned in the summer.

Two Feathers and Smokey sat in silence on the porch after the soldier left. Two Feathers wouldn't look at him.

"I'm coming back." Smokey's shoulders slumped, and so did his words.

Two Feathers didn't move.

"I work for Mr. Goodnight. I have to go."

No response.

"Don't you fret none, John. You are a son to me. I will be back."

Smokey left Two Feathers and walked to the barn to saddle his tall brown horse.

When the old scout disappeared into the barn, Two Feathers raced out of the yard and scrambled up to a ledge on the rock wall behind the cave house to sit in his favorite spot. He had found it the winter they arrived on the Pecos River Ranch, long before they built the adobe house. He could think there. In the silence. Alone. And now he thought about Smokey.

Piles of his heart's broken, jagged pieces filled his chest.

One pile—his parents' death.

Another pile—Yellow Hawk, killing his father and wanting him dead.

A third pile—losing Pa.

A big chunk—Smokey leaving, again.

Watching Smokey ride out of the ranch yard and cross the creek, he followed the progress of the tall brown horse, catching a glimpse now and then through the trees as it headed toward the Pecos. He knew where Smokey would cross the river and go north, toward Colorado, toward Mr. Goodnight.

Away from him.

Two Feathers heard Will scramble up the last few feet to sit on the ledge next to him.

"What are you doing up here?" Will curled his legs under him. "We got a letter from Mr. Goodnight."

"I know. Smokey read it before you got back. He left."

"We need to get ready for the roundup and get our steers branded. We have plans to make. I need to talk to Mateo and see when he and Cesar can help. And maybe his friend Lupe."

Two Feathers did not move. His stare searched the distant river. He wanted to catch a last glimpse of Smokey.

"Do you think he will come back?" Loneliness crept into his voice.

Will's business-like tone became puzzled. "Who?"

Two Feathers did not answer, only stared into the distance. Will studied his brother's face, then gripped his shoulder.

"Smokey? Yes. The letter said he'll be back in the summer." His voice mellowed, and he patted Two Feathers's back. "Smokey cares a lot for you. He'll come back."

Will leaned against the rock wall and shared his brother's silence. A speck appeared under the wispy clouds.

"Look, Will." Two Feathers pointed north.

A second speck joined the first, and a pair of red-tailed hawks flew toward them. The hawks veered off and landed on a ledge past the brothers and higher up on the cliff. Each held sticks in its beak. The birds disappeared and took Two Feathers's loneliness with them.

My puha made his home here, and so will Smokey. He called me son.

"They built a nest on the ledge." The jagged edges of Two Feathers's heart smoothed out. "They come back to this place." He jumped up. "Smokey will come back too."

Stepping from rock to rock, he half ran and half slid down from the ledge. At the bottom, he hollered at Will, who was still straining to see the birds.

"Come on. We have plans to make."

That night, Two Feathers, Will, and the twins sat around the kitchen table, where Tony spread the map of the ranch the four of them had drawn.

"Will, what would Pa do first?" A questioning lift in Two Feathers's voice replaced the usual confident tone.

"He'd move the first-calf heifers from the brush corral to make room for the steers. It's time to bring them close to the house to keep an eye on 'em. You never know how or when a heifer is gonna bring on her calf. We can put them in that little valley behind the barn."

Will put a finger on the map. "Here's the valley. Jake, you and Tony move all the beeves from the valley to the brush corral. Two Feathers and I can bunch the heifers and start them back this way. We'll do that first and then sweep the ranch for steers. Tony can take the section south of the corral to the river."

Two Feathers leaned over the map. "I will go north to Red Mesa, where Pa found the last stolen supplies, and then back east to the river."

"That leaves between here and the corral and then east across the river for Jake." Will indicated a wide area on the map. "I'll cover the area northwest between Jake and Two Feathers." He turned toward his brother. "If you don't find any that far north, come help me. My area has lots of deep arroyos and gullies."

Will stood from leaning over the map and stretched his back. "We can graze them in the corral until Mr. Chisum's crew comes to pick them up."

"Will, that's going to be a lot of steers in the corral. The grass is good, but it's only started to grow. I think we need to use the hay left from winter to help keep them fit for the drive."

"Good idea. I don't want to overgraze."

Two Feathers sat back in his chair and moved his gaze around the table. *Will I ever be a good cowboy like Jake and Tony? Or Will?* He sat for a few minutes, listening to the three of them make plans for the steers. Thinking. Wondering. *Do I want to be a cowboy?* Hearing them talk about rounding up the cattle turned his mind to memories of the men in his village rounding up the horses. He remembered their huge herds racing across the prairie, tails and manes flowing in the wind. *Horses—that is what I want. Many horses.*

A burst of laughter brought Two Feathers's thoughts back to the table. The others were arguing over leaving what they called "the best decision" for last.

"Who's gonna ride to Mateo's to see when he and Cesar can help with the branding?" asked Jake, sitting back in his chair and looking from person to person around the table.

"I think I should be the one to go." Will tried to speak with authority. "After all, I am the boss."

Two Feathers slid his fingers over his mouth, but they didn't quite cover the smile.

"Yes, you are the boss." Jake twisted his mouth sideways and cocked his eyebrows. "It's important that you be here to oversee the work. Sooo, I'll help you out by going to Mateo's."

Tony dropped his head in his hands. "Weak! Those arguments are weak. If you two can't come up with better reasons than that, I'll use the plain old truth."

"You are right, Tony," Two Feathers said, his tone teasing. "My vote is on you."

"Neither one of you cares two hoots about Mateo. All you want to do is eat Alma's good cookin' and visit with his pretty daughters. Sooo, I'll go."

Two Feathers's chuckle deepened when Will's face turned bright red, and Jake looked down in defeat. Will stood, slid his chair under the table, and folded their map.

"Okay, Tony is the winner. Leave first thing in the morning. And come straight back. Don't let *Elena*," mischief spread across Will's face, "keep you too long."

"Come on, ladies' man," Jake said, "I'm ready for my straw-filled feather bed." Jake hauled Tony out of his chair singing, "Elena, beautiful Elena."

Tony's face turned the color of a ripe apple. Jake's off-key notes warbled out the door and into the moonlight.

The next morning, Two Feathers saddled Gray Wolf and Buck while Will filled four bags with jerky, biscuits, and a pouch of coffee grounds. He doubled up on one bag because Two Feathers had decided to take two days to make a thorough search of the sizable area around Red Mesa.

The country grew more fractured as Will and Two Feathers rode west. Deep gullies and arroyos with steep sides made them zigzag and slowed their progress toward the outer areas of the Pecos River Ranch. After spending the morning riding around the deeper slashes in the earth, Two Feathers pulled Gray Wolf to a stop.

"Too much time wasted going around in circles."

Will stopped Buck.

"We have to go around." He pointed across an arroyo. "It's twenty-five yards to the other side and too dangerous to ride down."

"Not for a horse that has learned."

He tapped his heels to Gray Wolf, and over the edge they went. The walls were steep, and Two Feathers pushed his stirrups far ahead of him and lay back till his long braids hung down the horse's rump. Rocks tumbled with each leap down the steep slope, and dust billowed when Gray Wolf landed on the sandy floor about fifteen feet below.

"Are you crazy?" Will hollered from the rim. "How are you going to get out?"

"A horse is not the only animal that comes down. There will be a place. Come on. Make Buck come over the edge."

Will stood in the stirrups and peered over the edge at the path Gray Wolf made in the rocks. He backed away from the rim. Two Feathers moved Gray Wolf down the arroyo, and Will sat on Buck a good distance from the rim.

"What do you think, Buck? Can you make the jump?"

The buckskin walked a few steps toward the arroyo, shifted his weight, and blew.

"Let's get one thing understood. When we get to the rim, there's no changing your mind. Don't you stop at the last minute and send me flying by myself."

A sharp kick to Buck's flanks, a jump into a full gallop, and Buck exploded off the rim of the canyon with Will lying back on his rump, his boots high on the horse's neck. They hit bottom in a cloud of dust and flying rocks. Buck leaped over a cluster of rabbitbrush, slinging Will to one side of the saddle where he managed to hang on. Buck stopped, and Will slid the rest of the way to the ground and stomped around Buck, checking for damage.

"Dang it, Two Feathers. You and Buck are gonna get me killed." Will yanked his bandana off and swiped it across his face. "I've got grit all down my neck."

"You are here. I do not see any blood on you or Buck."

"I hope we can get out of here."

"The Comanche ride where they cannot be seen. Work with Buck. Soon it will be easy for him to jump. It may save your life."

A little farther down, they found a trail winding up and out of the arroyo.

After a quick lunch, the brothers split up, each going his own way. Two Feathers rode northwest toward Red Mesa. The afternoon wore on, and he found several groups of cattle, some with big calves, and headed them southeast toward the ranch.

When he reached Red Mesa, he stopped for a short rest. Last night's late planning session had left him tired, and the sun told him it would soon be suppertime. Even though the late April days were mild, the wind still held a bite. A small fire built under an overhang in the mesa wall warmed him. With his cup of water nestled in the coals at the edge of the fire, he dropped in some jerky. He liked broth better than the bitter coffee Will and the twins always drank.

Deciding to take a short nap, he untied his bedroll from behind his saddle and spread it on the least rocky spot he could find. He dunked his cold biscuit into his cup and decided, even cold, Will's biscuits were getting better. *That is something I will never tell him.* Putting his empty cup just outside the fire ring, he stretched out and cradled his head on his arm.

A sharp kick in the ribs woke Two Feathers. He rolled over and scrambled to his feet. A blow to his head sent him into darkness.

Pain. Small at first, like a wiggly worm, grew till it filled his head and threatened to split it like a blow from a sharp ax. He forced his eyes open, but the night was as dark with them open as shut. The pain in his head settled into a steady pounding rhythm that faded in and out with no sense of time or place. He slipped into darkness again.

The morning light stabbed at his eyes. He watched Gray Wolf's hooves step, step, step. Each time the horse stepped, his head banged. *How am I looking at Gray Wolf's hooves?* A pain stabbing into his ribs forced its way into awareness. He was not sitting in the saddle. He was lying across it. He kicked his feet and tried to sit up, but they were tied to his hands with a rope under Gray Wolf.

"You better be still, boy." A rough, gravelly voice came from in front of him. A voice he did not recognize. "You don't want to fall off that horse of yours. I don't think he'd be too happy, you hanging under him. He might start jumping and kicking."

Two Feathers lay still. He did not speak.

Time slowed to match each step of the horse's hooves, each bang in his head, and each throb in his ribs. After a while, the deep darkness returned, and he felt nothing.

The murmur of voices reached into the blackness and pulled Two Feathers back out. He did not move. He listened. *Comanche! The words are Comanche.* He opened his eyes and saw Running Wolf watching him.

"Be still. You have a wound on your head and your side."

Two Feathers did not move. He drank from a water pouch the man he had known all his life put to his lips.

"Yellow Hawk?"

"He is not here. You are safe."

Two Feathers looked around. He knew this place. Memories of camping there with Yellow Hawk and Weeping

Woman when he was a small child slipped around the pain in his head. A jumble of boulders a short distance from their camp hid a spring that gushed from under the rocks. It flowed around both sides of a flat slab of sandstone, dropping into a pool below. Spilling over a short waterfall, it disappeared beneath a shelf of rocks. Red Wing had chased him, and he had hidden in the rocks that concealed the sweet flowing water. It was good to be with the Comanche again. To speak the language, to see familiar faces. Even if one of them was Barks Like Coyote.

Two Feathers closed his eyes and slept.

When he woke, the sun had passed overhead and cast long shadows. His ribs were wrapped tightly with strips of deer hide, and a poultice of herbs covered the wound on his head. He felt better.

With slow movements, he sat up. Running Wolf and Barks Like Coyote brought him food and more water. On the other side of camp sat a man in ragged, dirty buckskins.

Badger! The man at the fort. The man with the chipped boot heel. Now Two Feathers knew for sure there was a connection between someone at the fort and Yellow Hawk, despite the Comanche's hatred of white men.

Two Feathers stared at Badger, then at Running Wolf.

The Comanche ducked his head and spoke in a low voice. "He came to see Yellow Hawk, not me." He spat on the ground.

"Where is Yellow Hawk?" Two Feathers dreaded the answer.

"He went to Palo Duro Canyon to see Weeping Woman."

"Tell me of Weeping Woman. Is she safe? Is she well?"

"She is good, but grieves for you. I told her you live with the whites. Her heart is heavy with sadness."

Two Feathers asked Barks Like Coyote, "What of Red Wing?"

His boyhood enemy grinned at him. "She will not look at me or any other man. Her heart waits for you. Weeping Woman is alone, so Red Wing stays with her."

Two Feathers leaned forward to rest his aching head on his knees—and to hide his happy smile.

"How did Badger catch you? I thought you lived with the whites." Barks Like Coyote spit out the last word.

"I do. I am blood brother to Will Whitaker. I am his partner on our ranch." He refused to admit that Badger had found him asleep.

"You own land like a white man?" Barks Like Coyote spoke the words as though he did not believe them.

"Yes." Two Feathers head hurt too much to boast.

"He been livin' too long with whites. He done lost his Comanche ways." Badger walked up and stood over Two Feathers. "I found him sleepin' in the rocks, knocked his head, and here he is. I knowed Yellow Hawk wanted those two boys pretty bad. So I brought him one."

"Yellow Hawk is not here." Running Wolf's words rumbled with anger low in his chest.

"I know. He's in the canyon." Badger nudged Two Feathers with his foot. "I may drag this youngin' all the way across these Staked Plains and drop him at Yellow Hawk's feet."

Will watched darkness fade from the ranch yard. It was the third day since he had left Two Feathers. His gaze stretched to the distant west, hoping to see Two Feathers ride out of the shadows, driving cattle. Should he wait longer? Or should he head out now?

"Will, come roll these eggs in the last of Señora Alma's tortillas and take them with you to the barn," Tony said. "I'll have supplies packed for you by the time you saddle Buck. Ride to Red Mesa. If he's comin', I'm sure he could use the help driving the cattle. If he's not, find him. You can do it. He's been teaching you to track, and you're gettin' pretty good."

Jake came from the sleeping room with Will's bedroll and ground cloth. He tossed the saddlebags on the table for Tony to fill.

"We'd go with you, but somebody needs to get the calves ready for market."

Will pulled his hat off and slapped it against his leg, again. Frustration, anger, fear—he felt like a calf that's been fresh thrown and tied.

"What could be takin' him so long? He knows there's work to do."

"Get goin'." Jake shoved Will's bedroll into his hands. "The sooner you leave, the sooner you'll get back."

Will stopped in the doorway and gave the twins a grateful look.

"Thanks. If the Pecos River Ranch survives, it will be because of you. Pa did right when he hired you two."

Will rode away from the ranch house, and the hours and miles fell behind with Buck's long-legged trot-walk-trot gait. Midmorning found him approaching Red Mesa. He stopped about twenty-five yards out and scanned the area around the base with its jumble of rocks and boulders.

No Two Feathers.

No Gray Wolf.

What had happened to them?

On the ride that morning, he'd seen bunches of cattle moving toward the ranch, which meant his brother had started them in that direction the day before. Where had he gone?

He's a Comanche! He's supposed to be able to take care of himself. How could he disappear?

Thoughts of losing his brother after losing Pa nudged their way into his head. Will slammed those thoughts to the ground, tied them tight, and shoved them into a far corner of his mind.

The tracks he'd followed all morning continued to the base of the mesa. He found a ring of rocks with the cold remains of a small fire inside, and sitting outside the ring was Two Feathers's cup. Will sniffed the contents and smiled with relief. *Jerky broth. Not coffee. This was Two Feathers's camp.*

Will walked a circle around the fire ring, studying the ground with deliberate care. Farther out, he found where Gray Wolf had nibbled on bunches of side-oats grama grass. A depression in the sandy soil and heel scuff marks told him where Two Feathers had stretched out to rest. And then—a boot track with a chip out of the heel.

Fighting his panic, Will searched a wider area around the fire ring and found tracks of a horse, a mule, and more chipped boot heel tracks. What happened to Two Feathers?

Will sucked in a deep breath and remembered what his brother had taught him. When something looks impossible, look closer. He went back to the fire ring and studied the ground again. The tracks going away were slightly deeper than those coming toward the fire. He followed the deeper ones to the spot where Gray Wolf had grazed. The man had walked back and forth behind the horse. Will moved a short distance out and found the man's more shallow tracks going to his own horse.

Will searched for any sign from Two Feathers, but found none of the usual markers. Now he understood. Badger had captured Two Feathers. He knocked him out and slung him across Gray Wolf's saddle, then rode off with Two Feathers in tow.

Anger at Badger filled Will, and he shoved his brother's cup into his saddlebag. With determination, he sighted the direction Badger had gone. Remembering how Two Feathers had rescued him from a Comanche camp, he set Buck on the trail after him.

He would find Two Feathers if he had to trail him into the camp of Yellow Hawk.

NEW EVIDENCE

Buck held a steady pace. Will followed Badger's tracks with little effort. He slowed only to search for the trail.

Will crossed the Pecos about noon and was thinking about digging out a few strips of jerky when an arrow whizzed past his ear, followed by the pounding of hooves behind him. He twisted in the saddle to see four Kiowas coming fast behind him. Sharp pinpricks of fear stung his skin. He smacked his boot heels into his horse's flanks.

"Run, Buck!"

The big buckskin leaped into a gallop, and they raced away, leaving a dust trail behind them. Will knew Buck could outrun any horse, but when he glanced back, the Kiowas bent low over their mounts and kept coming. Another arrow flew past. Will pulled his hat down tight on his head and shifted forward in the saddle. A firm pat on Buck's shoulder, a command in his ear, and the faithful horse found more speed.

The distance between Will and the Kiowas lengthened, but Will gave no command to slow Buck. A quick look over the horse's ears froze his heart. His eyes bulged. Ahead gaped a wide ravine. Buck slammed to a full stop. Will grabbed the saddle horn and mane to keep from sailing over Buck's head.

The Kiowas' wild yells grew louder. Buck spun in circles and then raced along the ravine's edge. The Indians whooped again and angled toward him.

Will pulled Buck to a stop, his fear of the ravine racing neck and neck with his fear of the Kiowas. His terror of capture won by a nose. Will pulled hard on Buck's reins. The horse reared, spun on his back legs, and raced toward the oncoming warriors. Startled, the Indians pulled up their horses. Will spun Buck back toward the ravine, leaned forward, and kicked him hard in his flanks. The buckskin bolted. At the rim, Will bellowed, "Jump, Buck!"

Will lay all the way back in the saddle—

shoved his boots forward in the stirrups—

and hung on.

They sailed over the edge.

Buck's forelegs slammed into the slope. Will clamped his thighs tight against the saddle till they burned. His heart beat thunderclaps in his ears. He gripped the reins till his nails dug into his palm, but dared not pull them. Buck needed control.

The horse's powerful hind legs pushed off the ground with every leap. Will leaned farther backward and threw his right arm high to keep his balance. *Don't fall, Buck! Don't fall,* screamed over and over in his head. Rocks tumbled before them and bounced to the ravine bottom. The last leap landed them on level ground.

Will jumped off, grabbed the reins, and pulled hard.

"Buck! Play dead!"

The buckskin dropped to the ground and rolled on his side.

"Stay, Buck! Stay!"

Will rolled in the dirt to stir up dust and stopped under a large clump of rabbitbrush. He stuck one leg out and bent his knee.

"Stay, Buck," he whispered.

He buried his head in the crook of his elbow, opened his mouth, and breathed in large dust-ladened gulps of air to calm his racing, pounding heart.

He watched the rim from under the bush. A head appeared.

His heart pounded in his ears.

Three more heads showed.

His heart hammered till he couldn't breathe.

They talked and pointed down at Buck and shook their heads. Will held his breath.

"Stay. Dead horse." He breathed the word just enough to reach his horse. *Please, Buck, remember the dead horse game we used to play. Don't move.*

The heads disappeared. Five minutes stretched forever. He heard the faint drumming of hoofbeats and hoped the Kiowas were riding away, not trying to find a way down. He watched the rim for a few more minutes. Buck snuffled his displeasure, and Will crawled out from under the bush.

"Buck, up."

The stallion lunged to his feet and shook himself. Will quickly checked his legs for injuries and hooves for rocks. The rim above him stayed empty. Will mounted Buck and followed the ravine east, his ears straining to hear the sound of hoofbeats. He heard none.

The steep walls leveled out to a gentle slope. Will left Buck grazing and climbed to the rim. A quick search found no Kiowa. He lay still for a minute, trying to stop shaking. When he thought his legs would support him, he stood and called to Buck. The horse scrambled up.

Will gave Buck a better going-over to be sure he hadn't missed any injuries. Then gave him a giant hug.

"You're the best horse ever. Let's get out of here before those Kiowas—or whatever they were—decide to come back." He searched for tracks to be sure the Kiowas didn't follow Badger. The Comanche and the Kiowa are enemies. The fear they'd found Two Feathers made his breathing deeper and rapid.

Satisfied his attackers' route would not cross Badger's, Will followed the seedy scout's trail again. Buck's fast lope ate up the miles. Will kept one eye on Badger's trail and one on the lookout for Kiowas. His skin prickled each time he saw or thought he saw a flicker of movement anywhere around him. *Nothing keeps you alert like an arrow whizzing past your ear.*

Their shadows stretched long and thin when hunger reminded him the Kiowas had kept him from eating lunch. A shallow arroyo choked with bunch grass, rabbitbrush, and mesquite veered off to his left. He rode to the bottom and found a spot clear of growth with an abundance of dry kindling and sticks and a small water hole.

"What do you think, Buck? Should we camp here tonight?"

His partner's ears twitched back. He rattled his bit and snuffled. Will dismounted and stepped to Buck's head.

"Does that mean you're hungry?" He rubbed the jowls and scratched behind the ears. "Thank you for remembering today. It's been a long time since we played the dead horse game. You're the best!"

He unsaddled Buck and with the brush from his saddlebag worked until the golden coat shined. Buck munched on the grain Will dropped into his feedbag.

Will sat by his almost smokeless fire, chewed on jerky, dipped cold biscuits into his hot coffee, and worried about

Two Feathers. What did Badger plan to do with him? Will hadn't seen a grave or body on the trail. Where was that sorry scout going? He had no answers, only worries.

The last color faded from the sky, and Will scooped dirt to smother the fire. He didn't want Kiowas or Comanche to smell the smoke on the night breeze and come hunting him. Warm in his blankets, with his head on his saddle and Buck standing guard, he closed his eyes. The *peent, peent* of a nighthawk circling overhead on its hunt for flying insects was the last sound he heard.

At first light, Will rode Buck out of the arroyo. The wind had blown during the night, dusting the prints with sand, and made the trail harder to follow. The rising sun helped, and by midmorning he smelled a whiff of smoke. Dismounting, he walked, leading Buck. The tracks led him down into a shallow gully. He heard faint voices.

Tying Buck to a creosote bush, he crept forward, each step calculated to make no noise.

No rattling rocks.

No snapping sticks.

No brushing against bushes.

The voices spoke Comanche. *Two Feathers!*

Will bellied down on the ground and peeked around the edge of a tall, angular rock. The three people in camp stared at him. A slow smile spread across Two Feathers's face.

"Hello, Will. Go get Buck and have some deer steak."

Will didn't move. There, sitting beside his brother, was the fierce warrior that rode beside him on the day Yellow Hawk captured him and Buck—Running Wolf!

Sliding behind the rock, Will dropped his head onto his arms. The world around him disappeared. He felt the pain of that long ride, belly down over a horse's back. He felt the pain and terror of Yellow Hawk throwing him hard against a tree.

He felt the despair of seeing Buck snubbed tight to a tree, unable to move. The air felt too thick to breath. He sucked in short gasps.

"Will?" Two Feathers knelt beside him.

"That's Running Wolf!" He forced the words through a throat so tight little sound escaped.

"I know. He was my father's friend."

Will slid forward to peer around the boulder again. His whole body shook at the sight of the Comanche lounging by the fire.

Two Feathers pulled Will to his feet.

"Yellow Hawk is not here. He is in the canyon."

They walked to get Buck and tied him beside Gray Wolf.

Two Feathers sat down beside Running Wolf. Will sat on the other side of Two Feathers as far from the man as he could get.

"Well, well, well. Iffin it ain't the knife stealer."

Will recognized the deep, raspy voice coming from behind him. Badger sat on one of two long rectangular wooden boxes stamped U. S. Army. He shoved himself up, walked past the boys, and squatted near the fire. With the tip of his knife, he speared a hunk of venison.

"Now I got me both boys to drop at Yellow Hawk's feet. He'll pay me a passel of skins for your hides." He shoved the big hunk of meat into his mouth, stuffed it in his cheek like a chipmunk, and talked around it. "That there buckskin you got, he'll pay real good for him. He wants that horse mighty bad."

Will pressed his lips tight. His muscles quivered, and his hands fisted with the desire to jump at Badger. Two Feathers laid his hand on Will's arm and squeezed. Badger sneered at Will and waggled his knife. Will jerked away from the sight and smell of broken brown teeth in his nasty smile. The man walked to his horse and picked up his saddle.

Two Feathers and Running Wolf talked low in Comanche for several minutes. With the little bit of Comanche he knew, Will understood Two Feathers wanted to take the scout to Fort Sumner.

Badger came back to the fire and bent over to cut another hunk of meat. With quick, fluid motions, Running Wolf stood, flipped his knife, and struck Badger hard with the hilt behind his ear. He grabbed the man by his shirt before he landed in the fire and ruined the roasting venison. Then he dropped the unconscious man at Will's and Two Feathers's feet.

The brothers fell backward and scrambled out of the way. Will jumped to his feet and looked back and forth between Badger and Running Wolf, eyes blinking, mouth wide open.

"Get a rope before he wakes up." Two Feathers's rare smile twitched the corners of his mouth. "Running Wolf gave us a present."

Will took his rope from Buck and tossed it to Two Feathers. He walked to the long boxes, opened one, took a quick look inside, gasped, and shut the lid. He returned to help his brother and Running Wolf heave the smelly scout over his saddle. Will tied his feet and handed the remaining rope under the horse to Two Feathers to secure his hands.

Keeping a wary eye on the Comanche warrior, Will whispered to Two Feathers, "Do you know what's in those boxes and where they came from?"

"Running Wolf said Badger gets rifles from someone at the fort. This is the first time he brought more than just a few. Yellow Hawk is waiting for them in the canyon. That is why Running Wolf did not go with Yellow Hawk. He had to wait for Badger."

"Come on. Let's load the boxes on the pack mule. It's going to be a hard trip with Badger and the guns."

Two Feathers stood still and cocked his head to one side with an I-can't-believe-you-said-that look.

"What's the matter?" Will asked.

"Running Wolf will not give us the guns."

"We need them. They're evidence. Tell him that."

"Who, me? I am not telling him. You tell him."

Running Wolf fired his steely gaze toward Will, then back to Two Feathers. Will swallowed a big gulp and shook his head.

Late the following afternoon, the three dusty riders arrived at Fort Sumner, stopping before they reached the wide gates. Long, heavy, high-sided freight wagons lined up outside the fort. Those headed into the fort stood empty, and those going out held crates, barrels, and tow sacks labeled flour, beans, or grain. Dust from the rumbling, lumbering wheels rolling in and out the gates filled the air. They waited for a team of six mules to pull a tall, loaded freight wagon through the gate. The teamster flung his long whip over the animals' heads, and when he jerked back, it cracked like a rifle shot. The loud sound startled Badger's horse. Will and Two Feathers kneed Buck and Gray Wolf close against the anxious horse on each side before the old scout slid off.

"Look at those wagons." Weariness and the dust that hung in the air dropped Will's voice to a husky half-whisper. "There must be fifty of them. I guess the Navajo are leaving."

The straining mules pulled the wagon past the gates, and Will tapped Buck. They rode through before another team blocked their passage. The Navajo filled the compound from the sutler's store to the colonel's office. They clustered together, and children ran from one group to another. Excitement flowed through the crowd like a fresh cool wind.

Will walked up the steps to Colonel Dowell's office. Sergeant Baker stepped around his desk and shook Will's hand.

"What's going on, boy? You look like you've been rode hard and put up wet."

"I feel like it. Are the Navajo going home? Did the army finally admit this was a bad idea?"

"Yes, they're going to Fort Wingate and from there west to Chaco Canyon country."

"We need to see Colonel Dowell. It's important."

"I don't know, Will. The colonel is busy getting this Navajo mess straightened out. He's pretty stirred up. I don't think he'll see you."

"We have the man who sold Yellow Hawk those Enfield rifles he used when he raided our and Mr. Goodnight's cattle."

"Who is he? Where is he?" The welcoming smile slid off the sergeant's face, replaced by the hard lines of a no-nonsense soldier.

Will pointed out the doorway. "Right there."

The sergeant followed him out of the office.

"Badger!" His tone harsh and his lip curled he said, "Why am I not surprised?" Sergeant Baker stopped two soldiers coming across the compound. "Get this man off his horse and bring him inside." He started to turn back to Will, but stopped to tell the soldiers, "And tie him to his chair. Then find the colonel and tell him he's needed here."

Loud hollering and boots scraping across the board walkway announced the arrival of Badger, struggling and fighting the soldiers every inch of the way. It took the help of Sergeant Baker to land him in his chair in front of the sergeant's desk and get him tied.

"Let me loose!" The scout's low growl sent prickles through Will's scalp.

Sergeant Baker leaned toward the bound man with a look of such twisted disgust and rage that Will never wanted to see it directed at him. Baker's lips rolled into a thin line. His eyebrows angled down and hovered over cold eyes.

Badger's voice quivered. "These two mangy pups kept me tied to my horse all yestiddy and all last night."

There was no reaction from the soldier. Only a long, silent stare.

Badger's whining complaints squeaked like a rusty hinge. "My arms is 'bout ripped offin my shoulders from these ropes. My hands is swelled up. Cain't feel my fingers."

There was no sign of sympathy in the sharp lines of Sergeant Baker's face or his flat, clipped words.

"Did you sell rifles to the Comanche known as Yellow Hawk?"

"Who told you that?" With eyebrows stretched high and eyes bugged wide, Badger's voice faked innocence. "Iffen it was these here rag-tailed boys, they got rotten, lyin' tongues. Don't believe them noways."

"Enfield rifles?" No change showed in Sergeant Baker's face.

Two Feathers slipped out the door and returned to drop Badger's worn, scarred saddlebags on the sergeant's desk. He laid a well-used Sharps .50 beside them.

The sergeant held up the bags and barked, "These yours? And this?" The big Sharps swung in an arc from the desktop to stop inches from the scout's face. The old man's head jerked back and to one side.

"Don't point that at me. It's got a quick trigger."

"So, it's yours?"

"Course it's mine. You seen me carryin' it."

The office door burst open, slammed into the wall, and Captain Stanaway stormed into the office. Sergeant Baker snapped to attention and saluted. The captain returned a quick half salute and roared, "What's so blasted important that I had to stop seeing about loading wagons and come over here?" His words bounced off the walls. "The colonel is meeting with Manuelito and Barboncito, Navajo chiefs. We've got Navajo scattered everywhere and all wanting what we don't have." He jerked to a sudden stop in front of the prisoner. "What's going on here? Why is this man tied up?"

Stanaway noticed Will and Two Feathers on the other side of Sergeant Baker, standing against the wall by the door to the colonel's office. His voice dropped to a growl.

"You two!"

Will's fists curled, and his face burned. He stepped forward, and Two Feathers gripped his arm, pulling him back.

"Stop." The word hissed in Comanche.

Two Feathers's hand squeezed tight. A quick, sharp nod to his brother, and Will stepped back against the wall.

"Sergeant, a report." The captain's angry gaze darted from the sergeant to Badger, to Will and Two Feathers, and back to the sergeant. "Now!"

"Sir, this man is a sometimes scout for the army. He goes by Badger, and his reputation is that of a thief and who knows what else."

The sergeant barked, "I know that. Get on with it!"

"Will and his brother, John Randell," Baker tilted his head in Two Feathers's direction, "captured him in a Comanche camp where he had Enfield rifles and ammunition for Yellow Hawk."

Will didn't think the captain's face could look any madder, but it did. It darkened to deep purple, and the muscles stretched taut over his cheekbones.

"So, Dan Whitaker, your Pa," spittle sprayed from his lips, "was not involved?" His stiff body jerked when he took a step toward the boys. "You took up where he left off. You and this half-Comanche brother of yours. Stealing supplies and selling rifles." The loud roar of his voice didn't send prickles down Will's back, but the calm chill of his next words did. "Why else would you be in a Comanche camp? And where are the rifles? You left them with the Comanche."

Two Feathers let go of Will's arm and stepped in front of him. "There is no truth in what you say. Our father was an honorable man. If we did these things, why come here and tell you about it?"

His strong, honest tone and manner made the captain's eyes blink and shift away.

Will turned his back to Stanaway and spoke to Sergeant Baker. His words stumbled through clamped jaws and thin, tight lips.

"Sergeant, if you will empty Badger's saddlebags, you'll find ammunition for his Sharps fifty and a half-empty box of ammunition for an Enfield."

Baker emptied the contents onto his desk, and the boxes spilled out along with hardtack and jerky.

Badger squealed, his voice ringing with panic, "Those ain't mine. I ain't never seen 'em."

Captain Stanaway's eyes narrowed into a bitter glare, directed first at Badger then at the boys.

"Sergeant, arrest this sorry excuse for a man."

"Yes, sir." Baker moved to untie the scout.

"And Sergeant."

"Sir?"

"Arrest these two gunrunners and lock them in the stockade."

CAUGHT

Will's head spun when the heavy wooden door shut and the keys rattled in the lock. His legs gave way, and he fell onto the narrow cot against the wall. Two Feathers's face drained to the color of sand, and Will dropped his head onto his knees.

"Sit down before you fall. I don't have the strength to pick you up."

Two Feathers sat on the cot across the small cell.

"What are we going to do? I do not know how to get away from here. I told you not to trust the soldiers."

The tremble in his always-strong brother's voice heightened Will's fear and panic. Tears pushed against the back of his closed eyes, and he squeezed them tight. With his mouth wide open, he sucked in air till his chest burned. He held it a few seconds and let it slip through his lips, blinking away the tears.

"There's nothing we can do tonight."

The muscles in his throat stiffened rock solid. No more words pushed past the ball of panic Will tried so hard to hide from Two Feathers. He closed his eyes again to block out the sight of the cell. *Breathe. Slow. Steady. In . . . Out . . . In . . .*

Out . . . The ball loosened. Clearing his throat, he managed to sound stronger, or at least he hoped he did.

"We're both worn out from the long ride bringing Badger in. Go to sleep. In the morning I'll tell Sergeant Baker to send word to Smokey and Mr. Goodnight. They'll get us out."

Two Feathers nodded and stretched out on his cot facing the adobe wall. Will watched him till he heard his soft, even breathing. Cradling his head on his arm, Will tried to find sleep. The lumpy cot, the smelly blankets, and his worries about Buck kept his eyes open. Sergeant Baker's promise to take care of their horses eased his mind a little, but Buck didn't like strangers. Maybe Gray Wolf would keep him calm. Maybe he was too tired to act up. Maybe.

The rattle of the key in the lock woke Will. The small window high on the wall let in a sliver of morning light. Sergeant Baker opened the door.

"Come on, boys. Let's get out of here."

The warm sun felt good on Will's face. The fresh air smelled far better than the stale air in their cell, and he filled his lungs with it. He watched the bright sunlight turn Two Feathers's washed-out face from last night back to its normal copper. The sergeant's arm felt good across his shoulders, and he decided Two Feathers must be enjoying the feeling as well because he didn't shrug it off. They walked with the sergeant toward the compound.

"I told the colonel about you two, and he wants to see you this morning. He's busy now. I don't have time to take you to the mess hall, so get something to eat at the sutler's store. Come to the colonel's office in a couple of hours." He patted both boys on the back. "Boys, I'm sorry about last night. I couldn't speak with the colonel until late, and by the time he learned what happened, both of you were asleep. Since you were in a warm place, we decided to let you sleep and get you out first thing this morning."

Will and Two Feathers nodded, and Will shook the sergeant's hand. The soldier headed across the compound.

The area around the Indian Commissary milled with Navajo. Will figured they wanted to know when they could start the trip back to their homelands of Chaco Canyon. Walking past a group of girls and women, Two Feathers spotted Na-es-cha and called to her. She ran to them, grabbed Two Feathers's arm, and dragged him behind the low-squat adobe building. Will followed. In rapid Comanche, her voice almost a whisper, she spoke with Two Feathers. He nodded, and she slipped around the other side of the building and disappeared.

"What's that all about?" Will asked.

"She found something. She said Mrs. Wallace is cooking breakfast."

"That sounds good to me," Will interrupted. "What's so important about that?"

"We need to come while she is busy and won't see us."

"Okay, but can we eat breakfast first? I'm starved."

Will decided Two Feathers was recovering from their night in jail when a glint of mischief flicked in his eyes and he said, "She makes tall, fluffy biscuits."

"Are you telling me you'd rather eat her tall biscuits than my flat sinkers?"

Will ran to catch up with the biscuit expert.

Licking butter and honey from their fingers, Will and Two Feathers waited for Na-es-cha behind the store. She opened the back door and motioned for them to come. They followed her to the Wallace's living quarters and made their way through packed and half-packed crates to a big chair in front of the fireplace. The mantel displayed beautiful intricately carved horses, all in different poses. Some running. Some rearing. Some lying down. A large one in the middle stood with its mane and tail flowing, as if in the wind.

Na-es-cha bent to the floor and scooped up wood chips and poured them into Will's hand. Two Feathers opened his pouch containing the wood chips collected from the campsite he'd found during his vision quest. They were the same sizes and shapes. The same type of wood. The same color as the horses on the mantel. Will untied his bandana from around his neck and wrapped the chips in it.

"Let's get out of here."

They ran across the wagon yard and into the barn. Will checked on Buck, and while he and Two Feathers fed and watered their horses, Na-es-cha talked.

"What's she saying?"

Will kept an eye on the barn door to be sure no one overheard them. He didn't want to get the Navajo girl into trouble. Two Feathers stopped her often to translate for Will.

"She said Mrs. Wallace never let her in their rooms before. Today she told her to pack all their clothes in a crate in the bedroom. She acted excited and gave Na-es-cha several dresses. She told Na-es-cha they were both going home soon."

Will and Two Feathers saddled their horses.

"Na-es-cha remembered me telling about the chips I collected and thought what she found might be important. She hoped we would come to the fort before the soldiers let the Navajo go."

Will finished tightening the cinch on Buck's saddle.

"Ask her if she ever saw Mr. Wallace and Badger talking anywhere besides the store."

Two Feathers spoke in Comanche to Na-es-cha, listened to her, and translated for Will.

"She said only the time they argued. She said when he came they talked long and stopped when anyone came into the store. Sometimes Mr. Wallace got angry and sometimes not."

"Ask her if he always brought skins to trade."

"No. Not much," Na-es-cha answered, and she ran out of the barn.

Will and Two Feathers led their horses around to the front of the store. They left the horses there and made their way through the crowd of Navajo to the fort headquarters. When they reached the steps to the colonel's office, Two Feathers stopped Will.

"I do not trust the soldiers. Stay calm. I do not want to go back to jail."

Will nodded. "You have to stay. No slipping out."

He took a deep breath and opened the door.

Captain Stanaway sat at Sergeant Baker's desk, his face a stone-hard mask.

"Come in. The colonel will be here soon. Sit down."

Neither boy sat. "We found something this morning the colonel needs to see."

"What is it?" His voice sounded like a knife striking flint.

"We'll wait and show the colonel."

"No, we won't. I've been investigating this problem, and I'm expected to evaluate all the evidence. Or what you think is evidence."

Will opened his bandana and laid it on the desk. "We found these chips in Mr. Wallace's room behind the store."

"So?"

Two Feathers opened his pouch and poured his chips on the desk next to the bandana. Will picked up a few chips and showed them to the captain.

"Two Feathers found these chips at a campsite where he also saw Badger's chipped boot tracks." Then, with the other hand, he picked up pieces from his bandana and stretched both hands across the desk. "They are the same."

Captain Stanaway stared at the chips in each of Will's hands for several minutes.

Finally, Will spoke again. "Mr. Wallace has a collection of hand-carved horses on his mantel."

Stanaway picked up a few chips from each hand and studied them. Watching Stanaway's face as he considered the woodchips, Will began to wonder if maybe the captain wasn't involved.

"What was Wallace doing out on the Llano Estacado with Badger?" The last word held contempt.

He dropped the chips in Will's hands, and Will dropped them on the desk. The door opened, and Colonel Dowell walked in, followed by Sergeant Baker. The captain stood and saluted, then moved out from behind the sergeant's desk.

"Hello, boys," Colonel Dowell said. "I see Sergeant Baker let you out this morning."

The colonel slid a withering sideways glance toward the captain. Stanaway stood rigid.

"Captain, I want to hear the whole story and all the evidence. Sergeant, bring chairs into my office for everyone."

When seated, he opened a file on his desk.

"I have Captain Stanaway's reports from his investigations at Fort Union, Las Vegas, and Santa Fe. Also," he cleared his throat, "I know you aren't going to like this, but I sent troopers to watch your ranch. They reported no suspicious activity. I'm sorry they weren't there when Yellow Hawk raided and killed Mr. Whitaker."

Will swallowed the lump in his throat. "I found army boot tracks along our creek bed and wondered why soldiers were there. Now I know."

The colonel shuffled the papers on his desk, but before he spoke, Will stood and approached Captain Stanaway.

"When you went to Santa Fe, did you plan on meeting Badger?"

"No. I didn't know he was there."

"Why were you in Burro Alley? Pa said an honest man couldn't be found there."

"I questioned the people, trying to find out if they knew of army supplies being sold. No one knew anything, at least that's what they said."

Will stood still, staring into the captain's eyes. His head dropped, and in a voice no longer laced with anger he said, "I was wrong that day. Thank you for helping me."

Captain Stanaway nodded, and a tiny twitch pulled at the corner of his mouth.

"Will, sit down, please." Colonel Dowell pointed toward Will's chair. "I want you and John to start at the beginning, and each of you tell me what you found and what you saw. I don't want to hear what you thought each event meant. I only want the facts."

Two Feathers started with seeing the rope hanging from the tree above the ledge along the river bank. Their story went back and forth with each boy describing their discoveries. Will ended their long tale with the chips he placed on the colonel's desk.

Colonel Dowell sat for a long time, staring out his window. Occasionally, he flipped through the notes in Captain Stanaway's file. Will began to fidget in his seat by the time the colonel finally stood.

"I think it's time we talked with Mr. Wallace and find out why he was carving horses on the Llano Estacado."

Colonel Dowell collected both sets of chips, and his boot steps echoed across the boardwalk. He took the steps at the store two at a time and made his way between the few crates of goods spread throughout the store. The others followed behind.

Reaching the counter, he called out, "Mr. Wallace, may I have a word with you?"

Will and Two Feathers stood next to each other. Will whispered, "How many times have we come here?" Two Feathers put his hand on Will's shoulder. "How many times did we get candy?"

Two Feathers squeezed gently. "And eat biscuits."

"How many times did he ask about Pa?"

Will's anger swarmed over him until he felt Two Feathers gripping his shoulder with a vise-like pinch. The big man walked up from the far end of the store.

"What can I do for you, Colonel? As you see, there's not much left here. You bought me out for the Navajo, remember?" His beard bounced with his grin at Will and Two Feathers. "Howdy, boys."

Colonel Dowell spread Will's bandana out on the counter. "Do you know what these are?"

Wallace stuck his big finger in the center of the pile and stirred them around. "They're carving shavings."

"Do you know where they came from?"

The man's black pointy beard bobbed up and down as he swallowed, and he shifted on his feet. His eyes darted toward the back of the store.

"Well, if I don't miss my guess, I'd say they came from around my chair in the back." A nervous laugh stuttered from his throat. "My wife fusses at my mess when I carve. Why? What's going on?"

"You're right. These came from the floor around your chair. And these," the colonel opened Two Feathers's pouch and poured out its contents, "came from a campsite on the Llano Estacado where Badger left his chipped boot track. We know Badger took guns to the Comanche. These chips prove you were with the scout when he had a loaded wagon where no wagon should be."

Wallace froze. No one moved. Will stepped to the counter.

"Did you kill my father? Did you tell Badger to have Yellow Hawk raid our ranch?"

Without warning, the storekeeper grabbed Will by the shirtfront and spun him around into a bear hug tight against his broad barrel chest, lifting Will off his feet. He jerked a gun from under his apron and shoved it against Will's throat.

"Get back! Move away from me."

He backed away from the group toward the door, dragging Will with him. Will held onto the man's huge arm to keep from choking. Two Feathers took a step toward them, and Will tried to shake his head. He mouthed, "NO!" and Two Feathers stopped. The men inched forward as Wallace moved through the door, across the porch, and down the stairs.

Seeing Will in trouble, Buck pulled on his reins at the rail where Will had left him earlier that morning. Wallace saw the big stallion, and with a heave of his giant arms slung Will into the saddle. Buck sidestepped at the sudden movement, but the man's boot caught the stirrup, and he swung himself behind Will.

"Hang on, Will!"

Two Feathers's loud yell reached Will a split second before Buck exploded. He shot straight up, spun around, and the kick of both back legs sent the colonel and the captain sprawling in the dirt. Two Feathers leaped to safety on the porch.

Buck twisted and jumped, dropped his head between his front legs, and shot his hindquarters high in the air. Wallace roared and tumbled sideways to the ground. Will landed on top of him, knocking all the air out of that big chest with a whoosh.

CONFESSION

Soldiers and Navajo came running. Will scrambled off Wallace, and Two Feathers jumped off the porch, grabbing the stallion's reins. Wallace, on his hands and knees, gasped for air.

Colonel Dowell picked himself up off the ground and swiped at his dust-covered uniform.

"Captain Stanaway, arrest this man."

"Sir?"

The scratchy tone of the captain's voice, as if drawn up from a dry well, spun the colonel around. The captain sat in the dust, his bleached face wracked with pain, and his arm twisted in an odd shape.

"Sir, I believe . . ." he sucked in a gasp of air, "you broke my arm . . ." another gasp, "when you landed on me."

"Oh, my!" Colonel Dowell hollered, "Sergeant Baker, arrest Mr. Wallace, take him to the stockade, and lock him up. Bring the boys to my office. I'll be there in an hour. I'm taking Captain Stanaway to the hospital."

One hour turned into three. Two Feathers paced and paced around the office, and Will talked and talked to make him stay.

"I'm not staying here." The pitch of Two Feathers's voice and the number and speed of the circles he paced increased with his level of panic. "What if they put us in that jail again?"

"That won't happen." Will tried to keep his voice steady. "You're safe here. The soldiers won't do anything to you."

"I'm going back to the Comanche. I do not like it here." Two Feathers threw himself into a chair, jumped back up, and the pacing started again.

"Settle down." Will's attempt at remaining calm dissolved and irritation made his words sharp. "You're not going anywhere."

By the time Sergeant Baker showed up, Will was about ready to bar the door to keep Two Feathers in the colonel's office.

"I bet you boys are hungry. As an apology to both of you for last night in the stockade, the colonel ordered the cook to fix a special lunch. It's not much, but he wanted to do something. He will join you in the mess hall."

"See." Will's exasperation vanished at the thought of food. "I told you we weren't going back to jail." He slapped Two Feathers on the shoulder. "I told you everything would be all right."

"Will you come?" Two Feathers asked the sergeant, his voice still shaky.

"Yes, I'll be there."

The mess hall was empty, except for the colonel sitting at a table at the end of the room. Will was surprised to see a white tablecloth and heavy china plates instead of the tin trays the soldiers used. And to see Captain Stanaway sitting next to the colonel, his left arm in a sling and his face a pasty pale under his desert tan.

The colonel stood, and the captain started to until the colonel put his hand on the man's shoulder. Captain Stanaway relaxed back into his chair with relief.

"Come, sit down. We have a lot to tell you. But first, let's enjoy our lunch. Then we'll go to my office to talk with Mr. Wallace and Badger. I've already heard most of their story. However, I feel you both deserve to know the details."

Will and Two Feathers sat across the table from the colonel and Captain Stanaway.

"I do have a question," Colonel Dowell said. "Why didn't you two tell anyone about the tracks and chips you found? We might have resolved this earlier if we had known all the facts."

Will snuck a glance at Two Feathers. His brother's face was stiff, and his eyes dropped to his hands. He wouldn't look at the colonel. Will knew what he had to do. His voice held no doubt or question.

"I knew a chipped boot heel and wood shavings weren't enough evidence to prove anything in the beginning. As time passed, I thought Captain Stanaway was behind it all, and I knew no one would believe me against him. Some of the information was given to Two Feathers by a Navajo girl. She is terrified of the soldiers and wouldn't have kept giving us information if we had gone to the army."

The colonel sat briefly in silence, his forehead crinkled in thought.

"I can see why you would react that way. Especially with John's history with soldiers."

Will looked at Colonel Dowell as though he'd pulled a coin from his ear, and suspicion once again clouded Two Feathers's eyes.

In a voice laced with laughter, the colonel reminded them, "Don't be surprised. Remember, I'm the commander of this fort. I know everything."

"Everything, Colonel?" Will cocked one eyebrow. "I don't know about that. We solved the mystery."

The man's laughter lightened the mood around the table.

"I guess you're right. I need to rethink that." He held his water glass in the air. "Drink up. What happened can't be changed. Let's be relieved the mystery is solved."

Two soldiers in clean white aprons brought steaks, bowls filled with fried potatoes and onions, and a platter piled high with fluffy golden biscuits.

"Private Peters, put those biscuits in front of John. I heard a rumor that he is particularly fond of them."

Now it was Two Feathers's time to be surprised. Throughout the meal, each time he reached for another biscuit, he showed it to Will and pointed out how tall it was, rubbed his stomach to show how good it was, and told Will he needed a lesson from the army cook.

Way too soon Will's pants began to squeeze his waist. He put down his fork and pushed back from the table. Two Feathers finished one more biscuit and did the same.

"Gentlemen, let's move to my office. The prisoners should be there by now."

They left the mess hall and walked across the compound to the colonel's office. Na-es-cha, with her mother, stood in the usual long line in front of the Indian Commissary. Her hand flicked in a small wave to him and Two Feathers. Will waved back and realized she would be leaving soon and they might never see her again. It saddened him. He shot a quick look at his brother, and that same realization showed on his sad face.

"Maybe we can find her before we leave."

Will tried to sound hopeful, but he wasn't sure who he was trying to convince. Two Feathers's mouth twisted down at one corner and one shoulder lifted in a small shrug.

"I hope so."

In the colonel's office, Mr. Wallace and Badger sat against the wall with their hands bound and a soldier on each side of their chairs. The colonel settled behind his desk. Sergeant Baker, Captain Stanaway, and the boys sat facing the colonel with the prisoners on their left. Colonel Dowell cleared his throat and began his long tale of events, his gaze moving from one person to another.

"Our Mr. Wallace is quite a master at keeping secrets. Like so many others, he came out west to make his fortune. He was a storekeeper back east and decided to operate a sutler's store. He became friends with Ed Franklin, who works in the quartermaster's office at Fort Union, and Franklin told him about Fort Sumner needing a sutler's store. That's how he arrived here.

"They devised a plan to profit from the large amount of supplies coming from Fort Union to Fort Sumner for the Navajo. Captain Inman is the quartermaster at Fort Union, and supplies are moved in and out of that warehouse to forts all over this territory. Ed Franklin is a bookkeeper in Inman's office. He adjusted the shipping orders to cover the stolen supplies."

The colonel fixed his stare on Mr. Wallace, who sat with his head hanging.

"Have I left anything out? Do you want to add any facts to my story?"

Will noticed Wallace's pointy beard that always bobbed up and down with his words and easy laughter was still.

"No?" The colonel waited. "Then I will continue. Between Mr. Franklin and Mr. Wallace, they managed to hire soldiers in need of extra money to deliver supplies to hidden places throughout the territory between the two forts. Through his contacts, Mr. Franklin made arrangements with a freighter to pick up these supplies and deliver them to Colorado to sell to the miners."

The colonel paused and asked Sergeant Baker to bring him a cup of water. After a quick drink, he continued.

"This is where Badger enters the story."

The old scout squirmed in his chair, rattling the handcuffs that bound his hands behind him.

"Badger located the hiding places and delivered messages to the freighter, who operates out of Las Vegas, telling him when and where to pick up the supplies."

"Sir," Will interrupted. "Isn't Las Vegas about halfway between here and Fort Union? Is that why they chose it?"

"Not exactly halfway, but close enough. I'd assume the main reason is because it's a good-sized town with a bank to deposit their money and enough freight companies so their activity would go unnoticed. Is that true, Mr. Wallace?"

Will watched the pointy beard make a slight up and down movement. He asked the colonel, "What does all this have to do with us?"

"I'm getting to that. So far, what I've told happened before you boys and your Pa came. From what we learned, Private Tucker liked to play poker but was not a good gambler. He lost more often than he won. So Mr. Wallace offered him money to meet the wagons from Fort Union and help unload in the places Badger located.

"Ed Franklin hired drivers at Fort Union. Tucker and Badger met the loaded wagon at the cave on the Pecos. They unloaded the crates into the cave, and I guess an argument broke out over a poker game and either the driver or Badger killed him. That was the grave you found. I've sent a messenger to Fort Union, and they'll investigate at their end."

"Sir?" Two Feathers spoke out. "Where were the crates we found? Who took them?"

"Evidently the freighter came before we did and collected them."

The smell of brewed coffee drifted in from Sergeant Baker's office. Heading that way, Baker stopped at the door.

"Coffee is ready. Colonel, would you like a cup?"

The colonel nodded.

"Will? John? How about some coffee?" Baker called from his office. "You boys might need a pick up before you hear the rest."

Badger sat up in his chair. "I could use a cup. Cut me loose so's I can stretch a bit and slurp it down right quick." Brown broken teeth flashed in an awkward smile.

Baker shot him a fierce look. "You won't be cut loose until you're locked in your cell."

Will took the hot cup in his hands. It burned, so he shifted to the handle and blew ripples across the dark surface. Even Two Feathers welcomed the coffee. He sat his on the corner of the colonel's desk to cool. Colonel Dowell took a careful sip and continued.

"Then you boys and your Pa arrived. When you came with Goodnight's cattle drive and set up your ranch on the Pecos River, you settled right in the middle of Wallace's and Franklin's operation. They couldn't move their stolen supplies as easily with you riding around over the area. So they decided you had to go."

Will nodded at Two Feathers. "We figured that out."

"Colonel," Captain Stanaway shifted his arm in the sling, "what about the Comanche, Yellow Hawk? How did he get involved?"

The colonel turned to Two Feathers. "He's your uncle, right?"

"Yes," Two Feathers answered.

"And there are hard feelings between you?"

"Yes."

"Then I assume he followed you here."

"I know he did," Will said. "He followed both of us here because he wants my buckskin stallion."

"My guess is he wants more than the horse. I hear he wants you boys."

"That's true, but how do you know that?" Will's puzzled expression seemed to amuse the colonel.

"I'm the commander of this fort. All information comes to me."

Will grinned.

"Well, most information." The colonel spoke to the scraggly scout. "Badger, explain what Mr. Wallace told you to do. And if you know what's good for you, make it the truth."

Badger sat up straight and wiggled his shoulders back and forth.

"Ole Wallace here was plumb upset when you folks settled on the Pecos. You sure ruint his plans. He knowed I was friendly with the Comanche, and he asked me what I could do to help him move you folks offin the Pecos. I'd heared 'bout that war chief Yellow Hawk and how he roamed around these parts, so I looked him up."

The nasty twist of his lips that showed Badger's rotten teeth disgusted Will. *Was that supposed to be a grin?*

"He told me he was huntin' fer two rag-tailed boys and a big buckskin stallion. When I told him I knowed where they was, he got right friendly."

Will's heart raced, and his throat squeezed so tight he couldn't swallow. He lunged from his chair. Two Feathers pulled him back, and Sergeant Baker stepped in front of the boys.

"Easy, Will." The sergeant pressed down on Will's shoulders. "We've got him now. He won't get away."

Will's knees locked. He forced himself into his chair and pulled Two Feathers down with him.

"Keep talking, Badger. Let's get this done." The colonel words hammered the scout.

The old scout's eyes skipped around the room, as if looking for a friendly face. There were none.

"Yellow Hawk and me made a deal. Iffen I could get a few rifles and ammo, he'd make sure there'd be nary a one of you left. Wallace here," he jerked his head toward the storekeeper, "said he could get them guns."

"Wait a minute!" Wallace tried to jump from his chair. The soldiers slammed him back down. "That's not all I said. I told him no one was to get hurt. He was to tell Yellow Hawk to only scare them, not kill them."

"Mr. Wallace!" Colonel Dowell's voice boomed through the room. "Stay in your chair. You came out here from Ohio. You know nothing about the Indians that live out here. When you told Badger to give the Comanche guns, you caused the raid on Charles Goodnight's cattle. It's a miracle no one was killed. You caused the raid on the Whitaker ranch that did kill Dan Whitaker."

"But I didn't want that to happen. Badger and I fought over it. We argued. I told him if anyone else was hurt I'd shut down the whole operation."

Desperation spit from his mouth with his words and his face swelled, turning blood red. Wallace's gaze jumped from face to face in a panicked frenzy.

Badger snorted. "Yur 'bout the stupidest man I ever saw."

The big man slumped and the blood drained from his face, leaving his dark beard a stark contrast to his white face.

"Sergeant Baker, escort the prisoners and their guards to the stockade and lock them up. The very sight of them disgusts me."

Will and Two Feathers sat stiff in their chairs. When the prisoners left, the colonel held his silence for a long while. The grim lines on his face made Will's heart hiccup.

"The danger is not over." The colonel's eyes softened a little. "I've come to admire your bravery and stubbornness. I don't want to read a report that something terrible happened to either of you. Yellow Hawk is still out there on the Staked Plains. He is still after both of you. He now has another reason to want you dead. His connection to a supply of guns has been cut, and by the two of you. You must be more than careful."

Will's stomach lurched, as it always did at the thought of Yellow Hawk. A glance at Two Feathers's face told him his brother had the same reaction.

Captain Stanaway cleared his throat and spoke to the colonel. "Sir, may I speak to Will and John?"

"Certainly. Say what you need to say."

Stanaway pulled his chair in front of the boys. Pain spread over his face with the movement, and he held his broken arm against his chest. Gazing from one face to the other, Stanaway spoke in respectful tones.

"I know this has been hard for you both."

Will took a deep breath and met the eyes that once held hate but now showed compassion.

"You have a right to be angry. I know your anger is at me. I was so certain that I knew what the facts were, but I was wrong. And I was wrong about your father. I know now that he was an honorable man, as you told me over and over. I hope you can forgive me."

Will leaned his hands on his knees, looking down at them. He sat that way until he sucked in enough air to clear his thinking. He glanced at Two Feathers, who sat rigid, staring straight ahead and not blinking. Will lifted his head to the captain.

"Thank you. You were wrong about our father. But I was wrong about you too."

Captain Stanaway smiled and held out his hand. "I think we all learned things are not always what they seem."

Will grasped the man's hand. They shook.

The captain spoke to Two Feathers. "Can you find enough forgiveness and trust to shake my hand?"

Will watched Two Feathers's eyes fade from the dark of shale rock to his usual soft gray. He put out his hand and he too shook the offered hand of a soldier.

TWO HEIFERS

Will climbed onto the boulder in the shade of the big oak tree between the adobe house and the creek. He settled himself and let his legs dangle down the rounded slope. All his energy flowed from his body through the toes of his boots to spill on the grave at his feet. *I'm so tired.* His arms felt weighted, too heavy to lift. He realized he'd forgotten to breathe and sucked in a deep breath. The air filling his chest felt heavy. The grave blurred, and a teardrop fell with a splat on his hand. He blinked several times and focused on the grave.

Grass poked little green heads through the soil. The snow of winter had settled the mound of dirt and broken up the larger clods. The leather strips Two Feathers wrapped around the cross to hold it together had shrunk tight. Speckled spots of shade and sunlight moved across the grave from the wind in the tree covered with the bright green of new leaves.

Thoughts of Pa filled Will's mind. He pulled his knees to his chest and wrapped his arms around them. The weight of his grief lowered his head to rest on them.

How did you know, Pa? How did you know we would be alone? So much has happened.

He lowered his legs, let their weight pull him off the boulder, and sat on the ground. His back rested against the cold of the stone.

"We made it through the winter, Pa. The bulls and cows survived, and we lost only a few calves. The ranch is doing good. We're collecting the heifers for Mr. Goodnight. Mr. Chisum will pick them up on his drive north in a few weeks. You would be proud of all we've done. I think Two Feathers and I will be okay."

Will rose and walked to the cross. He tried to wiggle it to be sure it was tight in the ground. It didn't move.

"We solved the mystery, Pa. And you were right. It wasn't Stanaway. It was Wallace. I would never have guessed him. We thought he was such a nice man." He pulled his bandana off his neck and wiped his face. "We're missing a couple of heifers, and Two Feathers and I are going to search along the river. They seem to like to go that way. If we spot another cave, I don't think I'll take a look inside."

Will and Two Feathers pulled Buck and Gray Wolf to a stop on the top of the tall banks overlooking the Pecos River Ranch. Will took in the familiar landmarks—the bluffs that ringed the brush corral, the little valley behind the barn, the trees that lined the creek that provided their sweet water. This was his ranch, his and Two Feathers's. Two Feathers sat still. Will watched him, not sure what he was thinking.

"Are you okay?"

Two Feathers nodded, speaking with care.

"I do not want to live on a reservation like the Navajo. I have a bad feeling that someday all the Comanche will be on a reservation. That will be a terrible day. I have decided to stay."

Will studied the banks of the river, then the rock walls on the other side. His gaze moved to the far distant horizon, and the muscles in his eyes stretched across the colors in this hard Pecos country. The sand, the rocks, the deep ravines, and tall mesas held every shade from pink to deep red, and their tans and browns flowed from the palest yellow to deep chocolate. He loved this country, even with its hard living. A smile spread across his face.

"Did you decide that just now? I figured that out a long time ago."

Two Feathers cocked his head sideways at Will. Peace rested in his eyes and in the loose way he sat his saddle. Will was glad to see it. A gust of wind fluttered the turkey feathers in his hair.

"I am still Comanche. I will always be Comanche. I will always ride better than you, hunt better, track better, and if you don't hurry up and learn to make better biscuits, I will do that better than you."

"Humph, not on your best day."

They sat for a while and watched the river wind its slow, sluggish way south.

Two Feathers pointed out two heifers ambling along the river's edge, heading north, away from the ranch.

"Look there, Will. See those heifers?" He pointed down the steep, tall banks to a sandbar where the wayward animals ambled upriver. "Do you think you are a good enough tracker to follow two heifers up a muddy riverbank?"

"I don't know, but I bet I beat you down there."

He gave Buck a firm tap. The big stallion plunged over the rim and down the steep trail. Gray Wolf sailed over the edge and followed in a cloud of flying pebbles, tumbling rocks, and billowing dust. They hit the river at a run, and water sparkled in the sun as the horses' hooves splashed it high into the air.

~THE END~

THE RIVER OF CATTLE

FOR READERS 8 - 12 | GRADES 3 - 7
by Alice V. Brock

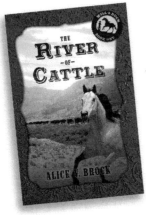

Winner!

Western Fictioneers Best Western YA/
Children's Fiction, 2017

Will Rogers Medallion Finalist for
Younger Readers, 2017

**Will Whitaker's eleventh summer is
one thrill after another.**

A cattle drive with a famous Texas Ranger, a Comanche trying to steal his horse, a buffalo stampede, thirst-maddened cattle crossing eighty miles of alkali desert to a dangerous ford on the Pecos River—it's almost more than Will can endure. He gets to work as a drover, riding his best friend Buck, a big buckskin stallion, until he is captured by a vicious Comanche war chief. And only his worst enemy can rescue him.

Two Feathers—half white, half Comanche—runs away from his tribe when he learns his uncle killed his white father. He sees Will's horse and knows he is destined to have him, this great warrior's horse. Camping alone and following the winding River of Cattle across the High Plains of West

Texas, he tries again and again to take him. Will foils him every time, but Two Feathers comes too close and is captured by the drovers.

The two boys, both fighting the grief of their mother's deaths, both without a true home, face death and danger separately, but eventually they must learn acceptance of each other's differences or their mutual mistrust could lead them to disaster on the brutal Texas-New Mexico frontier.

Will they become brothers or mortal enemies?

"A compelling and triumphant introduction to the colorful bygone era of cattle drives. Alice Brock entertainingly weaves fact and fiction into a dual tale of high drama, where diversity and friendship must meet head-on to determine who survives."

– Tim Lewis, Director of the Writing Academy at West Texas A&M University, author of *Forever Friday*

Get your copy today at

www.Pen-L.com/TheRiverOfCattle.html

or your favorite bookseller!

ABOUT ALICE

Alice V. Brock learned to love Western books as a child when her father brought home a Louis L'Amour paperback and she fell in love with the cowboys galloping through those pages. Mr. L'Amour's books, and TV shows like *Gunsmoke*, *Rawhide*, and *Bonanza* of the late 50s and 60s, brought the West alive to her. The history of Texas and the Old West is full of stories of those times. Her wish is to bring them alive for kids of today. The Old West has not disappeared, and Alice brings real people in history to her writing. Real people who lived during those times and have descendants who live today.

Her chance to see cowboys in action came when she married and moved to her husband's family ranch in Iola, Texas, where she watches the grazing cattle from her kitchen window. Her grandchildren are the fifth generation on the Brock Ranch.

Alice lives in Central Texas with her two dogs, Button, a shih tzu, and Quigley, a standard poodle, who keep things lively on the Brock Ranch.

The first book in the Will and Buck Series is the award winning *River of Cattle*, the Western Fictioneer's Peacemaker 2016 Award winner for Young Adult/Children and a Peacemaker finalist for Best First Novel of 2016. Also it earned the Will Rogers Medallion Award for Younger Readers, Fourth Place. It can be found through Pen-L Publishing, Amazon, and Barnes and Noble. Watch for announcements about book three, *Palo Duro Mustangs*.

To learn more about Alice V. Brock and her writing visit her website at www.AliceVBrock.com, her Amazon Author Page at Alice V. Brock, and on her page at Facebook.

Dear Readers,
If you enjoyed this book enough to review it for Goodreads, B&N, or Amazon.com, I'd appreciate it!
Thanks, Alice

Find more great reads at
Pen-L.com

Made in the USA
Middletown, DE
22 December 2018